HIDDEN PROMISES

By Annay Dawson

Hidden Promises

Published by Lulu.com

ISBN: 978-1-4357-0974-4

Prologue

Oh dear Lord, let this be the right decision, Maria fidgeted with her rosary beads. She prayed often and believed He heard, but right now she was terrified. She was totally out of her element.

As this young woman sat alone on the bench in a small border town in Mexico she had an old, small, multicolored bag and her long black hair was pulled back into a loose ponytail. Waiting on the bench at the bus station she contemplated what she was about to do. She was going to Phoenix. She had nothing left here for her. While scrubbing floors, the woman she had worked with showed her a letter from her bother. In his letter he had told her to go to Nogales and to wait at the bus station there, a coyote would find her. She would need to bring about two thousand dollars. Her brother had sent her the money, a little bit at a time. His sister wasn't interested in crossing to the US and had used the money for other things. Her feeling about the trip was that it would be too dangerous.

She had never seen so many different types of people in her life before. Maybe if she had made it into college, maybe if her family hadn't been murdered. Life was supposed to be much better, maybe she would find it in the States, according to that letter. It had been a hard decision, one she might regret, but after the decision was made there was no looking back. Now here she sat in the bus station with what could be thousands of people around her all looking for the same thing or plotting to take what they had left. Letting the rosary beads slip through her fingers she kept looking over the area.

From behind her a strange man threw his leg over the bench making her jump and then followed through with his other leg, stepping the rest of the way over. Making himself more than comfortable by sidling up close beside her, made her a little more than uncomfortable. Dressed in a fairly new leather jacket, dark glasses and a baseball cap turned backwards to hide all but a bit of his black hair did nothing to hide his slimy character. He was only about five feet ten inches tall, and he weighed in at about one hundred eighty or ninety pounds. She wasn't physically scared of him, but she wasn't positive about his intentions either.

"Where're you headed?" she sat eyes straight ahead, not sure whether or not to answer his question. "Wherever you're going, I can get you there. What's your name?"

"Maria, and I want to go to the States," he didn't look like any official she had seen.

"The States right," he leaned close enough for her to feel his breath on her cheek and smell the peppers he had eaten.

"Yes," she wanted to leave, run, he made her skin crawl.

"Five hundred dollars will get you across the border safe and sound," Maria fiddled with her bag. She had been told it would cost her nearly two thousand dollars and here was someone that would take her for five hundred. Doubt started to grow and show on her face, and she wasn't gullible. She looked at him again, "No catches, I just want you to get there. I can find you a job and then I get the first two months pay. Most of the time I make more money that way."

Even though she still had doubt niggling at the corners of her mind she couldn't help but think that she may need the money she had for other things. His offer of finding her a job could be useful since she would be an undocumented worker.

"Okay," she replied tentatively as he smiled and grabbed her bag. He stood up and turned before she had a chance to change her mind.

"Follow me," and he walked off with her bag not even glancing back at her. Maria got up and followed him, not sure of what was coming next, and she was too afraid to ask.

1

She sat on a rocky outcrop out in the mist of the ocean waves and waited. Maybe that wasn't the right word. It was the third day that week she had sat in the same place, at the same time, and was unable to meditate. Her ability to meditate had once saved her. The warmth of the sun on her face, the mist from the waves that cooled her and the steady beat of the waves on the rocks should have seduced her into a deep meditative state, but she felt nothing.

This had become her favorite spot over the last six months, but not anymore, and it was way past frustrating. She looked for a loose rock or shell to throw. Not seeing anything, she realized that she must have pitched them all off earlier this week. Turning, she looked back up the cliff and into the windows of the apartment that she shared with Ward. Low and behold there he was, on the balcony, and she realized that the source of her current problems originated with him. He didn't look down as Jan stared up at him, and he didn't smile. She couldn't quite read his mind, but she was sure he was reading hers. His range was greater.

'Damn you,' she thought as she unfolded her legs and slid down into the cool waves. Determinedly, she walked back through the surf, the waves pushing her back to shore. Jan marched towards the steps. It had been more than five months now since they had been on an assignment, any assignment. In fact, the last assignment they had worked on had freed her from the department that Ward had left over two years before. Leaving the department wasn't the plan, but as the events unfolded she saw an unfavorable pattern playing out before her.

It was that bureaucracy she learned she couldn't live with any more. Ward, her husband and true champion, had been caught in the department's web. Even though he had warned her, she allowed herself to become entangled in it as well. They both ended up leaving the department for the same reasons. She was no longer a mindless peon following orders ready to believe what they told her. The last assignment had almost cost both of them their lives.

The Paranormal Enforcement Department, or 'PED' for short, had identified and cultivated them both as mind readers in college. It had started out as an experiment by the CIA in the sixties, long before they were commissioned. Although all experiments had supposedly been stopped for lack of results, they hadn't. The PED had gone underground and taken on a life of its own. They were sure the department would go on for a long time.

The sad thing was that by joining the PED, they literally had given up their life, all aspects of it. Agents inside the department were removed from regular society, forever belonging to the department. After unofficially leaving, Jan and Ward could never go back to who they were, or live normally without the department looking at them like human guinea pigs. Until six months ago, Ward had been the only agent to live outside of their control. Instead, Ward and Jan had chosen to live life as hunted people. Their only crime was in wanting a life.

Now, fully recovered from the injuries that assignment had brought both of them, Jan knew she was ready, itching, to get back to work, and back into life. Although Ward had not talked about it to her, she knew that he had turned down three assignments over the last few months. Once Ward had left the department, he had set up shop for himself. Picking his assignments based on need and not always on payment. Sometimes they paid him; sometimes the results were pay enough. What she found out was that most of the time he took no pay.

Somewhere out there, there were three people that wouldn't get his help because he had said no, because of her. The people he chose to help sometimes existed only on the edge of society, with no other advocate to come to their aide; he was their last hope, their only hope. This was the part of the career change that intrigued Jan and finally drew her in.

She walked up the beach deep in thought. Jan knew that Ward had received another request three days ago. She wasn't sure, but from what she had picked incidentally from his thoughts, she knew the request had come from Eddy and he hadn't replied. Putting all the pieces together, it was no wonder that she could no longer meditate, and she wondered if he could.

Each time Jan had tried all she could see were faceless people still looking for someone to help, and what had they been doing the last few months? They sat here, hidden, doing nothing, safe from the world. Jan's thoughts twisted around to Ward, and what she hadn't been able to read. Was he afraid to lose her? Six months ago he almost had. What he needed to remember was that she had almost lost him as well. And how many other times had she nearly lost him without even knowing it? The thoughts darted through her mind, as she got closer to the cement stairs that wound their way up the cliff's side to their patio. What Jan needed to explain to Ward, was that he was at risk of losing her again, but this time from stifling her. She needed to do what she did best, and so did he.

Focused and intent on what she was about to do, she had almost gotten back to the steps when she heard Ward move through the foliage. Stopping, she read his mind, 'Running,' and knew what was coming next. Jan looked at the gap in the brush just as Ward walked through. Ward was about six feet tall, toned, proportionally perfect, and nicely muscled. Jan never got tired of looking at him, he was easy on the eyes, and with the time they had spent in Mexico, at their beach hideaway, he had become evenly bronzed as well. It wasn't his body she was tired of skirmishing with it was his mind.

He walked over to her and gently kissed her on the cheek. He knew there was a problem, and when she didn't reciprocate he read just enough of her thoughts to see what was coming next. He also read enough to avoid it.

'Ready to go for a run?' He silently asked as he completely avoided the issue. He had read that she had not meditated for the past week and the reasons why she suspected she hadn't. He had also not meditated for the last week, and his conscious was also bothering him, for the very same reasons. He had read everything in her mind and she didn't know how close she really was to the truth. Soon she would though. Ward knew he couldn't stray from his plan, no matter how much he wanted to. He had to be sure, very sure, before they took the next step. Ward left the subject alone for long enough, afraid that he would have to deal with the consequences of his actions, his conscious, as well as hers. It hadn't been the right time until now.

"Okay," and that was all Jan had to say. They went off down the beach at a steady pace for about ten minutes. The talent Jan and Ward shared, one that had been developed, used and abused by the government, was strangely not in use.

Jan and Ward had been empathetically sensitive all their lives. The government had harvested them, as well as others, in college to train them to become exceptional mind readers. Some had made it, others had not. Jan and Ward were now sure that the ones who had not made it into the department might have been the lucky ones.

Now, the tables were turned. They were the ones who were on the run from the government and society. They could live in neither and were needed in both. Today they ran for exercise and away from the people they had once been. And on this run, unlike the others they had taken on many other days, they chose not to share words or thoughts. They were avoiding the obvious, for the last five or so months they had been on the run from everything and everyone, even themselves. They couldn't run from themselves much longer.

Jan ran along beside Ward and started to wonder if they would ever work again. She questioned if he could make the jump from protecting her, back into working with her. Jan had not tried to discover how any of his jobs were presented to him. She was pretty sure that his network of friends, or associates, was fairly vast. She was also quite sure that only important jobs were presented to him. These were people in great need, with no one else to turn to, but he had chosen to stay hidden away for a lot longer than he had ever done before all because of her.

All of a sudden Jan could feel a gentle tug at her thoughts and knew that Ward had started to look in on what she was thinking. She didn't try to hide her thoughts. She watched his pace increase as he realized, from her thoughts, what was coming next. She had a bunch of questions; ones he didn't want to answer, ones he wasn't going to answer yet. Jan kept up pace with him as he started to pull away from her. They ran, slowly increasing the pace for another five minutes, before Jan finally said something.

"You can't run away from this, from me," Jan was keeping up with him and not even winded yet.

"I'm not running away from anything," Ward calmly stated as he continued to increase the pace.

"I know you read my mind, saw my questions," Jan took a breath, "We need to talk."

"No good conversation ever started with those words," and Ward increased his pace to a full run leaving her behind.

"You can fly, but not that high Eagle," she yelled from behind. Eagle had been his code name from the department. She followed in short order, this time mad as hell.

With one burst of speed, she caught up with him and leapt out tackling him from behind. They rolled a couple times on the beach then came to an abrupt stop. Jan was on top, effectively pinning him down, his hands above his head. Ward stared into her eyes for a moment about to say something, and then said nothing. Jan stared intently into his eyes.

"We need to talk," Jan stated again, with a firm hold on Ward.

"So I would guess," Ward lay motionless on the sand, not trying to get up, yet every muscle tense, readied.

"When was the last time you meditated?" Jan stayed on top.

"A few days ago, why?" Ward was surprised by this first question but stayed nonchalant.

"For the last week I haven't been able to meditate even though I have tried," she looked into his eyes, "Want to tell me why?"

"I have a feeling I won't have to. You're going to tell me," he said with a smug look on his face.

"Alright. You keep turning down jobs, and it's because of

me," Jan relaxed her right arm for a second. That was all it took.
Taking advantage of that split second, Ward was on top of Jan before
she had time to stop him.

"You're arrogant, you're right, and you're gorgeous when
you're mad. I have turned down jobs, but that was when we were
both still recovering," Ward shifted on top of her to get a better hold.
Jan knew part of what he said was true, but not all. He had just got a
job in the other day that was weighing heavy on his mind, and she
had the feeling he was about to turn it down as well.

"Have you forgotten? I can read your mind just as easily.
What about the job you've just gotten in?" Ward's face hardened
only for a split second before softening again. If Jan had not been
watching carefully she would have missed it. His grip relaxed, but
Jan didn't take advantage of it.

"How did you know about that?" he asked calmly, as his mind
betrayed the conflict within.

"It's been on your mind a lot lately, and I just happened to pick
up on it a few days ago as it floated through the air. What's it about?"
Her voice softened to encourage him to open up to her, the way they
used to before she nearly died.

He had known they needed to set these boundaries if they
were ever going to work together. Before now, whenever they had
worked together it had been by orders, never by choice. Ward
looked into her eyes, and then let his anger sail away on the next
wave that traveled back out to the ocean. Ward rolled off her and lay
quietly beside her on the warm sand of the beach. They stared up at
the blue sky and wispy clouds.

Jan wasn't going to rush him. If he told her now, or in twenty
minutes, it wouldn't matter. The only thing that mattered was that he
told her. This step would bring them even closer and she could tell
that as she lay quietly beside him.

'Eddy e-mailed the other day,' he chose to let her read his
thoughts so that if anyone was around they couldn't be overheard.
'Thought I might be interested in this job since no one else is doing
anything about it. Seems like there are a group of coyotes that have
found a new way of increasing their profits. After taking their fee to
get the people across, these coyotes just make these people

disappear, all of them women, and no one knows where they are going. Usually, in the past, the relatives would get ransom notes while they are held in a drop house, but they aren't getting any of those from the coyotes either. This is what has made some people nervous. There are usually bunches of people that go missing. Not too unusual as the people who crossover illegally would rather not be found by immigration.

'The underground network usually connects the families sooner or later, but a few of the relatives that have talked with Eddy say that they haven't heard from them since before they crossed the border. They are sure something has gone horribly wrong. They are hoping someone can find their family members that are missing, but it is difficult, as they have no one they can turn to for help. They can't go to the officials for fear of getting sent back and then they would be in an even worse situation than they are now. This group of illegals are pretty scared as a whole and even more so with what has happened,' now Jan knew why they weren't meditating. It was a pretty heavy case to say no to. It would mean saying no not just to this group, but also to Eddy. Not something that Ward would do.

'How did Eddy get the information?' Jan thought she knew. Eddy worked construction as a sideline and would easily meet up with lots of illegal aliens that were hired to work there as well.

'Works with some of the relatives. Overheard their worries while on the job. He started talking to a few of them. Not an easy task since he doesn't quite fit the mold of someone they would trust. He slowly got the information over the last week or so. Seems as if he might have some good information,' Ward knew that Eddy would never contact him unless he had enough information.

'The leads could be pretty cold by now,' there was no doubt in Jan's mind about that; 'It could make the job a bit more difficult. Not impossible, just difficult.' She looked at the passing seagull and then spoke, "Are we going to do the job?"

"No," and just as quickly as he said the word, his hand came up, effectively blocking the next words coming out of her mouth, as well as her thoughts. He had to play his cards right at this point. "To do the job properly your life would be put in too much danger. I can't choose to do that to you. Plus you're right, the leads are too cold," now he put up the blocks in his mind to keep her out as well.

"Isn't the first part for me to decide?" Jan turned onto her side balancing on her arm and looked at Ward, studying the line of his jaw. Jan already knew that Ward had closed off areas of his mind to her and she wanted to know why.

"Another time when there are no right answers, huh?" Ward closed his eyes. This was the hard part for Ward, but he kept his focus. He knew what he needed to do and he needed her to be sure of the path she was about to take.

'What do you mean?' She forced her thoughts back into his mind, 'The only right answer is to find these people and put a couple of coyotes out of business for good. It may not stop what's happening completely, but it just may slow it down for a while. It's bad enough people are forced to cross the border in this way, but to make the journey even more dangerous, that's why we need to stop it. And stop it now. Haven't we always said we wanted to make a difference? Isn't that one of the reasons why I'm here?' Jan looked into Ward's eyes as his head turned toward her, and made sure he was looking back into hers, neither one was new to the underground world and the risks. Without breaking her gaze, she needed to make sure he understood what she was about to say.

"If I had wanted to retire, I could have stayed at the department," Jan knew those words had hit the soft spot she wanted, it wasn't fair play, but then again he wasn't playing fair either. There was another agenda here she hadn't seen to begin with. She could feel Ward's mind tighten around that thought and then she felt how he let it go along with his anger. She just stared at him. He needed to know that by not letting her work, he just might lose her.

The problem was that Ward did know it, and didn't like it. He closed his eyes, he knew what was coming next, "And if you think I am going to spend my time raising a herd of children like Mama Garcia suggests, you need to think again. That's not us. We were meant to change lives for the better. We were given the skills to help and you're just going to throw that all away?" Jan sat up and crossed her legs, looking at Ward's closed eyes.

Mama Garcia, as they both affectionately called her, was the wife of the beach property's caretaker. Ward had once helped his family with a problem they had had with their son and a nasty group of people. Now, they took care of the house and apartment that Ward and Jan owned. Jan and Ward lived in the apartment, and the Garcias lived in the house and kept the secret.

Jan wasn't sure what bothered her most. Was it the fact that Ward might think he was in control of her life, or that someone needed to control it? Was it that he just lay there hoping the whole conversation would be washed out to sea? Or was it that there was still something else, something he wasn't letting her in on.

"Let's go," Ward's voice was flat, lifeless. He swiftly got to his feet and started down the beach again at a quick pace. He knew she wasn't there yet. His mind was filled with thoughts and emotions, all of which Jan was picking up on until she got a message, 'Stay out,' plain and simple, and that was the only hint she needed. He was focusing on a thought that she was not welcome to see. She followed Ward back to the hideaway at the steady pace he set and she let him keep his thoughts to himself for now. Jan worried that this may signal a change in the relationship between them, a change that she had been warned about by an old and dear friend.

Rob, her former partner in the department once told her that Ward would never be happy with any one thing, especially a relationship, for long term. As the years passed, Rob had become more of a father figure, wanting what was best for her. At first it had been her happiness, later, he got protective about the events and sincerity in her relationship. He had known about them, but he hadn't known about the marriage.

The Ward she had come to know and love, though, had never showed tendencies that would even lead her to believe he was anything but trustworthy and true. In days of old he would have been called a gentleman, but that was not a persona he had shown to anyone but her. Even after he left the department as a wanted man, he kept in contact with her, couldn't leave her. Each time they had met, it had been dangerous for him. In fact, he had begged her many times to come and join him, to work with him, to make her own choices.

Jan knew they worked well together, played well together, loved well together and that was a bonus. Jan knew that leaving the department and working with Ward was a big step, for both of them. In the department they had been told what case they were to work on and who they worked with. Would they be able to transition into this equal partnership, and share the risk? Now, was the first time that he had ever given Jan cause to worry about whether he was ready for this change as well. Jan was deep in these thoughts when she felt his thought drift onto the edge of her mind.

'If you want the job, we'll do it, but,' he couldn't bring himself to say it, only through his thoughts could he tell her. Even with the 'but' it was enough for Jan. Ward had spent the time on the way home contemplating just how he thought the rest of their lives would be now that the future, a future, had finally presented itself to them. It was hard. She was right; he really did enjoy working as a free agent, and the time he had taken off from it had been hard. He had missed the work. He had also missed working with her, even though he had enjoyed the time off with her. He smiled as he thought about the days, and the nights. Ward also knew there were things he could have done, maybe even should have done. Now that she knew the jobs were coming in, he was also sure, really sure, she wanted to work on them with him. They could now become a team. He had wanted this so much and now it was right in front of him, just one last step.

There were lots of ways to lose someone. He knew that more than any one else. One sure way was to stifle them. If he stifled her, he would lose her and not just for a while, but forever. He had thought about some of the jobs he had done after leaving the department. How would she have felt all those times if she had known what he had been up to? He didn't want to think about that. As he approached the steps she jumped in front of him, blocking his way.

"Do you mean it? I don't want to do a job, any job, halfway," Jan stood there and waited for his answer. Ward could see the spark of life in her eyes, the smile that just barely touched the corner of her lips, but what he really saw was the woman he had fallen in love with.

"Yes," although he couldn't bring himself to look her in the eyes after he said it. There was the last bit of realization she had to reach yet. He had gone through it, now it was her turn.

"Are you okay with this?" she could tell that something was bothering him. His eyes avoided hers, his muscles were taut and his face expressionless.

"About as okay as I will ever be with it. But you're right," he moved around her and went up the steps, "We've always thrived on this type of work, and it is what we do best, and we'll do it together," there, it was done. She still had one last step, and Ward would have to let her get there on her own. Soon.

Jan knew this was the partnership he had always promised and what she had given up everything for, but there was still something he wasn't telling her. That was bothersome. When would they get to that open and honest communication? They couldn't work together if he wasn't willing to share. People got killed that way. She took a deep breath, and the sense of calm that had escaped her for days began to creep in as she carefully followed him up the damp stairs. Jan remembered the mantra that Ward had needed and repeated as she had recovered, patience, but just how much longer could they wait?

Even as Jan and Ward walked back up the steps into what they called their safe place they knew that Mexico was not a place everyone would call safe. For many, braving the dangerous and illegal crossing into the states and leaving Mexico was their only hope. It would give them a chance at life, for them and their family. Over the last few years the borders in each state had been reinforced, all except for one, Arizona. The desert was a harsh and brutal place, even in spring. Daytime temperatures could reach into the nineties and nighttime temperatures back into the fifties. Without protection it wasn't the place to be, boiling and then freezing. Most knew this but with the stronger border enforcements on the neighboring states, it left them very little choice of where there were going to try and cross. Arizona was still the best place to make it across the border and not get caught.

Things were changing though and that meant using coyotes, or smugglers, to increase the chances of success to get across safely. Most coyotes were open about what they did here in Mexico and they knew the type of people to look for. Prowling the bus stations they could almost be assured of a couple of fares.

2

Once they were back in the two-bedroom apartment, Jan went toward the computer and Ward went toward the bedroom door. She needed to see the message; he needed to give her space. The apartment was small, but contained all they would ever need. In one corner of the room was a computer set up that rivaled the best seen in any governmental department and could be illegally connected to most. A small, but efficient kitchen led off from there. The windows of the living room opened like doors onto a balcony that overlooked the ocean and all the furniture in the room focused on the view out the windows and balcony door. Two bedrooms and a bathroom led off the other side of the living room. In the master bedroom, which was where Ward headed, the windows had a spectacular view of the ocean and beach. The on-suite bathroom was modern, the bedroom comfortable and large. The other bedroom and bath were just that, another bedroom and bath, not that they ever expected guests. Ward stopped just short of the master bedroom door, pausing to take a breath first, he then continued.

"I'm going to shower. I suggest that you read the e-mail from Eddy and then do your research. No one here is going to hand you a file that contains all the information you need to know," he turned to look at her. "Do your research. Then decide if it is a job you want to take on. Remember there are things to consider."

Jan watched as he went into the room and contemplated joining him in the shower for only a second. Glancing back toward the computer, she knew he was right; there was a lot to consider. Sitting down she started up the machine and waited. Pulling out paper and a pen from the drawer, Jan noted the date at the top of the first page. After the computer started she opened the e-mail that Eddy had sent. He seemed about as close to Ward as one could be without knowing who they really were, or as she now had to remember, had been. Only one other person, besides her, was as close to Ward as Eddy, only Eddy had no clue that they were mind readers.

After leaving the department one might think it would have seemed easier to let the secret slip. That was far from what the reality of it was. More than before the truth would need to be hidden in order to allow them any type of normalcy. Of all the people who had left the department, of which she now knew of only one other, each guarded their secret carefully.

Hey, it started out friendly enough, *Have you fallen off the edge of the world? Haven't heard from you for a while. Know you two might not be up for a problem yet, but I have one if you are interested. Seems like a few colleagues of mine are missing relatives (females) they sent money to, to have them brought to the states. Not all of it is on the up and up so they are afraid to go to the authorities to ask for help. Most likely wouldn't get any help from anyone else anyway, only a free trip home to visit the family if you get what I mean. This doesn't seem like the normal request. They have used chicken farmers before, so it isn't like they don't know what to expect, but something has gone really wrong. They say they aren't even getting ransom requests and they haven't been contacted by any of them at all. If you are inclined to help, send me a line,* and it was signed Eddy.

Jan knew the slang that Eddy had used in his e-mail. Coyotes were the people who transported illegal aliens across the Mexican-American border. Often the people they transported were referred to as pollos, chickens, no more than a meal ticket for the coyotes. It was an underworld ignored by most of the world and nearly impossible to stop. Coyotes provided a way for desperate Mexicans, as well as other nationalities, to cross the border into a world that they thought would bring them endless opportunities. Often, the situations they encountered were in actuality no better than what they left. Most are able to make some extra cash and send it back to their families in Mexico, but the human price they pay is high.

Treated as substandard humans, with pay and living conditions that usually matched, only a few were really better off. Over the last few years the patrols had gotten better on the borders of California and Texas. Arizona was the only place to get across with any certainty. The fee to cross was high, being somewhere between a thousand and two thousand dollars to take a long treacherous walk across a very unforgiving desert. A higher fee would almost guarantee being transported across the desert in some kind of vehicle that had been modified to hide people, but not always.

Jan jotted down a couple of items on the paper and closed the e-mail. Two things she would need to know would be where and how they contacted the coyotes. Had they contacted a coyote in the same town or had it been many different places? She would need a full description of each missing family member, a picture if possible, and the names of those missing. She then began to access the files available to her from the Bureau of Immigration.

Ward's computer set up was something to marvel. She had never had better access to files and information at the department. It seemed that no program locks or encryption codes could keep him out of the main frames of any computer. After Ward had unceremoniously, and without permission, left the Paranormal Enforcement Department, or 'PED' for short, he had managed to gain access to the data bases that the government had to offer. The ones that Ward had not gained immediate access to, he had worked on breaking the access codes; after all that was one of his talents the department had trained him for. Now Ward had a network of information that would rival the top officials in any US department; security clearances were not a problem for him, nor did he have to wait for permission anymore.

Jan looked at her notes and something made her skin crawl. If these people and others had disappeared, where did they go? Who did these coyotes meet up with after they crossed the border? These were not run of the mill coyotes. Jan wrote down a couple more questions. What types of things could these people be used for besides earning a few dollars for getting them across? Could it be drug related? Or was it worse? Was it slave labor they were selling these women for? Jan knew what else these women could possibly be sold for, none of which would be good dinner conversation. She wanted to know if any other governmental agencies were working on cases related to this. The last thing she wanted was to cross anybody else's path. Jotting down information she read and might need, she continued to read the computer scene. She now had two groups of people she would need to keep track of during this investigation.

Jan knew that finding a coyote and getting across would not be a problem. The problem that existed was to find the right coyote and try and follow the path the missing people had taken. The more information Eddy could get to her, the better. Jan suddenly remembered that she was not the only one that could work the case. Depending on the information they received, how they proceeded in the job would have to wait.

Jan looked at her questions again and tried to think of any other information that she would need to know before starting the case. First, exactly who, and how old, were the people they were missing? Next, did they know which coyote the missing people were going to use to cross the border? And, at what place were they going to cross? How much was the fee and was it paid up front? For now, that was what she needed from Eddy. Hopefully, he would be able to get some of this information for them, without it there may not be a case.

Now the next set of questions was more for Ward. Was there anyone buying people from coyotes for unknown or known reasons, or is this a new and dangerous trend? Some of the other information would have to be collected as the case went on. Jan decided that she may need to make a list of agents and agencies that could be working any related cases as she read through the list. This may be important; it wouldn't be good to run into anyone they didn't want to see while they were looking for the missing people. After all, they wanted to be missing people themselves. As she scrolled down the computer screen over and over again, she noticed that there weren't any names she recognized in any department working on any cases that would be related to coyotes, or illegal entry from Mexico. That would be a bonus for the both of them. That's when she understood what Ward had been waiting on from her.

Ward looked over her shoulder and nodded his head as he read the questions on the paper that she had written. A small drop of water from his wet hair dropped onto her shoulder. There was still one question she was missing, and it was the one he needed her to contemplate. He picked up the pencil and added that one question, 'Is it worth dying for?'

Jan contemplated this question. When working with the PED department, they were given jobs and there was never a question of if they would do the job or not. Safety was a concern, but not a choice, at least not theirs. It was calculated and weighed in some office, in some place far away from the agents themselves and once all the pros and cons were settled, the assignments were handed out. Now on her own Jan had to decide if the job was really worth all the risks? Could they get the results they wanted? Could they stay away from the people they needed to?

Maybe Ward was used to this but Jan realized she wasn't. The question took her off guard and she took her paper and walked away from the desk and over to the window. Looking back out to the ocean, she watched the waves play on the top of the water as she thought. This was what Ward was trying to get her to see, all this time. She hadn't come around to it herself; and he finally had to place it in front of her. The pelicans and the seagulls seemed to be dancing on the wind. Ward sat down on the couch behind her, not trying to disturb her thoughts, but waiting for the question he knew would come.

"How do you decide?" Jan didn't turn around.

"Babs, it's different every time for every job and it's never easy," Ward didn't continue. Jan didn't turn around, but simply stared out into the ocean. Time stood still for a while as the sounds of the ocean seeped in.

"Can you get Eddy to try and find answers to these questions?"

"Maybe, the illegals tend to keep a lot of the information to themselves because of immigration. They shy away from most people; afraid anyone could and would turn them in. Since they seemed to have opened up this much to him, I'm sure he'll get at least part of it as long as he can convince them they will get help with no strings. I'll send out an e-mail to see what he can get, or already has," Ward walked over and took hold of the paper.

"Good. As for the last question, I think I'll take a little time and think about it. Don't make any promises to Eddy," Jan still hadn't moved. She was not so worried about the dangers of the job, but the dangers from the agencies after them.

"Not as easy as you thought it would be?" Ward watched her move toward the door. He enjoyed watching her, but he didn't enjoy seeing the struggle she was going through. He had been through it, the transition from agent to free agent; she just needed to take the last step and he couldn't rush it. Until she made that decision he wouldn't contact Eddy though.

"Maybe the choice is not as hard as I thought it would be," and Jan walked out the door and up the small flight of stairs to the patio that was covered with red clay tile and adorned with all types of plant life to give it a cozy tropical feel.

On the way to the beach, Jan avoided thought. As she began to climb down the rocks, thoughts crept back into her head. Each step she took down the rock face seemed to add on another set of questions; all the questions seemed to have the same answer. It wasn't as if she hadn't faced death before; on some jobs that seemed to be the norm. It was more the fact that she now had the choice.

Taking the job Eddy had offered was not the question. Jan had to find an answer for the last question given to her. Her answer for Eddy had to be yes, and the dangers from the agencies would just have to be. Once they had the information then they could proceed how they saw fit. Jan was feeling something else and Ward was giving her room to experience it. It wasn't a totally new feeling.

She had felt it before, just once, as she had looked at people on the street after she had escaped from the department for the last time. It was a feeling of total and utter freedom to do and say what she wanted. The idea that she could run away and be free of all the things and memories that held her to what her life had been. The easy way would be to continue on as normal, helping others, taking on assignments and solving everyone else's problems. But no, Ward wouldn't allow her to mindlessly follow that path unless she truly wanted it.

Feeling the warmth of the sun on her face she realized that this was truly the question that needed answering. Was this what she really wanted? The wind brushed her long brown hair off to the side as she sat down and closed her eyes. Taking deep breaths she fell into a profound meditative state, one that she hadn't been able to achieve for what seemed like forever, and she let herself go.

When Ward felt her meditation begin he walked over to the phone and started to dial a familiar number. He couldn't wait much longer to contact him, it wouldn't be right. He listened to the ringing on the other end and then the familiar voice answered, "I'm here."

"I need more info," the conversation right now had to be direct; they would have time for small talk later.

"It doesn't look pretty. Called a friend, says that the market for women has reopened big time, both here in Phoenix and in a few other cities in the Southwest," Eddy took a breath. "Looks like these people may be involved."

"That's what I thought," Ward walked toward the balcony again. He could see Jan out on the rock. He could feel her; knew how relaxed she was.

"Going to take it?" Eddy didn't mince words, but Ward could tell that he wanted an answer.

"I'll get back to you on that," and with that he concentrated fully on Jan, "Jan wants it, but she has something to figure out yet. Same things we had to figure out. I'll be in touch soon."

The first thoughts that seeped in during meditation were centered on a time before she became involved with the PED. A faint smile brushed her lips as she remembered how excited she had been to get into college. She was going to study psychology. It had been hard to complete the first year, let alone four years. Money had been tight, but she had entered her fourth year at the university with a renewed feeling of success. She was sure she was going to make it. Her family had never been supportive of her choice and therefore they had never been a part of her college life. By the end of her third year, they had barely spoken to her.

At the end of her fourth year, when she was about to graduate with her bachelors, she was approached by a group of psychologists to join them in a study. At the time they had appeared to be psychologists. She had never heard of the group they worked for, but they offered her a job to do what she loved and had worked so hard to achieve. Assuring her that this work would become part of her masters, and later her doctorate, she signed on. The promise of conducting groundbreaking research, continuing her education, and make enough money to make this all happen had been too much to pass up.

It was with this group that all her experiences in her public and private life had started to change. Slowly, instead of being a college student on the edge, she had unknowingly started on a journey in which there was little hope of her returning to a normal life. Slowly her choices had been taken from her. In fact, it had been so slowly that she hadn't even noticed at first. All contact with her family had ended over a two-year process and in that time she did earn her psychology masters, as promised, but it had cost her.

When they told her she had no social life, no family life, no life to speak of except with the group of scientists that had once so long ago recruited her. She had watched her ability to assess people's feelings grow, but they promised more. With the carrot dangling in front of her, she took it, moved to Phoenix, and from that moment on, lived without a choice of her own. Completing over three different covert training camps she was well past trained and ready to move on. Over the next year Jan had learned the finer points of reading minds and working for the government as an operative. The more departmental work she did, the more she became the department. She thought it had been perfect, until she had met Ward.

Silence came over her mind as her mind returned her to the present. She sat just listening to herself breath for a while. The ocean lapping at memories that Jan had thought were long gone and buried. Slowly her thoughts drifted back to the first assignment and her first and only partner, Rob. They had developed an easy friendship, a father-daughter relationship, over the years. But the first assignment together wasn't that way.

Rob was new to the department, but not to the world of

espionage. He had been with another agency, and for reasons that later became clear to her, transferred to the PED.   On their first assignment, or test, together all they had to do was gather information from an organized crime group in Phoenix. Pick up some easy information and return to the office to report in. It sounded less complicated than it became. In essence, what it had been was a test to see how well they worked together. After the introductions, power struggles and the planning session they began.

They had chosen to go to the casinos and just listen in, both with Rob's ears and experience and her mind. Rob being a veteran of other departments was doubtful, to say the least, of listening to this 'young girl who thought she could read minds' as he had put it to their superiors. He had never said it to her, but she had heard it all the time from his thoughts. She had never shared that with him.

When they entered the casino they separated and began to work the room. Walking around the back of the casino and the near the private rooms, she got a lead. She went up to Rob and tried to encourage him to follow it with her. Without any other indicators, Rob refused to follow her lead in the casino.   They argued, but they stayed together as a team even if it meant losing that lead. What they didn't know until the debriefing back in the department was that it had been a set up, to test what would happen. They had passed. Once the information was confirmed, Rob began to change his mind about her abilities and their partnership began.

They were good memories, maybe not the ones she had planned as a child, but good memories. Jan slowly opened her eyes and understood why Ward had turned down the other jobs. Her future had to be her choice; it belonged to her and only her now. It was freedom, and even Ward wouldn't take that away from her if she wanted to choose another path for her life. Choice was something she had not been allowed much of. It was something she needed to have and understand before she could continue with her life, the way she wanted it to be. 'Shit,' she thought. She hated it when he was right.   Opening her eyes she turned and looked back up to the balcony. She saw him standing there again; and this time, there was a knowing smile on his face as he leaned, head tilted at a cocky angle looking down at her. He then turned and walked back into the apartment.

Ward had been watching Jan meditate. He often did this from the balcony as she sat on the rocks deep in thought. He found it relaxing just to watch her, and today was no different. He saw her laugh, felt her laugh, and knew that she had made the final leap into the present. She was whole. As he walked back into the apartment and over to the computer he knew that the last thing he ever wanted was to have her in danger. It truly scared him, but that wasn't the woman he had married two years ago.

He sat down at the computer and started up the links to the departmental computers. He wanted to see if there was any information on coyote activity. He knew that Jan had already done some of this work, but he also knew that double checking information was a necessity for safety. As he sat and waited for the links to connect, he remembered the first time he had seen her.

He was about six years younger. He had just finished an unscheduled overseas assignment and was coming back to the United States. Both Ward and his partner had reentered the country in L.A. on separate planes, and as Phoenix was the closest office decided to go there for a while until all the reports were completed. Over the years he had spent with the PED, he had two partners. His current partner, Gregg, thought that Phoenix would be a good stop. That way they would be able to catch up with some old friends. Gregg would never have guessed what came next.

Walking into the office and over to claim an uncluttered desk was when he caught his first glimpse of her. She was hunched over a desk. It wasn't as if he was a novice, but something about her was different and he hadn't even seen her face. He could only see the back of her head and the brown hair loosely tied in a ponytail. It wasn't reading her mind, he wasn't even about to try that here, but there was a connection, an attraction, even without reading her.

Ward didn't know if he had stared too long, or if his thoughts had slipped somehow into hers. He didn't even know if she could read minds, but she turned to look at him and smiled. It was a smile that spoke volumes. Their eyes locked, his breath caught in his throat, and that was all the encouragement he needed.

From that moment on they had taken every chance they could

to get to know each other, in all senses of the word. It started with coffee and lunches, and as the relationship progressed it led to late night desserts and more. It hadn't been easy, they were usually on assignments in opposite directions, but there was something between them, something that neither one of them could escape from.

Later he had transferred to Phoenix to be closer to her, although that's not what the official request said. His move had been a good fit. It meant a change of partners for Ward, and that had been a positive. Ward and his partner had not been getting along. It hadn't been a good fit in the beginning and it was getting worse. Gregg and Ward had not been seeing eye to eye for a quite a while and the jobs had been not been going well. The department had approved Ward's transfer papers and moved him, silently thankful that Gregg stayed in Virginia.

He had been reassigned a partner in Phoenix, and it seemed to have worked for a while. It also gave him a chance to work with another friend that he had gone through training with. He had been stationed in Phoenix as well. The most important thing to Ward was Jan. It was when he had been reassigned that he got to know her more intimately as well. They even worked a few jobs together.

The more they were together the more they wanted to be. It was not only the fact that they had achieved the ability to freely roam through each other's minds, communicating without words; they had connected even deeper. They became inseparable any day or night that they could afford to be together, but they didn't allow anyone to know about it. Later, when the department learned of their growing involvement, they had surprisingly encouraged it, for a while. But it wasn't long before they began to frown as they saw their control slowly slipping away. They were forbidden to see each other, and they complied, at least until the department thought that it was over.

After that, Jan and Ward met in secret. They never again worked together. He finally left the department under unfavorable conditions and officially charged with criminal activity. Even that didn't stop them. At first Jan thought that maybe the charges were true; but as they continued to meet in secret she learned without a doubt that he was not guilty. She never really knew just what had happened until a couple of months ago when it had been necessary for her to learn about it. They had married in secret and now lived together in secret away from the department that they had been entrapped in. Deep in his thoughts, he never heard her come in. He never heard her move soundlessly across the room behind him.

She was skilled and he was distracted by his thoughts. She had seen his thoughts, carefully picking at them so that he would not detect her. Slowly she came up behind him and when her hands touched him, tracing the muscles in his back, he turned off the computer and stood up in one fluid movement unalarmed and totally aware of her now. His arm reached out to grab her. She ducked just as quickly, slipping away into the bedroom knowing that he would follow. With the information he wanted from the computer pushed aside; he walked toward the bedroom, removing his shirt in the process.

3

It wasn't until the next morning that either Ward or Jan got back to the computer. Without any thought, Jan opened Ward's e-mail account as he finished up in the shower. When the program finally opened, a letter popped up on the screen. There, in front of her, was a note from Eddy.

"Glad to see that you two have decided to join the world again," as she read down the note she could almost hear Eddy saying it. "Got a bunch of good descriptions, information and even some names. Give me a buzz and I'll let you know the details." Jan closed the e-mail before Ward could enter the room and she walked into the kitchen to fix a quick breakfast. This news would be better on a full stomach she decided. Hearing Ward come out of the bedroom, she called him over to eat breakfast before he got a chance to read the new e-mail. Ward sat down at the table and picked up the spoon. When he saw that she had boiled eggs and made toast he knew that something must be up. Jan never did anything more than toast for breakfast, or something that might resemble it, when she made breakfast. Although when he cooked she was always happy to finish off eggs, bacon and any other fixings that might come with it, if he made it for her. He gave her a knowing smile. Letting her stew a moment, he began to eat.

"Eddy e-mailed. Sounds as if he has what we need to get started," she took a breath and looked at him. "Ward, we're taking the job," her voice held an air of confidence. Ward continued to eat and didn't look her way. "Did you hear me?" she had expected some kind of reaction and when none came she was surprised.

"Yes, and okay," Jan looked at him confused and Ward finally stopped eating and looked back at her, "I always knew you would want to, you're just like me, but you had to know that yourself. You had to have the choice. You see it took me a few months away from the job to want to go back and then nothing could stop me. I figured you wouldn't be any different; just wanted to give you and us, the time first," he continued with breakfast. "I also had to be sure that's what you really wanted," Jan made a face he didn't see and took a sip of coffee, choosing not to respond to the last comment he made.

"Eddy wants you to buzz him to get the information. Now we just have to plan out the details before starting," it was routine procedure, and that's one thing Jan knew would never change. There was a plan, always a plan A and B. The plan was there for safety, for routine and for each other. It was the routine paperwork and research that made all jobs safer.

After breakfast they sat at the table with paper and pencil determining their roles and options for this job. As the plan began to develop, Ward could have told Jan that he wasn't happy with the risks she would need to take; but the risks on any job like this usually never changed. They had always taken risks and that was one of the many hazards of what they did. It was also what they liked to do, and they had the best training. And after all, she was probably not going to be too pleased with the risk he was going to take either. Both being in the same emotional boat made it easier, as well as more difficult, but they tried only to focus on the job, not each other. Jan realized that she had never asked Ward the most important questions before she had decided to join him on his, and now her crusades. She had only just assumed the answers. Being on the other side herself now, it was time to find out the answers. She had to wonder just how they would get justice for those who had been wronged? Who did he call? Just how did he do all of this?

"What do you do after you find and catch the bad guys?" Jan rested her elbows on the table, folded her hands and rested her chin on them. She tried to look casual. His left eyebrow raised a little as he raised his head to look at her straight in the eye.

"What do you think I do?" he had issued her a challenge. Looking at her sarcastically, he awaited her answer. Jan looked back into the eyes of the man that she thought she knew.

"Well, I would hope you find some way of turning them, or the information, in to the correct authorities," Jan was beginning to feel a bit uneasy as she tapped into his thoughts, not sure of what she might find there. Knowing that it might not be the answer she would want to find, she stopped and waited.

"I'd like to tell you that every job ends up with the bad guy in jail, but you know differently even from your past experiences with the department," he let her into his thoughts now, sharing their past experiences, and then just his past jobs after the department. "Most of the time it works out the way everyone would hope. I can get local authorities, or friends to help out. But there are those times when the goal is the most important thing to keep in mind and the bad guys go free." Jan could feel his pain from those experiences that had not worked out the way he planned. She didn't miss the clouded thought in the back of his mind that her last assignment in the department had been one of the ones that had caused him pain. Knowing that, she decided to let it go and get out of his thoughts for now. As always, the mission was what was important. Determine the goal and plan the mission; the rest of what happened was, of course, the icing on the cake or the fly in the soup. Some things in their lives had changed though; now they decided the goal and what was important. This case was promising to be as big as some jobs they had worked in the past, not the biggest, but substantial. No one in the official world would take it on yet, not without some more proof or people who could fight for their right to be heard. Ward had watched her face and her thoughts, as all the worlds collided in her head, and the crystallization of who they were now, became clear in her thoughts. Ward smiled as he saw the realization dawn in her mind and in her face that they were the vigilantes, the ones who fought for those who had no one to turn to. They returned to planning out the mission with a renewed sense of vigor.

It wasn't easy for them to work together. There were now two leaders with no one to hand them their orders. Jan noticed that it had been a while since Ward had coordinated with others or equals. He was definitely used to running the show. Many times, Jan needed to remind him that she was also capable of making choices, not just taking orders, as to how they were going to gather information, roles they would play and in what directions the investigation was going to go. In the end, after their roles were set, they planned most of what they were each going to doing separately; only occasionally checking with the other to make sure their plans would mesh together. It seemed an amiable relationship, and as they picked at each other's minds during the process, both consciously and unconsciously, they were able to keep the goal in mind, as well as keep the plan on the same track.

After they finished the planning stage, and the job was recorded on paper, it was clear that Jan would be in need of a completely different wardrobe. Ward looked her over and decided the tan that she had gotten would help. They looked at each other, and Jan knew that the best person to help her shop would not be Ward, but on the other hand, she did know who to call on for the stylistic flare she would need. Ward nodded at her and she left the table without a word. They both knew where she was headed.

Jan didn't fancy the idea of who she was about to talk to, or have to get by. Jan left the apartment by the patio entrance that hid them from the rest of the world. Knocking on the Garcia's door the person she least wanted to answer the door did, Mama Garcia. Most of the time Jan was always happy to spend a few moments talking with her even if the same question would always come up, "When are we going to see some little ninos?" In her fluent Spanish Jan would always say they were not ready for them yet. She didn't say that they would probably never be ready for them. As always, Mama Garcia would just 'tsk' and shake her head at Jan. This discussion was just not in her plans right now. Mama Garcia envisioned a house full of babies and more on the way. Somehow, they were not looking through the same glasses. Mama Garcia would have liked them to settle down, to stop all this nonsense. Without really knowing who they were, she would never completely understand why they could never stop what they did, and did so well. It was a programming that could never be undone, now, or ever.

"Is Manuel around?" Jan spoke fluent Spanish and sounded like a native. She had always been good with languages. Being able to pick up on the subtle nuances of a language by reading other people's minds had always just polished off the edges, and made her sound like a local. Mama Garcia gave her an inquisitive look.

"Porque?" why, there it was, the question she wanted to avoid. There was plenty going on in her head, and most of which Jan picked up on whether or not she wanted to.

"I need to discuss where I might find some specific items to buy," Mama Garcia was about to ask another question, and then realizing she already knew the answer she just turned to leave. Jan noticed that as she turned, her shoulders drooped just a bit more, and for a moment Jan did wish she could be the person Mama Garcia would want her to be. But as quick as the moment came, it left.

When Manuel entered the small living area, Jan waved for him to come outside, knowing that the conversation was about to take a turn that Mama wouldn't like or approve of. It would be better, easier on all, if her ears never heard it.

"Manuel," she spoke in English to him just incase there was anyone close by listening in, she didn't want to make it too easy for Mama to hear and understand, "I'm in need of some clothing that would make me look more like a native. To be a bit clearer; a native that is about to illegally cross the boarder."

"Why?" it was an honest and question, "You are an American, you can go across any time you want. Even Ward does it and he is wanted. Planning something?"

"Yes. Now, where can I get some clothes?" she wanted to bring him back to the topic and away from the job. Manuel just gave her a look. Manuel was not a person that could be of much help to them, only cover if necessary. It had been Manuel that Ward had had to save ages ago, and at times he was too eager to try and return the favor. She knew that Ward had also promised the Garcias that Manuel would always be safe from the trouble he was in, and this is why they took such good care of the place for them. It was also one reason that it was easy for them to stay quiet about the location of the apartment, they didn't want Manuel ever put in danger, and they knew that Ward lived in a constant state of danger when he was away from this place. Right now though, all Jan wanted was the clothes she would need to complete her transformation.

"It will be hard, you don't look Mexican," Manuel folded his arms and looked her up and down quickly, and then again slowly. He wasn't totally being honest.

"I'll deal with that later. Will you help me with the clothes or not?" she just needed him to give her a location of a shop, but she could see that it wouldn't be that easy as the next question came from him.

"I will go. What size?" Jan decided not to fight it. It would save her time.

"Eight or small, and make sure they are realistic. A small old bag as well to pack in, one with a wide strap if possible," she waited until he met her glance again, "By the way, the sooner the better. Can you have them to me by tonight?"

"Do you need them to be from any particular region of Mexico, or other Central American country?" Jan shook her head no. The only thing she thought would really be important on this job was that she was female, "Then I can have it here by tonight."

"Thanks, I'll be by later to get them," Jan turned to leave then stopped. Turning back toward Manuel she asked, "Wait, can you drop them by so your mother won't worry?"

"I understand. Yes. You are planning on crossing the border illegally? It is dangerous," Manuel was still looking at her, this time with just a hint of concern in his mind. Jan smiled, letting his concern for her touch her heart.

"That's what I'm counting on," and Jan, turning, went back through the patio gates. This time as she walked through the beautiful garden patio back to the apartment, she hardly noticed the beauty around her. She was busy thinking about just how she was going to pull off the rest of the costume. She felt alive again. There was an excitement she felt when she thought of working again, and as she bounced back into the living room of the apartment her thoughts were interrupted.

While she had been up talking with Manuel, Ward had been talking to Eddy. It had been a conversation that left him just a bit unsettled, and Jan picked up on this. Eddy had given the information they had wanted and more to Ward. His conversation had been a good one with the day laborers that were missing relatives. It hadn't been the first time that people had gone missing, but like Eddy had said, and they had known, the other leads were too cold. The migrants had known it when they had told him stories of their relatives that had disappeared, so he had left the other information out. Mostly it was about people who had never wanted to meet up with them really. What they needed to focus on were the ones that they knew were missing for other reasons than ones of their own.

Ward had discussed his plans with Eddy and arranged a meeting place back in Phoenix. Running down the list of what they would need, Ward checked that Eddy would be able to handle a change of clothes, and even a change of cars. Eddy assured him that he would have no problem with either. Ward also let Eddy know whom he would need to contact for him before he got back into Phoenix. Those people existed on both sides of the law. Last, Ward asked Eddy to arrange a place for him to stay for a night or two, explaining that the apartment he had for emergencies was no longer available. Ward refused to stay with Eddy, knowing that it would put him at a higher risk than either one of them were willing to take. If for some reason his place was watched, or checked on, Ward would be a risk, and not a good one.

There were positives. He would not have to dodge the department anymore to meet up with Jan. They would both have to avoid contact with anyone who would inform the assistant director of their whereabouts. Neither one of them wanted to be invited for a lengthy stay at the department by the assistant director because there would be no way to ever leave. In one way it would be easier, in another, there was now no one in the department to run cover for them anymore. Ward thought for a moment, maybe he still would for Jan's sake? Things had changed when Jan had left and maybe not so much for the good. With this feeling still on the fringes of his mind, Jan had walked into the apartment. He handed her the papers that he had made notes on, and left the room to be alone with his thoughts.

Jan watched him walk away, and didn't question him. Looking down at the papers she saw all the information that she would need, the names of the missing women, their ages, the dates they were at or near the boarder, where they crossed, and where they might have met the coyote they used. The name of the coyote that had been used by the people already in the US had not been included in the information. They were probably trying to protect them. Then she read the information she needed most, the descriptions of the missing women. Strange thing was that the age of the women didn't seem to matter much. One of the missing was only sixteen, one was twenty-five, and one was even in her early thirties. There seemed to be nothing in common except the fact that they all crossed from the same place or at least that was what their families had assumed. The only conclusion that Jan could make was that whoever was making these women disappear wasn't picky about the age of the person he took, just the looks. This would help her out. Even though she wasn't bad looking, in fact she was good looking, toned, and evenly tanned, but she was no where near the age of sixteen anymore, and was definitely looking at thirty in the rear view mirror age wise. She would be able to look the part of a twenty year old, but there would an added advantage if they weren't picky.

The next page contained all the information that Ward had gathered for himself, and who he needed to contact. He had made an assumption as to why these women disappeared. From that, he planned where he was going to start his part of the mission. Most of the information he had collected led in one direction, and it wasn't a direction that either one of them liked. All the information that Ward had gathered was written straightforward, in list form, without any emotion, and in a style very familiar to Jan. Jan was glad to see that he still used the same format that they had polished between them over the years. This would make working together easier as she would know just what to expect, and how to read through it efficiently.

While Jan would be busy gathering the information that she would need to hopefully locate both the missing people and the coyote, Ward would be investigating the other side of the coin, or what they feared was the other side of the coin. As they both were well aware of, most of the illegals, and even American nationals that were missing women didn't have a happy life. They had been treated more like slaves and less than human, they could only hope they would be able to find them before it was too late. Assuming that they were still alive, that would be their goal. The only way to know for sure was for Jan to illegally cross the border, and Ward to approach this investigation from the marketing side as the leads steadily grew colder and colder. Ward had made a list of people to see, on both sides of the law, in the Phoenix area. The list was gotten from the files of Border Patrol, the CIA, and the FBI. Some of the names on the list she recognized from other times and crimes when both she and Ward had been with the PED department. Some of these people had been watched for many years. Almost every department, at one time or another had some kind of records on most of these people. The only thing that they had not been able to do yet was to bring them to trial for anything but minor offenses. They had been put on a list of other probable crimes, such as drugs and weapons running, but to Jan's surprise, nothing had ever transpired. These were the people that would be the most knowledgeable about new comers in the field and the most arrogant, as they had never been caught or burned by any department. They may also be the most helpful with information in order to preserve their territory.

Ward also listed, when possible, the people he knew who worked for each of these organizations. By knowing some of the names, it would make getting into or dealing with the organizations that much easier. This is the side of life he would try to infiltrate hoping to pick up any leads about the missing women. At this point, Jan was unsure of whether he would pose as a middleman, or a new player. Most likely it would just be a quick decision he would make when standing in front of someone depending on what he could pick up from reading the minds around him. His way in was not going to be as clear as Jan's. Neither role was without danger, and neither one of them dwelled on that fact.

Jan's goal on this mission would be to put at least a couple of these groups out of the business of selling women, and catch the coyotes as well. Keep the goal in mind she thought, no matter what else they discovered. Faceless people with no advocate, migrant workers who only supported the economy of the US, and they were their only hope right now. They needed to return all three of these people to their families, whether or not they were legal residents of the United States they were part of the human race and had basic rights. They, at the very least, needed to find out what happened to them.   In the best of circumstances, they would be able to do it all. Jan didn't want to dwell on what the worst could be. She had never dwelled on it before and now was not a good time to start.

Ward had been listening in on her thoughts undetected from the other room for the last five minutes, and he could tell that Jan had finished digesting the information on the paper. Ward had also come to some conclusions himself that he was not prepared to share. He came back into the room quietly. At first no words passed between them, only random thoughts, feelings, and a few fears. Each knew the risks that were involved in this puzzle. If they were honest with each other, they would have to admit too that they were each more worried about the other than themselves. They stared at each other, still no words passing their lips, and now no thoughts being shared. There was nothing else to share; it was like old times, and the beginning of brand new times. There was no safety net on this one, no one for backup besides each other and anyone in Ward's network. Ward was the first to move and he walked into the kitchen.   A moment later he came back out and handed her a cold cola from the fridge. He gave her a peck on the cheek and Jan took the cola and smiled back at the man she had loved from the time they had met. It was funny, but they were finally at peace with the decisions they had made and with that unspoken understanding. Jan broke the silence.

"Nice work," she held the papers up. It broke the ice, and that is all she wanted to do.

"Still think this type of work is for you," Ward walked over and sat down in the overstuffed chair looking out to the ocean. As he leaned back, he casually crossed his legs. He took a sip of cola, looked back smiling at Jan, and waited for the answer he knew was coming. She walked over to the corner of the couch closest to the chair and sat down, propping her legs up on his.

"Were we ever meant to live any other way?" She let his smile spread to her lips. Both sat and finished off their colas without finishing off the conversation. Staying in the moment they just looked toward each other, sharing nothing but raw feeling. Slowly the thoughts changed over to the problem at hand. They sat letting their plans formulate in their minds separately. Slowly their minds started to wander together again and in an easy exchange of information each knew everything the other had planned. Reading minds took energy, but they had found that reading each other never did. Still, they didn't move for about half an hour and they didn't talk. It wasn't until Ward took out a piece of paper from his pocket and handed it to her that the verbal conversation began again. Jan read it. It contained one name, number, code and address on it. He watched her read the paper as Jan's one eyebrow raised. She had a look of amusement on her face when she stopped reading and had digested the information.

She had always known that Ward must have had contacts within the departments, but this one was special, different. As the question began to formulate in her head, Ward answered it before she could even voice the question.

"He's one of my contacts in Phoenix. He's still in touch with the agency, and he will pass any information on to the appropriate departments without any questions if he knows you're with me. He never believed that I went bad and still trusts my judgment. His information base is large enough as you can see, so he just doesn't let the authorities know the information is from me," Jan read the address again. It was an interesting cover. Not unexpected, but interesting. Memorizing the address, code name, and given name she handed the paper back to Ward and he continued the conversation, "You won't have a phone. Nor can you count on keeping hold of any of the money probably, and Eddy may be busy with me. I also make it a policy to never stay with Eddy. He doesn't need that kind of trouble. If you need to contact someone, he's a trustworthy contact. He can make calls to any of the people you may need, and have the bad guys picked up. And, if you need, he will put you up for a few days. He will also know how to get a hold of me. Just give him my code name, and he is familiar with yours as well."

"Does he light up the bat signal, send up flares," Jan could hardly contain the teasing sound in her voice as the next set of words came out, "or is it your superhuman hearing that he relies on?"

"I prefer the red phone," his mouth twitched up at the corners as he answered. He grabbed at her legs as she pulled them away playfully.

Jan knew that she didn't have any contacts, which she knew

of, in the department right now. She had burned a few too many bridges herself for any of them to willingly stick out their necks for her. She also didn't have enough time to contact any old friends who may be willing to work with her, given time. Over the years they both had a network of names on which they could rely. She could have always contacted Rob to have him arrange for an arrest, but not if he wasn't in the Phoenix office. There was also the problem of him associating with her. She knew that Rob would be no help, if she needed someone to stay with, it just wouldn't work. When she was still with the department, Ward had never once asked her to do anything on his jobs. She knew that it kept her reputation clean. She couldn't risk getting involved with the department again. Neither of them had left on a favorable basis. Maybe this was because one really was never allowed to leave. If the department found either one of them, they would be kept, jailed within the department of course, for an undetermined amount of time. No trial, no lawyers, and no one they could count on. She was told on the last job with the department, it could be a lifetime. If she were jailed with them this time, she would not find it easy to get out, and she didn't want to have to try.

"Interesting contact. Is he still on active duty?" Jan placed her feet back on the ground and picked up the empty bottles. Getting up, she began to walk to the kitchen.

"Not really, but I wouldn't put it past anyone that retires to still have connections within any department. As you know, no one really ever leaves," Ward smiled as he said this for they both knew they had left, and were now being hunted by the department that they once had worked for. Ward sat and watched her pick up the soda bottles and walk away. There was a knock on the door, and as Jan went into the kitchen Ward went to the door. Jan could barely hear the voices, but could tell the conversation was in Spanish, and knew who had to be standing there. She walked back into the room in time to see the door close and Ward holding a small, old, tattered bag filled with what she could only assume would be her clothes for the next week or more.

The bag was nothing more than an old cloth backpack that had seen many other good uses. As she looked it over she saw that it would suit her needs quite well. She could clearly hear Ward's thoughts in her own head, 'Want to try them on now or later?' Jan only smiled, trying to erase some of his fears, and took the bag.

"Let's see how I'll look," she took the bag, and went off to change into who she was going to become.

4

Jan had gotten dressed long before the sun had come up and Ward had packed the Explorer quickly as neither one needed very much, just the one packed bag each. Ward needed to get across the border before changing his identity. He had packed a couple items he would need for his role change. It fit into a small bag, no bigger than the small bag that they had always carried for the jobs they used to work on. The idea of the small bag had been both a habit and a necessity when working with the department. It would be less to lose on an assignment if it were left behind, expendable. Important items needed to be kept on the body, or in relative safety, and anything that was needed for daily routines usually could be gotten wherever a person was. It also made an agent more portable getting through airports and across borders, as well as quick.

Jan walked over to the window in the bedroom that overlooked the ocean and opened the curtain to see the last rays from the moon bounce off the ocean in the distance. Looking out to the deepest depths of the ocean she wondered where the dolphins were at this moment. Closing her eyes she made a silent wish, a prayer that they would both return here safely and quickly. Not something she normally did, but now was as good a time as any to start a new superstition. Ward walked out of the room without saying anything. Jan turned and followed Ward out the door and out of the apartment.

They got to the top of the stairs, crossed the patio, and went out the ancient gates, to where the Explorer sat waiting. They got in and closed the doors without saying a word, both mentally preparing for the job ahead of them. As they drove away from the relative safety of their hideaway, Ward popped a CD into the player. It was soft and eerie music that seemed to fill every corner of the vehicle. It was the CD Ward played when he needed to reach a level of calm and consciousness that seemed to be beyond his ability at the time. The sound of the Native American flute filled every crevice of the vehicle, calming and soothing their nerves, as it worked its way into their very beings as well. Jan was unsure of what problem he was grappling with; and decided that waiting until he was ready to discuss it with her would be the prudent move. Letting the music again fill every spot in her brain she nonchalantly placed her hand on his leg to reassure him of her presence as they drove. She could feel Ward's muscles begin to relax in response to her touch, and she could feel some of his tension fall away.

When the first two songs had faded to the back of their memories and the third was about to begin, Ward turned off the CD and glanced over to see if Jan was still awake. Jan, without turning her face toward him, opened her mind to let him know that whatever the topic may be, she was willing to discuss it with him. At first they didn't talk, at least not out loud. He started to slowly share his thoughts with her, mentally letting his mind wander into hers, and hers back into his. There were fears. Crossing the border illegally at any time would be dangerous, but there was an added danger for both Ward and Jan every time they crossed. They now had to be careful every time they crossed the borders. Ward had made it easier to cross with the casual friendship he had achieved with one group of border patrol officers. His fears for Jan were different. Crossing illegally left a few more items to chance. They had planned and emotionally prepared for their identity changes and for the dangers they would both face, except for one. Jan had half prepared for it, but the danger still existed and there was no way to make it all better. Who they were and what they had done in the past had always been dangerous. The criminal elements were never nice, but there was now an added group of people actively looking for them, always looking for them, and it wasn't only the criminals that they had to be careful of, it was also the department. This was what was truly worrying Ward. One slip could cause the entire operation to fail, and their lives to be ruined.

"Don't get caught crossing the border. If they get your prints I don't have to tell you what will happen next. Gregg and the guys will get to you before immigration can even walk you back to the bus for Mexico," his voice a lackluster tone as he referred to the current department head of the PED, and his previous partner. "He won't ever give up, not until he gets both of us now." Ward would know better than anyone else what would be in Gregg's head. Over all the years that she had known him, he had never shared why they had split up as partners. It was unusual to request a change, but not unheard of. Ever since then, though, Gregg had been almost out to get Ward, catch him on anything he did wrong. He had even tried to get Jan to lure him back to the department in exchange for her freedom and future at one time.

"I don't plan on getting caught, and with any luck, the name I'm using will give me just enough cover if I do. Most of the time the border patrol just sends you back without getting your prints completely processed first, or at all. Not a good policy, but with the amount of traffic that crosses the border here, and is caught, it is understandable," the conversation was over as quick as it had begun, and they drove on in silence. Jan's mind wandered back to the arrangements they had made if she were to get caught. She was going to use the name Isabel Garcia Lopez. If there were any problems, the phone number she would give them would be Manuel's cell phone, in Mexico, or a phony address in Hermosillo. Ward arranged this when Manuel had dropped off the clothes, and then later shared it with Jan. He was to pose as her brother if she called. Most importantly, he was not to let Mama Garcia know what was happening, they didn't want to worry her anymore than necessary. Manuel would be good cover, and would come to meet the bus if necessary. Ward left a vehicle available for him to use for just such an event. Ward and Jan tried hard not to involve the Garcias at all if possible, but sometimes they would use Manuel as back up.

The drive through what could only be described as a dusty, sandy, low scrub desert was fairly boring if one was not in love with the desert. They didn't talk for hours and barely shared their thoughts. Jan watched the scenery as they traveled down the nearly empty roads through the countryside. As they passed through the small towns she would watch the locals walk along the streets and glance unnoticeably at the Explorer. She drifted in and out of a restless sleep, and when it was about noon they stopped to grab a couple of sodas and a taco with everything, from a vendor on the corner. The place looked as if it was well kept even though the wood that held the stand together was well worn from the years of weathering, and the paint was almost nonexistent from sun and wind. There seemed to be a lot of people enjoying the food and just as many waiting to be served. They finished eating quickly and got back into the Explorer. As they got back in, Jan and Ward started a small conversation that had nothing to do with the job they were about to embark on. It was just simply small talk. The small talk seemed to loosen up their minds as well as their muscles. As they talked about nothing of importance, the tension seemed to drift off on the wind that passed through the vehicle. Most of the drive was done, but they needed to get to Hermosillo before the last bus left for Nogales. Jan had printed out the schedule yesterday to make sure they didn't miss it. One more day could mean that they would lose a lead. It could also mean that there would be more people preyed upon and lost. On this job, time was everything. They also knew that the full moon was tonight, and for the next couple of days crossings would be favorable, and frequent.

Ward drove for another hour and a half. He then pulled over to the side of the road on a dusty and sandy turnaround that barely existed. Off to the side there were the remains of a table and what might have been a trash container at one time or another. The Explorer jostled to a stop and he turned to look at Jan. They were just outside of Hermosillo. Ward wanted to ask Jan if she had everything she needed, but he already knew she did. Words would not serve his purpose right now. Instead he just stared at her and she returned his strong gaze with one that was equally as strong. Knowing what he was thinking without even reading his thoughts, she allowed her thoughts to mix with his to let him know that she was feeling the same. To ease the tension and create a diversion, in her thoughts she went over what she had in her bag, and going over the premise of the legend, or persona she was about to adopt.

Jan had placed two thousand dollars in the bottom of the bag, and had a bit of extra cash sewn carefully into the straps of the bag where it would be hard for anyone to know it was there but her. It was a less likely place for someone to look, and even if they did, she had it well disguised within the folds of the fabric. She had carefully packed the bag to look like it contained nothing important. A couple changes of clothes, a few bread rolls bought from the local bakery, a bottle of water, a ragged old pad of paper, a pen, and an old rosary that Manuel had tucked in the bag before he gave it to her. The bag looked old, shabby, and lacking in the many items she may be in need of to protect herself, but in all reality it contained all she would possibly need or want. Ward had always been baffled by her choice of items. It wasn't standard equipment, but it always seemed to get her out of trouble when she needed it.

She had taken the time to hide the other items in both the straps and in the lining of the bag that she was carrying. They would not be things easily detected, found, or if found, that anyone would care about. In one part she had put her favorite item, a small package of rat poison. It had gotten her out of quite a few fixes in the past, easy to hide, easy to use, and easily replaced. Inside the bag she had included her favorite lock pick that she had once loaned Ward. When Ward had returned it to her, she had placed it in her apartment and left it there. On her last assignment she was almost sure she had lost it forever, but somehow, Ward had gotten it for her. To anyone else it would look like an old pen, but it had been a lifesaver for her many times, and a keepsake given to her by an old, and dear friend. Jan had taken the time last night to haphazardly sew the bag with one package of dental floss, twenty-five feet long, which only added to the authentic look of the bag as well as adding to her supply of tools that she may need. She had been careful not to cut the floss, as she never knew just how long of a piece she might need. After glancing at the bag, Jan gave Ward a quick affirmative nod to let him know she was ready. Before he put the car back into drive, Ward leaned over and let his finger gently trace her face and then cup her chin with his hand. His hand rested there for only a few moments before his hand moved farther down her body and at the same time he kissed her with a passion that she could feel deep inside both her mind and her body. Then, pulling away from her, he put the Explorer back into gear and drove back onto the road without a word. The transformation between lovers into working partners was just getting started.

Ward and Jan pulled into the small town of Hermosillo early in the afternoon. Hermosillo was where they had decided that Jan should catch the bus up to Nogales, the border town in which she would try and hire the right coyote to take her across. Being dropped off in Hermosillo would cause less suspicion than if he dropped her off in the border town itself. This way she looked as if she was on her own, and alone. It made her a much better target. It had been a long ride from the cool Pacific coast of the Baja to the warm dry mainland of Mexico, but a necessary trip that they both hoped would prove profitable.

As they pulled up to the small, old and dirty building that served as the bus stop, ticket booth, and information desk, she turned to look at Ward. His thoughts were open to her. She could tell that there was a plurality in his thoughts. This was not a new feeling. The one problem all mind readers faced was that people could, and often did, think of many things at once. It wasn't something that was planned, but weeding through it was the skill, not reading the thoughts as some people presumed. He was beginning to prepare himself for his transformation into his legend, character, as well. Ward was both exhilarated and worried about what was going to transpire and it wasn't something that Jan was surprised to read from him, she had the same feelings. The idea of working again was intoxicating to her in one way, but on the other hand it would mean that the person she most loved and trusted would be in danger. She had the same plurality going on in her head. His thoughts were also busy going through his plans for the rest of the day, wondering if he would make the small, informal border crossing he used before the officer he had become the most friendly with went off duty. They sat stopped for a few minutes watching the people around them before Jan got out of the Explorer. Leaving the personality of Jan behind, and adopting the role of Isabel completely, she walked the ten feet up to what was left of the old iron bars of the ticket window. Ward watched as she talked to the man on the other side of the barred and glassless window. Ward listened in to both Jan's and the attendants thoughts, and quickly knew that all was going well. The guy on the other side of the window had already decided that she was in a business type relationship with Ward, the oldest business most likely by his thoughts, and now she needed to get back to where she worked out of most of the time.

Jan's thoughts were predictable, focused on duty. She was amused by the attendant's thoughts, but careful not to let on. She was also glad that they had decided on this as the drop off place rather than the border town where they would have drawn even more attention, and suspicion. After she completed the transactions for the ticket, she then placed it all in her bag.

Jan turned and returned to the Explorer. Getting into the passenger side of the vehicle she wore the little smile on her face that Ward knew so well. It was the smile of satisfaction of being on a job. What was on her thoughts she didn't say out loud, but she did share them with Ward and found out that he had picked up on the entire conversation she had had at the ticket window. She could feel the eyes of the man who had sold her the tickets on her, so she leaned over to Ward and French kissed him. Not wanting to waste the moment Ward returned the kiss, and after a couple of minutes they pulled away. They stared at each other lost in the moment. It only took a couple of minutes before Jan broke the silence, her voice sounding just a bit out of breath.

"The bus will be here in twenty minutes," she didn't finish the thought out loud, she didn't need too. Jan leaned back on the seat, mentally preparing to step out of the Explorer and into the world of Isabel until the job was complete. Ward turned to look at her and what he saw never ceased to amaze him. They had learned how to blend into any situation, or any environment, when they had been trained, but Jan had always had a special knack for it, and he loved to watch her prepare for her role in the moments before she left. He didn't know if it was her college studies that had made her so good at this, or if it was just a talent she had. What he saw before him was not the Jan he knew. She was there, but buried deep inside, keeping her feelings safe from others, and only barely accessible to him. Of all those people that could and would see her, all would truly believe she was a native of Mexico. She looked the part, her clothes, her hair tied back into a ponytail, and although she would be considered a light skin Mexican of mostly Spanish decent, he knew that when she got out of the car, she would put on the rest of the act for all to see. There would be no question if she was authentic or not by anyone outside of this vehicle. By reading the minds of those around her, she could change her actions, mannerisms, and expressions all in a split second to fit with the area or to adjust the character as needed. She could tweak her role to fit anything she would need. That was one of the many reasons why mind readers were so valued, and a top-secret commodity within the government. The government had put a lot of training into each of them and wanted to reap the benefits of it. With the training each reader had received and continued to get, they could work with any military or clandestine service that had access and knowledge of their department, maybe not the skills, but the department. That's one reason they were not happy to have two leave the fold. The numbers of readers weren't that great to begin with, and the years of training a costly investment.

"You know my number if you need me. My phone number is the same as always and I'll keep it on. Don't hesitate to use it," he knew she wouldn't need it. She was as good as he was at this, if not better, "If you need to contact any of the departments or local authorities, remember to go through my friend, it will keep your identity safe. If you aren't in Phoenix, give me a buzz and I'll see if we have anyone friendly near," with that said, he took a good look at her. He looked through her facade and reached back into who she really was. Their minds touched and what was expressed could never have been said with words.

"I'll be fine," she knew that he was worried. Not about the job at hand, it was something else, "With any luck we will have some good leads in a week and we'll finish early. Time is everything in this mission and getting in will be easier for me than it will be for you." Jan watched as he turned away and looked out the window. He watched the lazy life-style that they had grown accustomed to and the people, carrying their small bags of groceries, going by. A few school kids in their uniforms were on their way home, and he watched them laugh and joke with each other. Jan was picking up on his thoughts and was unsure of what she was reading. It seemed to her that he had no doubts that he could easily get into the underworld. For a moment, Jan wondered just how many times he had done this before. Ward interrupted her thoughts, "Don't get too many ideas, okay. Eddy and I have a few friends," the last word was emphasized.

Unsure of who thought of it first, they suddenly both looked at the ring on her hand. Even though they both wore the wedding bands on their right hands, not the left, they also knew that Jan couldn't leave hers on. Jan looked back at Ward, and in an instant knew just what she wanted to do. Carefully she removed the bracelet from her arm and the necklace from around her neck. It was a matched set that Ward had picked out for her. The bracelet Ward had given her on their wedding day, and except for one really bad time in her life she had never had it off her wrist. The necklace, that was an anniversary present, but it had ended up as a late present because of her and the PED department. Ward watched her hook the two together with great care. She then carefully removed the wedding band from her finger and threaded the chain through the ring. Placing her arms and the chain around his neck, she hooked the chains together again at the back of his neck, and slid the ring inside his shirt gently pressing it to his chest. She felt the warmth of his chest under her hand, and the warmth of his breath on her cheek. The beating of his heart quickened. Ward felt her warmth from the ring against his skin and he moved closer to kiss her, softly at first, and then they let the kiss deepen and their minds mingled making the most out of the last minutes they would have together for awhile. It was only seconds before he pulled slightly away from her lips knowing their time had come to an end.

"Take care, Babs," was all he could whisper in her ear before she slowly pulled away and got out of the car. Jan started to walk over to the bus depot, stopped and then started again.

She hated 'Good-byes,' so she had always chosen not to say any, ever. In all the time she had known Ward, she had never once said good-bye to him, not even on their first unofficial date. At first it had been just a bad habit of hers, and then after joining the PED she intentionally never said good-bye to anyone. She never even said good-bye to Rob, her old partner, when she knew it was most likely the last time she would ever see him. Jan thought that goodbye's were for those who were trying to close doors, and hide behind them. She preferred to leave her doors open, just in case. Or was it that she just never had the nerve to say the word? The only time she had ever said goodbye to anyone was to another agent. On the next job he went out on, he was killed. Now was not the time for her to struggle with those issues. Right now, not saying the dreaded 'good-bye' word to Ward was more of a superstition, a habit she didn't intend to break. If they never said it, they would have to be back together, and if not, then there would probably be only one of them left with regrets. With any luck it wouldn't be her.

Even for Jan it was a silly superstition, but lots of silly things keep people going through life, and this was only one of hers. Don't step on a crack, don't walk under ladders, don't break a mirror or it will be seven years bad luck, none of these she believed in. She smiled inside at the times she had broken a mirror and had never once associated it with bad luck. Most of the time luck was what you made it. Sometimes you have it, sometimes you don't. She began to read the people around her, truly leaving herself behind now. This would be a necessity, throughout the entire job, to survive.

The engine of the Explorer started up. She heard the transmission engage, and didn't stop. The sound was present for only a second. Jan turned, just so slightly, as Ward drove away. Jan watched Ward from the corner of her eye. Ward never once turned back to look at her. This was his superstition. He silently smiled at her in his thoughts. She held onto it as long as she could, and then slowly lost her connection with him. She stared at the road filled with cars, the smoke, the dirt, and the commotion, not seeing any of it. It was time to start the game, and to play for keeps. Jan turned back toward the benches made of old half painted wood, and she picked up on the thoughts of those around her. Slowly, she walked closer and closer to the benches leaving the persona of Jan behind her. With each step that she took, anyone that could see inside her head would know that she had become Isabel.

5

Jan had been bouncing along for about an hour with the hot dusty air flowing through the bus. It was the same road that she had just traveled along. There wasn't anything different about the drive except that it was a couple hours later, Ward was not with her, and it wasn't as comfortable. Jan stared out the window as the short man next to her snored, his head bouncing up and down against his chest. Outside all she could see was dry dusty desert once again. The mountains in the distance were the only things that broke the horizon, and they did little to make a desolate place look any better. It didn't seem possible that so many would choose to cross in such a bleak environment. It was hard to image that things could be so bad that people would chance conditions like this just to cross.

No one spoke to her; conversations were difficult on the old bus with the windows open and the air streaming through. The sound of the twenty-year-old engine rang in her ears and reverberated in her brain. The puff of exhaust that should have been leaving through the nonexistent tail pipe filtered into and through the bus. Add some chickens and it would be like any bus found in many third world countries. Luckily, Mexico was not so third world in this area. The ticket she bought was one of the cheapest you could buy to get back up to Nogales. No one about to cross the border illegally would be traveling in any kind of luxury to get to the border. All would be saving their money to pay the coyotes to get them across. Jan shifted her weight. The seats, also twenty years old, were just as uncomfortable as the rest of the ride, but to a lot of people on this bus, it would be their first steps to a better life. For some, she feared, it would be a ticket to what was still the unknown, not the American Dream. This was the side of life Jan was hoping to infiltrate and uncover.

It would have been the perfect time to practice her mind reading skills except that it would be intruding on personal moments, and memories in these people's lives. Mind reading wasn't something that was done just for fun; it was difficult and tiring. The bus was also packed with people, which at times made it difficult to sort out whose thoughts were whose. For Jan to try and figure out just who might be trying to cross, who was going to see relatives in Nogales, who had jobs, and so on and so on would be a daunting task if she only relied on her mind reading skills. If it was necessary, she would not hesitate to read anyone's thoughts to accomplish the goal, but now, with the ride just beginning, it seemed a waste of time and energy. Jan decided on a more old fashioned way of gathering information and to let her mind rest a bit.

The first thing she needed to do was to assess visually who might be the most likely people planning to make an illegal trip across the border. There wasn't a set type that went across. Those that were alone were always a good possibility, but there were many families on the bus as well that might be trying to cross. It wasn't unheard of to have whole families crossing with children as young as six months old. For what Jan was looking for, families would be of no help. She started to look at how people were dressed. Dress wasn't always the biggest clue either. Some very respectable looking people chose to cross. Not the ones with business suits, they were not riding on this bus, but the ones dressed in newer clothing were also a possibility. The coyotes Jan wanted to find were looking for women who were traveling alone, who were desperate. She only looked at the women who seemed to be traveling alone on the bus, because they would be the targets. She casually let their thoughts bounce off of her, paying only half attention to what she was seeing and just half looking for a thought that might become a lead.

Half an hour later, Jan had identified about five good candidates that might try to attempt an illegal border crossing. Now the specialized work that their group had always been known for would begin. She had to choose who to focus in on first, and who to wait to read until later, if at all. If the thoughts she wanted were not at the top of their minds, then getting to them would take a lot longer, if she could reach them at all. It was a more invasive technique to get to those memories that were not readily available, a possibility, but an intensive as well as invasive one. It was like building a house of cards. Sometimes making it to the upper levels were easy, sometimes all the work collapsed into a pile with nothing to show for all the work already done. Each time Jan looked through someone's thoughts, the whole process could easily be demolished by a random thought from the person she was reading or even another person nearby. An unexpected event that would completely change a person's train of thought could knock the house down and she would have to start all over again. All in all, it was truly easier to read those people who were thinking about the information she wanted, but not always a possibility.

Jan began to take a deeper look into the minds of the people she had picked. Hoping to find what she wanted right away, Jan quickly glanced at the thoughts of the five people she had singled out. Of the five, she identified two of the women that she wanted to take a deeper look into their thoughts. Of the two women she targeted, only one of them would make a good target for these coyotes. She was a young woman, about the age of seventeen. She was about two inches shorter than Jan if she had to guess, and she weighed in at maybe one hundred pounds, a little on the thin side. Her long, black hair was pulled into a loose ponytail at the back of her head, and she wore clothes that just fit her. In her mind Jan could see that she was alone and wanting desperately to get across the border to see her brother. She would make the perfect target. Her thoughts were almost transparent, too easy for someone else to pick up on even if they weren't mind readers.

As Jan sifted through her thoughts she discovered her name was Gabriella. She had been sent money to get across the border by her older brother in Phoenix, and she seemed to be worried. It was the worried part that Jan focused in on. She wanted to befriend her, and the fastest way make a friend was to have something in common. Fear was a good thing to have in common. It was one thing to find the lost women, but Jan also wanted to keep another one from disappearing. Taking a deep breath and closing her eyes, she continued her construction of the house of cards that made up Gabriella. One thing Jan was sure of was that Gabriella was scared. She had come a long distance, Oaxaca maybe, and was now unsure of where she was and just what was going to become of her. Her brother had told her to get to Nogales and then wait in the bus station near the border, or in one of the small taco stands just near the bus station, a coyote would find her there. She wasn't sure where she would spend the night, or if she needed to, or if she should just sit and wait. The idea of any of those choices was what made her nervous. If she tried to stay somewhere, how would she know where to stay, and did she have enough money? Was it safe to stay in the bus station at night? Just how long would she have to wait? Jan smiled as her questions continued to poor through Jan's mind. This may be the person that could help lead her to the coyotes she needed. Gabriella sat only three seats in front of Jan and there was no one beside her. Jan began to move toward her on the bus. When she was able to sit down beside her Jan closed her eyes and waited for about ten more miles before starting up a conversation.

"Hola, my name's Isabel. I'm going to Nogales. This is my first time there. Have you ever been there?" Jan started to display some nervousness for Gabriela to see when she didn't answer right away. She fiddled with the strap of her bag and didn't quite meet Gabriella's eyes when she looked her way, "I've not been there before, and I'm not sure how to find what I want."

"No, I've not been there," Gabriella was in no mood to talk. She turned and looked out the window again. Jan worried only momentarily that she would not be able to make a connection with her. On one hand she really didn't need to, but on the other it could be helpful. This coyote could approach anyone, and it might not be Jan to begin with or worse yet, not at all. If she made a connection with someone else, then she might be able to meet up with more coyotes than just the ones that approach her, doubling her chances of finding the right one. If the coyote group she was looking for approached Gabriella, then she could bring Jan to their attention; that would make her job a lot easier, and faster.

"My brother told me to go to Nogales. He's living in Arizona right now," Jan used Gabriella's details as her own to start building common ground between the two of them. "Says the work is good, and I need to come."

"Oh," Gabriella sighed her response. Jan could tell that she was slowly becoming more interested. Her mind was now not as fragmented as it had been, "How are you going across the border?"

"Um," Jan pretended to be a bit on the cautious side now. She began to twist the strap of her bag even more, "I have some money he sent me. He told me to go to Nogales and then some people would help me across."

"Coyotes," looking out the window, Gabriella didn't meet her gaze. Jan could tell she was beginning to close up again even though there was a little part of her that was interested. She had to break through this time or start again elsewhere. This time she used Gabriella's fear to try to strengthen their bond.

"Yes, coyotes. I have no other way of getting to the United States. But I worry I won't make it. So many have told me stories about their brothers and sisters dying in the desert; but my brother says it is a good thing to do," Jan turned and looked out the window on the other side of the bus giving Gabriella time to think.

"My brother says the same thing. Use the coyotes. He says it is safe, but I worry like you." Jan's face was turned away from Gabriella's, and although it didn't matter, she had been well trained not to ever let her emotions show, Jan thought bingo.

"A bit, but so many people do it, it must be safe," Jan knew it wasn't, but she also knew that by keeping this one close to her, she had the possibility of keeping one more person safe. They rode in silence for a while. Jan spent this time assessing Gabriella's thoughts and feelings.

Jan had never been a fan of illegal immigration, and in fact had worked a couple cases for the INS, or what is now called ICE, on it before only from the other side of the border. Illegal immigration was a problem, but not the way many people thought it might be. Most of the people who came into the country were looking for a better life. Looking for what could be called the American Dream; some found it, most did not. These were the people who lived their lives as migrant workers, traveling from one place to the other, never having a permanent home, and continuously worried about being discovered by the authorities, any authority, and being deported. If they were lucky enough to work in only one area, then they were subject to hiding in the groves and fields out of the sight of any type of officials, or living in housing that could be substandard and even dangerous with no resources.

Many illegal immigrants who made it across the border waited in substandard conditions in what were called drop houses, for transportation to other parts of the United States. For those that did make it, they forever lived with the thought that it all could be gone in a matter of hours if they were discovered. All of these people were the ones who considered themselves out of the loop of help, or protection, from the local authorities. They felt that if anything happened to them they couldn't call the police, they were running from them as well. That kept most of them vulnerable to all who would take advantage of them. As Jan looked out the window, she just hoped that she would be able to take care of at least one group that seemed to be preying on these people right now. Jan noticed that the bus was close to Nogales and she let out a silent sigh as she saw the poverty, pollution and criminal elements increase. Border towns anywhere were about the same. The people who lurked in Nogales were those people who waited to cross the border, who never made it across the border, and who could not afford the price and decided on a different type of work. Usually it was illegal activities that could fund their way again for another one, two, or twenty more tries at a later date. There were also the people who preyed on them, who tried to sell drugs and get them to take them across the border in exchange for a reduced rate. The list went on and on. Jan's concentration was broken, and she sensed it before she felt it. A hand touched her arm. Gabriella's comfort level was vanishing as she fiddled with her bag and her ponytail.

"Can we go together?" it was the words Jan had waited to hear. The words she had not only expected, but had wanted to hear from her.

"Yes, let's go together. It will be safer that way," she turned to see the smile on Gabriella's face, and it made Jan happy to know that yes, it would be safer for her, probably not better, but safer.

"My name is Gabriella, Gabby for short," Jan smiled back at her. Since Gabby was younger she looked to Jan for advice like she would to an older sister, "How do we do this?"

"We will have to find someone we trust to get us across. We will sit at different places, and then when we find a good coyote we will get the other and we will go together. With any luck it won't take us too long to find one," Jan reached out to Gabby, "My brother said that there are many that we can find, just to be careful of the ones that just want your money and will steal it from you. He said to pay only part of the fee until after we get across safely."

"Thank you," and Gabby turned again to look out the window, "I will worry less now that I won't be going alone."

The bus jumped and bumped along the rough road and into the small town as they traveled along about half an hour outside the border into the heart of Nogales. Jan looked carefully at the other person, a woman, which she had pegged just in case she couldn't break through with Gabby. Jan wanted to be able to remember her face; it may be necessary later to be able to help her as well. She couldn't risk losing her contact with Gabby, but she also didn't want to risk any more people than necessary.

Traffic increased, as well as the smell and pollution, as they got closer and finally pulled into the Nogales bus depot by the border. People crowded the streets, tourists, and locals, pick pockets, drug runners, and thieves. It was hard to tell who was who, unless she took the time to read each of their minds. Gabby was excited and was looking at everything with new and innocent eyes. It was just after sunset when the bus had pulled into the stop, opening its doors to the dangerous world that waited. Jan grabbed her small bag and helped Gabby with her bag that was about the same size.   From the look and feel of it though, she had a few more items in that bag than Jan had in hers. They got off the bus together and Gabby took a deep breath of polluted air. Jan could smell the car and bus exhaust, the sewage, and the cooking smells of the local eateries. It was not a mixture that was uncommon to the third world, but it still did nothing for Jan, or her appetite.

They walked into the sitting area together through the crush of people, the gangs, the poor and desolate until Gabby looked her way, waiting for Jan to tell her what to do. Jan already knew what she would tell her. She needed her to wait in another area so that they could both work the stop for coyotes. Jan also needed her to be close enough to read her, and anyone with her easily. If Jan found the coyote first she had already decided that there would be no way she would bring Gabby along, so she positioned Gabby just out of her sight. Gabby would have a better chance if she never met up with these people, and she was too young not to get that chance. Jan smiled as she walked up to her and gently directed her to a bench to wait at. They both knew that if they waited long enough they would be approached. What Gabby was most worried about was the cost of getting over the border. Jan worried about the cost as well, but it wasn't the same price tag that Gabby was thinking of paying. Jan walked just out of sight of Gabby, and sat down. She began to fiddle with her bag for something to do, all the while keeping a watchful eye on the people around her.

Jan wanted to reach out with her mind, but knew that she would need all of her energy later to explore the minds of those coyotes that approached each of them. She needed to be sure she got the right coyote. There was no way she would risk making that mistake. Jan also knew to keep a mind's eye on Gabby, as she was more impressionable than she was. That might make all the difference of who they would be approached by first.

Jan took a deep breath and focused in on Gabby when she sensed a man sit down next to her. He leaned in to talk with Gabby in hushed tones. From what Jan could read, they were discussing crossing the border to the States. Jan turned slightly so that she could both look at the man and read his thoughts. The man was in his late twenties, and his hair was slicked back and tied in what was the shortest pony tail Jan had ever seen and it stuck out of the back of his head instead of laying flat. He wore dark, mirrored sunglasses, which obscured his eyes from everyone he talked to, and a sports coat that was in good condition about five years ago. He smiled and chewed gum, and leaned back on the bench as if to say he was something special. As he discussed price with Gabby, Jan started to shift through his thoughts. With his attention on someone else, it made the process faster. She started looking for those he had approached before, faces first, and then names if he had them. He had seen at least one of the girls, Jan could see the face of someone that fit the description, but there was no name or other connection attached to it. Frustrated by the noise around her and the fact that this did not seem to be the right coyote, she continued to delve deeper into his thoughts, and ignore her surroundings. Her eyes went a brilliant green and small beads of sweat appeared on her forehead. Jan had forgotten about her surroundings for only a split second, and a split second was all it took. A man sat down beside her and touched her on the knee. Jan nearly jumped, but stopped herself in time. She turned to face the unexpected guest.

"Where're you headed?" he was a coyote as well. All concentration had been broken with Gabby and the man she was talking with. Jan turned to get a better look at the man who had approached her. Dressed in a leather jacket, fairly new, dark glasses, and baseball cap turned backwards, hiding all but a bit of his black hair. He was only about six inches taller than she was, but he had a good sixty pounds advantage over her. Jan never worried about being out weighed; she had learned ways that would make the odds equal if necessary, and things that would make even a three hundred pound bouncer beg for mercy. It was the newness of his outfit and the surety of his gaze that sent up the red flags for her. Leaving the mind of the coyote that had caught Gabby with little to believe that he was the one; she decided to look closer at this one.

"The States, to see my brother," Jan spoke, and his smile only grew wider. It was a smile Jan would have said belonged more to a lion preparing to devour his prey, not a coyote looking for spare cash.

"I can get you there cheap," he leaned back against the bench, turning to rest his arm over the back of it, and placing the other arm around Jan's shoulders. Jan knew that his attitude was too self-assured, slimy.

"How much will it cost?" Looking past his exterior and into his head she began to find just what she was looking for. It was merely under the surface of his thoughts. It was the names and faces of the people she wanted to find, it was easy, almost too easy. Jan had entertained the idea that she may have lost her touch when she was reading the other coyote, now she was sure she hadn't as the thoughts she needed to access were all right at the tip of her fingers, or her mind. He was too sure of himself, and she knew whatever the price, he was the one she was looking for to get her across the border. Given more time, probably a lot more, she would be able to see what had happened to these women she was looking for, but for now, she had to keep him on the hook.

"Let's say five hundred," the going price for crossing the border was at least a thousand five hundred, so to most people this would sound very good, or very suspicious. To Jan, this just assured her that she was onto the right coyote. Knowing that he was making money off the women he picked up and taking money from the women as well, made her blood boil and want to uncover his scam even more. Jan tried a quick look deeper into his head, and confirmed what she had thought. He had sold the other women into slavery. It wasn't just one type of slavery though; it was to anyone who had the money to pay for his cargo. She didn't have time to see was just who his clients were. A little more time and she might be able to discover this, if he actually knew who they were. He might only be the first step. A mind readers primary job was to collect the information they needed and then collect the evidence to support it. Without the evidence, there would be no prosecutions, or happy outcomes. She just nodded an affirmative as he leaned in toward her. "Meet me here in two hours," and he patted her thigh.

"Yes," but that was when the problem began. Out of the corner of her eye she saw Gabby walking toward her. With a quick look inside her head she could see that the other coyote had been too expensive and she seemed tired of waiting alone. When Gabby had seen Jan talking with this man she had assumed that it was a coyote. She had seen Jan give an affirmative nod and it was then that she had started to walk over. Jan was trapped. She couldn't hide Gabby's presence, and she couldn't shout a warning without blowing her cover. She had no choice, no options to turn to, so she pushed her emotions to the side as Jan had done so many times before.

Jan checked the thoughts of the coyote. And like any predator scoping out its next meal, he was ready to pounce on another one. His eyes seemed to almost glisten behind the sunglasses when he thought he could pick up another one so easily. His smile stretched across his face, and even though his eyes were hidden, she could tell they were looking her up and down. There was no way to stop her from coming up to the bench, no way to protect her from this madness now except to keep Gabby close to her and pray for the best.

6

As Ward approached the border between the United States and Mexico, he gave a wave to the border patrol officer he had always dealt with. As he pulled up to the booth, they exchanged a little small talk and within minutes he was across and on his way. It was not Ward's first choice to leave Jan in Mexico, alone. That's not how things were supposed to work, not even outside of the department. First rule of thumb, always have backup. Very soon he would take care of that. He wasn't planning on leaving her without backup for long. It was a matter of making the right contacts. Picking up his cell phone, he dialed a very familiar number.

"'Lo," it was a smooth deep voice that Ward had heard many times before.

"Hey, I'm back on this side," Ward announced to the voice on the other end of the phone. This man was a good friend of Ward's, as well as a-one-time talented crook and hit man. Eddy Darling, a large and well-muscled black man with an attitude about both his life and name, was once under Ward's watchful eye when he worked with the department.   Eddy had been relocated by the witness protection agency to Phoenix. To this very day Eddy swore that they had given him the name he now lived with as a joke, a bad joke. Ward had gotten the assignment to watch over him as a side job while he was in the planning stages for a larger operation. All Ward had to do was to make minimal contact to be sure he stayed on the straight and narrow. Developing a friendship, Ward had gotten to know and like Eddy. It was only months later that Eddy discovered that Ward worked for the government, and why he had gotten to know him.   Eddy had never been mad about what had brought them together; he knew there was something else to their friendship besides the fact that Ward had been assigned as a baby-sitter.   In fact, Eddy had taken Ward in when he suddenly, and under departmental suspicion needed a hiding spot.   Eddy had chosen to balance on the edge of the law by hiding him, but he knew it was the right thing.   It was soon after Ward moved in that they started working together, not only to right wrongs but also in business adventures to build the funds to support them.

Eddy had no idea that Ward, or Jan, could read minds.   It was a piece of information that Ward thought was better not known, by anybody outside of the PED.   What Eddy did know was that Ward, and Jan, wanted was what was morally right.   He found this to be more appealing than what he had done to earn a living, and signed on with them.   The cases they took weren't always what others would agree to focus on.   Ward chose the hard cases, the underdogs, and the unwanted.   Eddy admired this and this was how their partnership had begun.

"Good timing.   I'm off for the next couple of days and I can prolong that for as long as you need me," Eddy and Ward were also partners in real estate.   Eddy occasionally did construction on the side just to keep busy when there wasn't anything else for him to do. He didn't really need the money, but he enjoyed the associations with the other workers he got to know by being on the job.   Ward was his silent partner in real estate ownership, and they made a very good living off of it.   "Where's Jan?"

"Mexico," Ward didn't need to say anything more, Eddy would know what she was doing.

"With anyone?" Eddy sounded a touch worried, but didn't want to let on.

"She's fine and we'll get to her soon enough."   Even Eddy could tell that the conversation was over at that point.   He had known Ward long enough to understand that some things could not be changed, or even controlled.   "We're going to need a nice car to make an impression for this one I think," Ward passed the old and beat up Chevy truck in front of him as he continued the conversation, "Got one in mind?"

"Got one I've had my eye on. Meet you with it in let's say about three hours at the regular spot?" Eddy understood what Ward needed.

"Good. I'll need to make a van call on a friend. Want to ride along?" Ward knew who he would need to talk to in the Phoenix area. His contact had information on the matters that went on under the police's radar. With Eddy's next words Ward could almost hear the smile.

"You think I'd miss that? I always like to see him squirm," Eddy called out instructions away from the mouthpiece to the group he was working with. "Do we need anything else?"

"I have an extra bag, but you may want one knowing what we may walk into," Ward had brought his 9 mm with him across the border. "Also, what apartment do we have open? I need a place to stay. My place is no more."

"Got yah covered on that one. Later." The phone call ended there and Ward placed the cell phone back on the seat, Jan's seat. Giving himself a mental shake, he let it go and pulled it together as he pulled into the diner that he always stopped at. It was old and out of the way. The dusty parking lot was calm, as always, and the only people that would be in there right now would be the owner and a waitress. They hadn't fixed the missing lights in the sign; and he really couldn't remember a time that those lights ever worked. As he pulled to a stop, he got out of the Explorer and locked it. Being anything but professional would cost Jan her life. Walking into the diner with its yellowed lighting trying to brighten the darkened room, he smiled and waved at the waitress. Smiling and waving back, she knew what to bring him, a bowl of chili and a cola. Eating anything else at the diner might mean taking his life in his own hands. He finished it quickly and was on his way.

Fifty miles down the road, Ward changed his appearance at a small gas station that was on the way to Phoenix. He walked into the restroom unobserved and locked the door. Walking over to the sink he started to pull out the items he needed from his bag. On the edge of the sink he placed the bottle of hair dye and the gel. Pulling out paper towels from the dispenser he then leaned over and damped his hair. Watching carefully in the mirror, so as not to miss a spot, he began to apply the black coloring. His hair quickly changed to a jet-black color. Ward routinely and methodically, almost hypnotically, worked on his appearance, as he had so many times before; his thoughts began to drift back to last night. The reflection in the mirror slowly changed. His mind was replaying last night, when he had helped Jan alter her appearance. In the mirror he didn't see what he was doing at that moment anymore, instead he saw himself walk into their bathroom and take the bottle of color from her. He then carefully put the coloring on her hair, working it through her hair with his fingers, watching its light brown color change to a dark dull brown color. Earlier, she had applied a bit of a relaxer so that her natural curls would disappear. Ward could see his hands moving through her long hair as he rinsed out the excess color. He saw his fingers mixed in with her hair and the relaxed look on her face, eyes closed, as if she had no cares in the world. It had led into a long night together. As the image in the mirror began to fade, he now refocused his attention in on what he was doing, and started toweling off his hair and applying the gel. It was time to get dressed and move on in many ways. His hair was now jet black and neatly brushed straight back, held into position with gel. Ward put on a black leather jacket over a pair of black jeans and tight black tee-shirt. He put the bottles of coloring and the used paper towels in a bag and pushed them toward the bottom of his bag. He'd burn it later. Picking up the small pack he had carried in, he checked his appearance once more in the mirror. With a gentle tug on the corners of the jacket and checking on the position of his gun, he turned and left the bathroom.

It was early evening and still light, when Ward pulled into the Valley of the Sun, Phoenix. He pulled into a donut shop in the large shopping mall where two freeways crossed, and parked about twenty feet away from the door where he could see Eddy. He didn't see Eddy's truck so assumed that one of the cars in the lot would be what they were driving. Ward got out of the Explorer and hung his dark sunglasses from the neck of his shirt. His gun was in his specially designed holster, and out of sight. Eddy sat just inside the shop and picked up his donut and a cup of coffee as he got up and walked outside.

Eddy had also changed the way he normally dressed.

Picking up on Ward's earlier cues, he had dressed the part of a well to do businessman that made his living on the other side of the law. It wasn't hard for Eddy; he had been down that road before. Eddy was dressed in black tailored slacks, a black light weight sports coat that was also tailored for his bulk and his gun, as well as a dark blue, almost black shirt, collar open. He had trimmed his hair so short that he looked nearly bald, and it gave him the overall desired scary look to all who didn't know him. The large diamond that was normally in his ear was still there, and this time looked more appropriate for the way he was dressed. He was nearly done with the donut and about halfway through the coffee, when he walked out of the shop. He gave Ward a nod when he saw him walking toward the door, then took a quick look at his watch.

"Want anything?" It was less of a question and more for polite conversation. Eddy knew that Ward hardly ever ate donuts, coffee was another thing, but indulging in a donut was rare. Ward gave a shake of his head indicating he didn't want anything, "Sun's heading down, so we probably need to get going; otherwise he will be on his way back to the sewer." Eddy threw a set of keys at Ward and started to walk over to a solid black car. Ward looked at the vehicle and smiled. He glanced at Eddy for a split second and then back at the car. Eddy's face showed no emotion, but Ward knew he was happy to be riding around in this one for a while.

"Sweet," was all Ward could say as his fingers skimmed over the hood. It was a black BMW, Z3 with the top down. Ward knew that an image of money, and a bit of arrogance, might be necessary in this case, and was more than pleased with what Eddy had found.

"Found a great deal, and thought that this might fit the bill," they got in the car and Ward started her up resisting the urge to rev the engine. Pulling out of the lot, they both knew where they were headed.

The BMW that pulled into the poor South Phoenix neighborhood only got a few stares. Most people wouldn't want anything to do with what it symbolized. A man in his late thirties, looking more like he was in his early fifties, was selling popsicles from the old van that he had been using for years as an ice cream truck to children that stood in line in what seemed to be stifling weather even for Phoenix. Not that his looks instilled any type of trust, but that didn't matter because it was a rare commodity in this neighborhood.

He was about five foot ten and a very slim build. He seemed to always be sniffling, but that was from another bad habit that he had never chosen to break. His hair was black with greasy streaks of gray in places. It was uncut, unkempt, and pulled back into a raggedy ponytail. His clothes were old and in need of a wash. The years he had lived had not been kind to him, and the lines that were etched in his face made him look at least ten years older than he was. He noticed the black BMW turn down the street and slowly come to a stop behind his van. First of all, there was never a good reason for a black BMW to be in a South Phoenix neighborhood, and second, it was never good to have one pulling up anywhere near to where a person was. He didn't have many friends in this life and none of the ones he did have could even afford that kind of car. The only people he knew that drove those things were the ones he didn't want to talk with.

He started to close down the ice cream window under the wailing protest of the waiting children and even before the last kid was up to the window. He didn't look to see who got out of the BMW, just tried to shoo the kids away. Ward got a lock on his thoughts as he sidled up the side of the van, sunglasses in place hiding his eyes effectively. Once he reached the window, he slid the sunglasses down for only a second and smiled as he made eye contact with him. With the other hand he pushed the window back open.

"Now, now, you wouldn't want to keep these kids from having their sweets. Go ahead, I'll wait," pushing the sunglasses back into place, Ward leaned against the side of the van. He knew the van was a shoddy cover for all the other items, mostly drugs; he was selling from inside this bacteria ridden slushy machine. Ward had warned him once not to sell to the kids, or all bets were off and he would find a way to make the charges stick, or solve the problem himself. He was pretty sure with the information from his sources that he had kept his word.

"Hey, why don't you just go away, I don't know anything and I haven't done nothing either. I've changed," Rubber sniffed and rubbed his nose with the back of his forearm. Ward just smiled.

"Now Rubber, why should I believe that?" Ward had used Rubber as an informant many times before. In fact, it had been Ward that had given him this unique nickname. So many police charges had bounced off of him that Ward had started to believe that he was made out of rubber, hence the name. His real name was Carlos Nunez. Even if the police charges had never stuck, the nickname did. The only reason none of the charges never stuck was that he was an informer, for both sides of the law. Rubber was always on the streets, had many different contacts, and heard a lot of things. As long as he treated both sides equally they left him to his meager existence. It was the one place Ward knew he could start looking for information, maybe even get some answers, and avoid suspicion. He also knew another thing. If Rubber could avoid him, he would. As Ward waited he gave a nod so discretely that no one watching him would have been able to see it. Ward didn't want just anyone to see it, it was meant for Eddy. With that nod, Eddy moved away from the car and down the other side of the van, out of Rubber's sight. Ward had already seen into Rubber's mind. He had no clue Eddy had been in the car with him. After selling a popsicle to another child Rubber quickly turned to try and slip out the passenger side of the van. He, unluckily, ran into an immovable force, Eddy.

"Mother F...," Ward interrupted him before he could finish the phrase.

"Now, now, there are kids around Rubber," Eddy turned Rubber around, and Ward, now leaning on the old counter attached to the makeshift window of the van, smiled like a Cheshire cat. The last child had left knowing that he would never get anything if he waited and there were no other children near enough to hear the next part of the conversation. "I need some information Rubber."

"I don't know anything," he tried to give Eddy a push, "and tell your mountain here to get out of my van." There was barely enough room for one man to stand in the van and with Eddy behind him Rubber had no room to move.

"Now you're being modest. You always have something I can use, information wise, and if not you know where to get it," Ward ignored the comment about Eddy, as Eddy leaned into Rubber making it impossible for Rubber to do anything else but face Ward, "I need to know about some coyotes and pollos." Ward started to pick away at his mind just to save time.

"Oh, is that all," and Rubber let out a sigh of relief. "Just right down the road here," Ward interrupted Rubber with a wave of his hand and he stopped, afraid of what was next.

"No, I need to find a particular group of coyotes."

"Got a name?" Rubber rested his hands on the counter, as there was no room to place them anywhere else. Ward could tell he was feeling a bit more confidant.

"That's what I was hoping you could give me," not waiting for Ward to continue, Rubber started in.

"Are you nuts! Now who's sniffing something. You'd win the lottery faster than finding someone when you don't even know who you're looking for," Rubber started to laugh and the mountain moved closer, if that was possible, pushing Rubber into the counter and his breath right out of his lungs. "Hey, back off. If I yell for cops around here I could have you picked up for assault," looking right at Ward he continued, "and I know you're wanted for other things also." Rubber smiled and Ward could see the holes where teeth used to be. It was then that Rubber thought he had the upper hand, and Ward knew he was right. What Rubber didn't know was that Ward had also read his mind and knew what stash he was afraid they would find in the bottom of the freezer. Returning the smile, he answered the threat with a threat.

"I'm wanted by people who would lock me up in a nice little apartment, away from people like you," he left out the part that he still wouldn't like it. "You, on the other hand, must have something back there you wouldn't want them to see; and if my friend here just happened to knock it onto the floor by accident, you would end up in a not so nice place, with some new, very close friends. Plus," and Ward addressed Eddy this time, "didn't you see him dealing to the kids?"

"Yes I did," Eddy's deep voice rumbled from behind him.

"Shit. Who do you want me to find?" Rubber tried without hope to push Eddy back. Eddy never budged.

"Shouldn't be too hard. We need to find some coyotes who

are either new or have changed what they do with their pollos," Ward waved at Eddy and he moved back to literally give Rubber some breathing room. "Some women have gone missing lately. Traveled across the border with coyotes, maybe the same ones, maybe not, not too sure that's why we need your help. We want to find out who these coyotes are and what they are doing with their pollos. Easy right?"

"Oh yah, sure, could probably make one phone call and get all that information," the sarcasm hung in the air. He saw that Ward was not impressed, as his expression never changed. Wiping his nose on the back of his arm again he continued, this time without the sarcasm, "It's a very closed community. How long do I have?"

"I need this as soon as possible," Ward looked into his mind deeper and deeper. He could tell that he wasn't lying. It would take him a bit of time to come up with this information. They needed to be sure that there was only one group right now selling their hostages.

"What do you want this information for? Planning on changing professions?" after saying this, Rubber knew he had made the wrong comment. Eddy leaned back in, and if it hadn't been for Ward, the amount of pressure he used threatened to separate Rubber's top from his bottom using his own counter as the splitter. Ward on the other hand, waved at Eddy and dismissed the comment. Eddy let up, not completely, but he had dealt with people like this before and now each time he had to, he found it rather displeasing.

"Can I trust you to meet up with me here tomorrow, or do I need to leave my friend?" Rubber's comment had angered Ward, but it was nothing new. These people lived in defiance of the law and anytime they could try to rattle someone they would. Ward just refused to sink low enough to become infected by it.

"I'll be here, but I don't promise anything in just twenty-four hours," Rubber turned and looked at Eddy.

"You'll have something, I have faith in you," now it was Ward's turn to give a sarcastic smile. He nodded at Eddy and just as fast as Eddy got in the van, he left. "Remember, sooner not later," and Ward walked back to the BMW with Eddy beside him, never turning to look back. He didn't need to; he could read his thoughts and knew that the only thing Rubber wanted right now was to leave. Even before

Ward could get into the car, the van pealed away from the curb and sped off. The music box tones emanating from it as it sped off seemed completely unsuitable.

"That was fun," Eddy sat relaxed beside Ward staring at the back of the now quickly disappearing van, "Think he'll get anything?"

"Maybe. We'll make a few more stops tonight before getting a few zees and I have a message to send. I made a few phone calls earlier and located a few people and where they were going to be tonight." Ward pulled the car away from the curb and handed Eddy a piece of paper with a list of names and places on it. There was a bit of tension in the air, and Eddy had known Ward long enough to know what, or who, it might be about, Jan. In fact, he was feeling a bit of it too. Eddy wanted to tell him not to worry, but knew enough not to say anything. He had worked with her only once, but in that time knew he would never want to be on her bad side, or for that matter, Ward's either. Eddy watched the road in front of him as they headed back to pick up the Explorer and get it hidden away. Ward eased the car onto the freeway, not commenting on Eddy's thoughts at all. Some things were better left unsaid.

It was about two hours later when Ward was ready to meet up with the other contacts. Back on the freeway with the top up he looked over at Eddy and saw the same strong face he had gotten used to relying on, and truly the best partner he had ever had. Ward couldn't help but think that it was too bad that the first part of Eddy's life had been so screwed up or maybe both of their lives would have been different. Night had settled in and the lights of the city were quickly being put behind them. It was a starless night, yet not late enough for an empty road. The BMW slid easily around a sedan that was going about ten miles an hour slower than they were. In early March the days were warming and growing longer, but the nights were still chilly. Perfect weather in the desert for many things; perfect for golf, running, hiking, and perfect for crossing the border illegally. This thought was always near the top of his mind never too far away. Leaving someone completely without backup was unheard of in any scenario, but now they didn't have a group of people to draw on to help serve as backup when needed.

Eddy didn't have to be a mind reader to know what occupied

Ward's thoughts as they drove down the road; they had worked together too long. He was sure that Jan would be going across the border soon and like Ward, he didn't want to miss her on this side either.   He had been briefed on the plan, and even though he had worked with Ward many times, he felt a bit concerned about how this plan was to play out. Jan was to get picked up on the Mexican side; Ward was to find the buyers that they knew had to exist on this side. Once found, if they posed as prospective clients, or somehow got themselves on the payroll they would soon meet up with Jan. If plans went the way they should.

They were on their way to a casino located outside of Phoenix on a Native American Reservation just south of the city. It was about half an hour out of town and this casino was nothing like the ones found in Vegas. During the daytime they were filled with the over sixty crowd looking for entertainment, a quick dollar, and a cheap meal.   Later, at night, they were filled with hardworking people looking to make it rich on games of chance that had been fixed long ago to take their money and only lure them into a false sense of hope. What that meant was that some did win a few dollars, or even a few thousand, but compared to the amount of money taken in, it was only a drop in the bucket, chump change. These establishments also attracted other groups even later at night. It wasn't the type of people they encouraged, or even owned up to being in their establishments, but it was where they came.   Being out on the reservation avoided one set of laws in exchange for another, and sometimes a less enforced set of laws for some organized groups. It was an easy place to make and complete deals, and it was an easy place to get lost and be unnoticed. In this way alone, it was very similar to lives lead in Vegas.

Ward was certain he would find a couple more of his acquaintances out there, and if not, maybe even make some new ones. Rubber had been right about one thing, it was a big town and they were looking for a needle in a haystack, but that had never stopped him before. Most of the time he had found the needle he was looking for, it just took persistence. This time there were two different needles he needed to look for, one more important, but that couldn't distract him. If he wasn't careful, and didn't abide by their training, it could be a matter of their life, or death. Ward let his mind wander to another topic as he drove down the interstate. The car was quiet and the company good. Ward began to slide easily into his new character. Eddy sat quietly, never asking a question, and was simply there ready to work. The closer they got to the casinos the more Eddy started to fidget, his jaw tighten. Ward knew all too well that going into casinos was Eddy's least favorite thing to do and he avoided it at all cost, most of the time.

Eddy had never meant to get involved with the wrong crowd in high school back on the east coast. But once he had, it sent him down that path, and he had a hard time escaping it back then. The money was good, easy, and he was good at what he did. Eddy had moved up in the operation quickly to become the bodyguard, the muscle, the one handy with a gun. It was what had gotten him into trouble as he moved on from the high school bunch, to the local gangs, and then farther. Not sure of just how many people he had ever eliminated, no one ever asked, and he had never kept count. When he was told to make a hit he did it quickly and without question until the last one. It was that one in Vegas that caused him all the problems. It was a sloppy job from the get go and Eddy had known it. They hadn't given him time to set up and do the job right. If he had taken the extra time he needed, someone else would have been after him. It didn't take much to know that he was the one being set up, and Eddy had known it.

Eddy did the only thing he knew to do. He did the job, got caught, and turned states evidence on the entire bunch. He had been smart enough to know early on that the Vegas job was to set him up, to get rid of him one way or another, but he was too good and too smart for that. He had managed to complete the job and to turn them all in. Once under the watchful eye of the government and in their protective residential facilities Eddy had decided to do the only thing that would save his life, and possibly give him a second chance. It wasn't as if he had had an epiphany, he had just come to the realization that the friends he had made were ready to sell him out, so he had talked first. If it was going to be them or him, it wasn't going to be him. Once he started, he didn't stop. After the trial and sideshows, he had been hidden away in Phoenix, given a new name and job, swinging a hammer. Not a great new start like he had expected.

When he first arrived he nearly fell in with the gang crowd there. It wasn't until he met up with Ward that everything started to come right. It hadn't been until then that Eddy was sure of what a good friend was. They had met at a bar one night and begun to hang around together. Eddy never asked questions; in general Ward was able to get him better work and a fair apartment. In fact, it was better than the government had done. Eddy had no clue that Ward was just supposed to keep an eye on him and not interfere. It was one thing that Eddy had never figured out; why Ward had chosen to help him out and not just follow his orders. Funny how fate steps in, Eddy only learned later that it wasn't part of the government's assignment for Ward to help him out; the cash he had given or loaned Eddy had been from his own pocket. 'Who knew why people did what they did,' Eddy thought. They had been friends for a while before Eddy knew Ward worked for the government. All he knew was that Ward hadn't asked for anything in return for his friendship, a new experience.

Ward had only ever asked one favor from Eddy. When Ward left the department in haste he had needed a place to stay and someone that would keep it a secret. Eddy could relate to hiding out and being hunted. That was when their friendship had truly been cemented. To this day it was the only favor Ward had ever asked of him. Ward had never asked him to become a vigilante with him, it just happened. Eddy knew they made a good team. What was even better was a feeling Eddy had never known before, that he could and would make a positive difference when he worked with Ward. It was a different type of feeling, and one Eddy enjoyed. Ward had never asked, but Eddy had requested to help out. It seemed to do his karma good.

Now, Eddy had all he could ever have imagined out of life; only it was free and clear of crime, the wrong side of it at least. He sat in the BMW he had paid cash for and mused at the thought of what he would have had to do to get a car like this if he had still been living his other life. Best thing he would have ever gotten to drive would have been something like Ward's Explorer. Eddy watched as Ward pulled off the interstate and turned to go into the casino.

Yes, casinos had bad memories for Eddy, and whenever they had to go to one it was never any fun. As they approached the casino entrance, Ward felt Eddy's mental squirm. Ward pulled into a parking space and still looking out the windshield started up the conversation.

"You don't have to go in. I won't," Ward was interrupted. He didn't need to read anymore of his thoughts.

"I'm going in. They're only ghosts now," Eddy got out of the car and stood waiting for Ward to get out. Ward got out and smoothed his gelled hair back and slipped on the leather jacket to ward off the cool breezes that still existed in the midst of spring in the Arizona desert. His face set and stern, he looked every inch of his part and someone you would not even try to mess with.

Eddy looked the same as Ward, except the look in his eyes was even darker, more menacing, and scarier. Ward's gun was tucked safely away where it would be hard for anyone else to find, he looked back at Eddy.

"You're not carrying are you?" Ward preferred it when Eddy left his gun at home. According to law, and his conditions that had been stipulated by the government, Eddy was not even supposed to own a gun. Ward had to look the other way at times knowing Eddy had changed his ways completely. At times it had been a necessity for Eddy to carry a gun if he wanted him to be safe as they worked some jobs. This was not one of those times though when he would need a gun.

"Just my wallet. I'll know when I'll need the other," the conversation ended and they walked toward the door of the casino, shoulder to shoulder. Once they were in the casino, they separated quickly. Eddy walked to the left, Ward to the right; both sets of eyes carefully looking over the gaudily lit floor for who they might want to hold conversations with. Ward was looking for a friend, at least he had been a friend at one time and he was hoping that he still was. He was his only hope for any backup. Eddy was looking for the criminal element; the underworld that existed and brewed just beyond the reach of most law enforcement agents. Both spotted who they were looking after about five minutes of entering the building.

Ward sat down beside a man at the slots that looked about

ten years older than he was. He was about the same build, a little less fit and had more gray to his hair. He had on a white shirt and a tan pair of pants that Ward recognized right away. Ward didn't look over at the man next to him as he sat down; and the man didn't look back at Ward as he continued to play the slots. Ward began to be bombarded by questions and accusations right away from the other man's thoughts, even before he could start the conversation. This was a man used to dealing with mind readers. Ward pushed it out of his head and put a quarter in the machine.

"You're playing the wrong machine. It only gives you one chance to win," Ward kept his voice low, but knew that Rob heard it.

"The one you're playing doesn't give you a second chance either," Rob's words and tone hit their mark.

"You might want to give me a minute to explain," Ward watched as the machine rolled out only a pair. The other man chose not to respond verbally, but continued to push the questions mentally; knowing Ward was reading everything he was thinking. Ward mused at the fact that he had chosen the quarter slots, before he dropped another coin in the machine he was on, only to have it come up all lemons this time, "She's happy."

"And alone, and in danger," the other man didn't say anything more. Ward had expected this from him. He was good at what he did; after all, he had been Jan's partner when she had been with the department. They had worked well together, a good team.

"Not for long," Ward stared at the machine not seeing it at all, "Thanks for coming alone."

"That's how you do all your work right, alone. It's not right, or safe, or how you were taught," it was sarcastic, and after it left his mouth he regretted it, "Sorry, I'm afraid I don't have much information for you. Not too many new places on the list here in Phoenix, at least that we know about, but you already know that I'm sure. If they are selling them to the highest bidder, they could be anywhere by now."

"Thanks," Ward changed the topic. "Let's clear the air. As for the department, I see they didn't believe you either," no one had believed Rob's story after Jan's final assignment. Jan had gone out on a limb to save him, and if she hadn't, he wouldn't be sitting here right now. She had risked her life to save his, knowing that the department wouldn't believe who was really involved. They hadn't believed Ward a couple years before. That's what drove Ward out of the department; that and being criminally set up by the same man to take the fall, "Would she have been happier there?" Rob gave no answer to Ward's question. They both knew the answer. Rob wasn't happy anymore either, but knew of no other life, and was too close to retirement to lose it.

"There are a couple people in here tonight you should visit with, but you probably know that. Looks like you're dressed for the part," Rob had gotten a cryptic message earlier in the day on his e-mail, and after reading it decided that the best choice would be to follow the directions. That was why he was here. Not for Ward, but for Jan, an old friend, a partner. Rob had wondered what Jan had been up to since the last time he saw her. He hadn't been in good shape, and she and another person that he couldn't remember had taken him back to civilization after she had rescued him and given some much needed emergency medical treatment. That was when he had learned Jan and Ward were married, and had been for some time.

He had often wondered since then, how he had missed all the signs. Now that she had truly decided to follow in Ward's footsteps, he didn't know how he felt about it, but at least Ward had offered her some kind of commitment, something Rob hadn't thought he was capable of doing.

He didn't blame her, no, he just worried about her, her and Ward. Ward took on risks, like now, and Rob wasn't sure Jan had thought it all out. He also knew that if she stayed with the department, what she had loved doing she wouldn't have been allowed to do anymore. Her reputation had been dirtied; they had lost their confidence in her. She was burned. Either way she would be in a losing situation, if she had truly thought it through, maybe this way was best for her. Even Rob had been taken down a notch by the department. He had never been reassigned a partner, or even given fieldwork again. For the last six months he had been retrained and then given a desk job. It was ironic though; he now matched partners together.

There had been a small policy change. Partners were no

longer partners until one requested a change, or other grave circumstance occurred. Partners were changed at what seemed to be the director's whim. Rob had tried to talk to Gregg about it; had explained how partners needed to be together longer in order to be able to complete assignments efficiently and effectively. They needed to get to know each other, read each other's actions, and learn to use the skills of the mind reader to their highest potential in the most desperate situations. Somehow, Rob knew his opinion meant very little. He was seen as part of the problem in Gregg's eyes. It was a wonder to Rob that he was doing anything of importance at all. If Gregg could have gotten away with it he was sure he would be doing the filing.

"As for the people in here tonight, I've got that covered. I don't think these coyotes are selling out of town yet. I don't think they have had enough time to get that good or that confident from the information I've gotten from family and friends. We want to keep it that way. I'll get the information to you in the usual way so you can act on it if I find anything for you."

"Fine." There was no feeling in his voice.

"There is also another problem," Ward hesitated. He didn't like asking for a favor, especially not one from him, "With the extra border patrol assigned to the area recently, it makes crossing even more dangerous. I just need you to watch the computers for her and keep her out of the system if she's picked up and detained," Ward waved a waitress over and ordered a cola. The other man was silent for a while. He picked up his drink, an ice tea, and took a sip. Ward thought he smelled a bit more than ice tea in the glass, but wasn't sure.

"That's a lot to ask," Rob put down his drink, and continued to play the machine.

"I wouldn't expect you to do it for me, but for her," Ward was in his thoughts and knew what his answer would be before he could say it. Rob also knew he was there, even though he was no mind reader, and didn't bother to answer. In some small way, he enjoyed being able to communicate his thoughts again to someone without having to say anything at all. He missed that part of the relationship the most. Ward continued, "It was her choice. I know what you think, but I've never pushed her to do anything she didn't want to do, she's had to make those decisions herself. And believe it or not, I would have lived with whatever decision she made."

At that, Rob got up and not even glancing in Ward's direction he turned and left. Ward didn't dare turn to watch him leave, but he did look into his thoughts where he knew Rob would put his last words for him. All Ward could read was, 'I hope you know what you're doing.' What Rob couldn't read from Ward, and didn't know, was that Ward had had that same thought today. He had come to one conclusion. He wasn't going to try and change who Jan was making her into something that she would never be happy as. He had also come to the realization that it wouldn't make him happy if she wasn't the person he had fallen in love with. Ward dropped a couple more coins in the machine and then started to look for Eddy.

When Eddy walked into the casino he knew where to look. He went straight to the blackjack tables and sat down next to a Hispanic gentleman. This man looked like any other Hispanic gentleman, short spiked hair, and a tight shirt with a couple of gold chains around his neck. The only thing different about him was that Eddy recognized him. Eddy started to play, and waited for him to start the conversation.

"Good to see you," and he flicked his card to get another hit, "Want to get back into it, huh?"

"Been out too long," Eddy signaled to stay, "I'm bored."

"You don't start small," as the cards were played out, Eddy won and his associate lost the hand.

"Got enough money now that I don't have to," they placed their bets and got their cards.

"I set up a meeting for you in the back, room three," both signaled to stay with the cards they had, and both won their bets this time. Eddy got up and started to leave the table.

"Thanks," and he walked away hoping to never see him again.

As Ward got up from the slots he looked at the people as well as the room. It was strange what types of people were in the casino at this time at night. It wasn't yet ten, but the criminal element had already started to crawl out amongst the regular people and only a very few people would be aware of the difference.   He moved through the casino toward the back rooms, letting his mind quickly touch all that he passed looking for Eddy or any other clue. When he got to the back rooms he found what he was looking for. There were a few doors that led to rooms where all types of private games were held. What type of games, no one ever talked about. The rooms were also available for meetings, and as he started to mentally listen in at the different rooms, he noticed he was drawing some attention from a six foot six Hispanic man dressed all in brown leather and staring right at him. Ward did a quick mental scan of the room the man was near and found exactly who he was looking for inside. As he walked closer to the door, so did the guard. By the time Ward reached the door, the bodyguard was in front of it.

"This room's busy amigo. Try another," nothing about his attitude said friend, only go away quickly or face the consequences.

"Amigo, my friend is inside, if you would be so kind to check," Ward could tell that nothing about his mannerisms or words seemed to be convincing this wall. He also knew that the guard had no intention of checking with the occupants either. Deciding on a course of action that would surely get him in, Ward made a quick, although foolish, attempt at the door. He knew that he wouldn't get past this man without a scene, and a scene was the last thing he wanted, but he could get taken into the room forcibly if he played his cards right. Better to be taken in physically, than not at all. Ward made a move for the door and ducked just low enough to catch the handle making the door swing open. The guard grabbed Ward by the arm and twisted it round to his back. Ward felt his hand touch his shoulder blades with a twist. He felt the pain shoot up his arm and his hand go numb. He was good at what he did; Ward had to give him that. Ward kept his fingers crossed, so to speak, that this guard wouldn't end up breaking anything as the spears of pain continuously shot up his arm and then down through his torso. Eddy, being the first one to hear the commotion, turned to look toward the door, and in impeccable Spanish was the first to speak.

"Let him go, fool. He's my partner," with that Ward's arm was released and just as a final snub, he was given a shove into the room. Ward took a second to gain his balance and rubbed his arm to encourage the blood back into his fingers.

"Nice," Ward took the cue and spoke only in Spanish as well. Looking past Eddy, he then saw what was on the table and knew why the guard had been so vigilant.

7

She could sense Gabby's fear and panic filling the darkened room. She hadn't wanted Gabby with her, but once Gabby had approached them it was hard to keep her from getting involved with this coyote. Now they were in a concrete shed with a steel roof located in a small compound with an old house at the center just outside of Nogales proper. Imprisoned by a flimsy wooden slatted door that allowed only small bits of lights to peek through and was padlocked from the outside, all they could do was wait. Jan sat crouched down, ready to move at a moment's notice if necessary, and working hard not to absorb Gabby's tension. Switching her weight to the other leg, she adjusted the strap of her bag on her shoulder, and began to wonder what was going to happen next. Earlier, when they had been driven into the compound, she had noticed the house. She wanted to do a sweep of both the house and the area to get all the information she could, but if she were to do that it would blow her cover with Gabby. She was still unsure of just how well Gabby would be able to keep her secret. Later, she may need to trust her, but not just yet.

Jan knew from experience that they could sit here for hours, or for days, no one had told them anything, nor were they planning on it. It had been the last thought Jan had read from the men that put them in this box. They had been put in this shed to wait late last night after having paid half of the fee for being taken across. The one man who had picked them up at the bus station had taken a Polaroid picture of each of them before he had put them in the shed. As the door closed, he told them that someone would be here soon.

Soon could be anytime, at least the shed had been warmer than sleeping outside. Closing her eyes she concentrated again on what she could feel from the outside. She had already done as much as she could on the inside.

When they had first been locked in the shed there was enough light from the headlights to allow a quick glimpse of what was inside. There was little more than a dirt floor littered with cigarette butts and other assorted trash. The smell inside the shed made it a bit suspect as to how long they were really going to be kept imprisoned in these walls. Gabby had made her way to the far corner of the shed and wedged herself into it. Jan had slowly made her way around the outside walls to determine the length and width of the place, as well as the construction and condition of the shed. Without breaking through the door, which would be fairly easy, there was no way out. The shed was sturdy, well constructed, for what she would have expected to find most coyotes using. She even suspected that the door might have been reinforced from the outside somehow. Since she wasn't trying to escape it didn't matter, she just needed to do her best right now to collect all the information she could. Later the information could be turned over to the Federalies to do with it what they would. There was no one guarding the shed that she could tell. Her mind kept searching in patterns to look for anyone near that might give her a bit of information. It would also keep anyone from sneaking up on them. Jan hated surprises and with that thought in mind she smiled weakly to herself in the darkened room.

"Isabel," it was a very small, frightened voice from Gabby's corner.

"Here Gabby," Jan had been grateful that she hadn't found anyone else in the shed, waiting for transportation. Jan knew what she needed before she even spoke. She was also pretty sure that you didn't need to be a mind reader to know what it was either.

"Where are they? Are we going to get across?" She wanted to ask more, but didn't.

"We will be fine. We will get across. They have to wait to take us across until the best possible time. I promise we'll make it." It was a promise she intended to keep. Jan felt responsible for Gabby's situation even though it went against all her training.

Jan's ideas of what she did and who she was were changing, and if it was a bit uncomfortable at first, it had steadily grown easier in some ways and harder in others over the time she had known Ward. Jan also understood that she couldn't control everything. If she hadn't met up with Gabby this coyote may never have picked her up. Then again, he may have. Predicting the future was not her talent, hopefully just affecting it was.

"Good," and that was the end of the conversation. Gabby retreated back into the corners of her mind. Jan went back to looking for minds that could be close. She began to breath very slowly as she reached out about as far as her mind could go and still got nothing. She let out a little sigh and rested her head back onto the concrete wall. "I'm sure someone will be here soon."

"Yes," although Jan now knew very different. They were alone, and they sat like that for another two hours, both in silence, and with Gabby's tension increasing with every minute. They had sat in silence as Jan could do nothing to alleviate Gabby's fears of what was to come. The waiting was hard; it had never been easy for Jan. She used the time to meditate, not deeply, but enough to give her a rest, and a break from the monotony. Jan also used the meditation as a way to release from the worry she felt about what was happening with Ward.

She took a simple stretch and did a few Tai Chi moves to loosen her muscles; Jan wanted to be ready for anything. As she finished the last move, Jan now realized that she was no longer worried about Ward. It was like old times, and that thought comforted her for some strange reason. She knew that two women would be good money, but three, four, or more could be great money and that was probably one reason they were still waiting.

It was in one of the mini meditations that she felt it, another thought drift across her mind, and it wasn't Gabby's. Slowly a smile crossed her face, even though no one could see it, and just as quickly it was gone. They, yes she could sense more than one person, were coming closer to them with the intentions of taking them out of the small shed where Jan and Gabby had been trapped.

Their thoughts were all over the place, they were thinking of the route across the border as well as the party they would be going to in a couple of days, their girlfriends, friends, food, and all the other clutter that bounce around in their heads. One of the coyotes was making a phone call to someone in the States about the transfer they were about to make. Jan didn't have time to get a name. What Jan did have time to read from their minds, was that there were more, more women that would make the journey with them. She was not altogether sure, but she thought she could see three more faces in their minds. One of the faces she had seen before on the bus. Ready or not the journey was about to begin.

Jan was a professional and had been in situations like this many times before. She didn't warn Gabby of the men's approach, she just sat still, the same as before. At the first sound of someone at the door Gabby jumped, Jan was still. They could hear the padlock being pulled off and Jan turned her eyes to look down, she was the only one ready when the door flew open. The sunlight glared into the shed, blinding Gabby and only half blinding Jan. As the two men entered the room, the man they had seen at the bus station gave the orders to stand up. The other man moved toward Gabby and pulled her off the floor and out of the corner. Next, he grabbed Jan by the arm and began to half drag; half walk them both from the shed they had been confined in.

The man who had a hold of both of them was half a head taller and had a third more muscle to him than the man they had first met. The man from the bus station had never told them his name. It wasn't until Jan read it through the taller man's thoughts that she discovered at least one of their names, Hector. Hector seemed to be the leader, at least on this side. Without a lot more work she wouldn't be able to get a last name, and now was not the time to do it as she was being pulled out the door and toward an old dusty jeep. As Gabby's fear lessened, Jan's concern was beginning to rise. They were thrown into the back of the jeep with the other women and Jan looked in the direction of the sun to check the time of day. Jan guessed it to be close to five in the afternoon. Soon their light would be gone and if she could be thankful for anything, it was the fact that she had always been an amateur stargazer. All the maps she had memorized and her familiarity with the area in general would come in handy so long as she could navigate by the stars. Nothing was discussed with them. Listening carefully Jan picked up the name of the other man. It was just the first name, but it was all she needed. Hector and Emilio were holding a conversation of their own in the front seat. It had nothing to do with the trip they were about to take, just the party they were going to in a couple of days.

As Jan read through their minds she could see that this would not be a short ride. They were headed for a part of the fence that was only patrolled occasionally. They knew when and where the patrols were the weakest. The crossing point was located on Indian land, specifically the Tohono O'odham Reservation. This was not a surprise, it was the weakest area, the least patrolled, and they would probably not run into any volunteer militia looking for illegals. Jan had read this information when she did her research to begin with. She had studied the maps of the area and memorized them, along with a couple of other likely places.

The fences there were designed only to keep out the cattle, not illegal immigrants. It was a rough part of the desert, but an area where they could get very close to the border on this side, and the walk on the other side should only be a couple of days at most; it was only about forty miles by foot to a major road. If they had other plans, like Jan suspected, the walk would be a lot less than two days. Jan looked harder to find more information about these two that she could later pass along to their people. No matter what others may think, she was still on the side of the good guys who were just trying to make a difference.

What she read as they were traveling along an old dirt road was interesting. Both men were Mexican Nationals, both were in their mid-twenties living in Nogales, both were originally from the Mexican state of Chiapas, and both were street thugs that were pleased about what they did for a living now. Their partnership hadn't been for long, only about six months. Jan mentally made a grimace, as it had been only about two months since the first person had disappeared. They had known each other for a while before Hector had started in the transportation business on his own. Later, when business picked up, he had called on his old friend to help out to increase their chances and their profits. Hector made the connections at the bus stations, Emilio made the connections at the local bars.

It had been a good arrangement until two months ago. Hector needed more money and he couldn't get more any more people across or raise the fares. With the price they had to charge now for crossing, it made it nearly impossible to keep up on the expenses and the extras. Emilio was the one to suggest the change in occupation; Hector had only wanted to hold them for ransom once they got them into the States. Emilio had assured Hector a good profit if they worked through some people he knew in Phoenix.

He had been uncomfortable with the idea at first, but had gotten used to the money and the ease of getting people across without one of them having to take them into the States. His comfort level had readjusted. Jan had just reached into the part of Emilio's mind where the names and locations of his connections were stored when the Jeep went off what Jan had graciously called the road. The bump jarred Jan to the point that she had to try to grab the roll bars just to keep herself from being thrown to the floor of the Jeep, or into the others. With the link broken, Jan was now keenly aware of the strain and effort she had put out, and decided to concentrate only on where they were going. Hoping she would get another chance to read Emilio later, she looked around the desert they were traveling through.

When these two had first picked them up, they had been taken out of Nogales by the back roads to get to the small compound that they had been housed in. This trip was different in many ways to that one. They were now headed out across the desert. It was a dirt road of sorts at first and didn't seem to be used too often by the condition the road had been kept in. The scrub bushes, rocks, and cactus that were scattered through the desert encroached on what passed as the road. The landscape surrounding them mirrored the type found in Arizona. She was again reminded of the absurd reality that it was only a line in the sand that separated two areas that were once and still linked through cultural and time. Hector, who was driving, had followed the road, or path, as it turned toward the south, away from the border. Jan hoped that what she had read in their minds, as it had only been a glimpse, was the reality. Many other types of crimes happened in border towns, and ways to take advantage of those who tried to cross were many. Jan hoped that this adventure would not be the kind that would not even get them close to the border. Jan had faith in her abilities, but she sometimes lacked faith in humanity. They had been traveling on this road for about forty minutes, but it wasn't until Hector made the unexpected turn onto and into the desert towards the northwest that Jan was able to relax once more.

He seemed to be piloting the Jeep by the shadows, speed unchanged. They jumped and lurched through the desert. She sensed a bit of urgency in the air, as if they were late, and that it was necessary to take a bit more risk to get them there on time. Looking toward Gabby she could see that she also was hanging on to anything she could cling to. The others in their party of five seemed unconcerned about where they were headed and just held on as well. Jan noticed that Gabby's bag had slid to the back of the Jeep. Jan had placed the strap of her bag over her head and shoulder before the ride had begun. Bracing herself, she leaned over the seat to get the bag. Just as Jan's hand was almost on the bag Hector hit another large dip and her ribs hit the small seat with enough force to audibly knock the wind from her lungs. No one took notice and as soon as she recovered her breathe, she handed the bag to Gabby taking care to place the strap over Gabby's head and shoulder. She was rewarded with a smile. Jan carefully felt her ribs and was thankful that nothing was broken. Gabby was turning green and even Jan was unsure of just how much longer she would be able to take all the bumps and jerks to get to the crossing point without tossing something herself.

After about half an hour more of bouncing and lurching, they came to a stop. The sun had just set no more than ten to fifteen minutes prior and now the desert was becoming dark, intensely dark. Emilio pulled out a flashlight and got out of the Jeep. He handed them both a quart of water in an old, well-used bottle, a tortilla with some unidentifiable filling wrapped in wax paper, and a large black garbage bag. To most the garbage bag would have seemed odd, to Jan, she was thankful to have it. The desert got cold at night and when they stopped to rest the bag would be helpful to keep them warm by climbing inside it. Jan just wished that they had given them more water, as this would never be enough for any of them if they had to hike the full forty miles. It was insurance that they would do what they were told to do though.

"This way," was all he said.   They followed Emilio as he walked through the desert, Hector bringing up the rear. It was hard enough to walk through the desert during the day, but at night it was treacherous. The desert came alive at night, animals that hid from the heat of the day came out and those that had been out now rested. Predators like coyotes, the real ones, and wolves also came out to look for their meals. Animals that thought they had found a quiet resting spot could not be seen, and even though Emilio had a light, Hector did as well; they didn't use them to shine a pathway for Jan, Gabby, or the others. Without light the needles of the cactus and the rocks that covered the ground could easily make any of them turn an ankle or cut them open. Jan carefully picked her way behind Emilio who was in the lead. It worked well for her in many ways. She wanted to stay close to him to be able to read his mind easier.

His thoughts were clear. They were walking to meet up with someone. She could read that in his thoughts. She could also see the pathway they were following through his mind as well as some other interesting information that they hadn't been told. Right now Emilio was concentrating on just getting to the border, but Jan was very interested to learn that he wasn't going across. She had sensed that before and thought she was wrong. They would be told where to cross and that they would be met on the other side by someone that would take them the rest of the way. It was a nice set up; none of them could be arrested for transporting illegal aliens across the border. Jan looked deeper into his thoughts trying to see what their final destination was, but when the rocks slipped under her feet and her muscles responded accordingly she lost his thoughts.

Jan had to give more and more of her concentration to the path that grew fainter and fainter and harder to follow. She had less of a chance to see just what was in store for them as the path suddenly took on all types of slants. Jan wondered if they were ever going to be told about the jobs they had been promised. She was pretty sure that the jobs that were waiting wouldn't be ones any of them would have chosen to do, nor would they be able to escape from them once there. Jan wasn't worried about her situation. She was worried that she would fail these women. Her training nagged at the far reaches of her mind. She should leave emotion behind and move on but she couldn't. She knew that she could pay a high price for caring. Jan tried again to focus in on just how much Emilio might know about the U.S. side of this operation.

She had been concentrating so much on Emilio and the path she hadn't noticed that Gabby had fallen even farther behind. She heard Gabby gasp as she tripped and fell behind her, and heard Hector mutter something unpleasant and demeaning to her as he pushed her, making it even more difficult for her to regain her footing. Jan stopped and turned looking both with her eyes and mind. She used the other minds in the traveling group to quickly locate where Gabby had fallen. Quickly she walked back, avoiding the others, to help Gabby stand up. She moved her along this time so they would not anger Hector, again, and chance her being left behind. If she was hurt or left behind, her chances of survival this far out in the desert were next to nil.

Jan wondered just how much longer they were going to be walking before they would reach the chosen part of the border. They had been on foot for almost thirty minutes in the dark, walking almost parallel to the fence. Emilio abruptly stopped and shined the flashlight into everyone's' eyes. Again Jan had already turned her head to protect her eyes from being blinded by the flashlight. She saw Emilio give Hector a nod. Hector turned his flashlight off and went into the darkness.

"He will signal our contacts on the other side. You will walk across the desert and through a small opening in the fence in that direction," Emilio pointed with the light. "Take too long and the Federalies will be here, then you will be caught and sent back." He was very matter of fact as he spoke, "Get across without being caught, then you will need to quickly find my friend, or die in the desert." This Jan knew to be true; many Mexican Nationals died each year in the Arizona desert as they tried to get into the U.S. The paupers' graveyards were filled with numbered graves of those that never made it to civilization after they crossed. Some groups were just starting to do DNA cataloging for any relative that came looking for a lost loved one. Not something that would happen too much.

The fact that the desert was cruel and hard along the border between Mexico and Arizona was a fact that had been in the news all too much as of late. Sometimes the only water to be found was in the cattle troughs and even those troughs were not easy to find. At times even the troughs they could find didn't have enough water to help starve off dehydration from these desperate travelers. Not many illegal aliens took advantage of these dirty oases because they didn't want to get shot by a rancher or picked up by any number of others that wanted them back on the Mexican side. Least of all they didn't want to be turned in to the Border Patrol.

In her research, Jan had read about all the small militia groups that had been organized by the ranchers, in some cases, along the borders to help protect the ranchers, their families, and their investments. Not only did these groups patrol the area to send people back to where they came from, they also provided first aide, water, and food for those who got lost or stranded in the desert. They did turn whomever they found over to Border Patrol, but they kept a lot of people from dying out in the desert. It was a double-edged sword, and not one she was going to fix when the government couldn't even agree what to do.

All of a sudden they heard what sounded like a coyote; it didn't sound like any coyote Jan had ever heard and Emilio answered with another coyote call. With that, Jan knew they would soon be on their way across the border. There wasn't much to read from him right now, and as far as Jan could tell, there wasn't much more he knew about the operation on the other side. They were just supply, and the less information they had, the less they could give out if caught. Unless they crossed the border, it was unlikely that they would be picked up as they could claim they were breaking no laws, just providing sightseeing trips through the desert. She hoped she, or her team, would be able to break the supply line.

"Don't we get a light?" She asked knowing that they would be walking the rest of the way without Emilio.

"Sure," he smiled. The smile was not a pleasant one, it was lopsided and nearly a snarl when he handed her the light, "you just don't want to use it. You'll be caught for sure." Jan pushed the flashlight back towards Emilio. He was right; any extra light would bring attention to them. She looked to the sky, and just as the sun's rays had slowly faded from view earlier, the rays of the full moon had started to fill in as best as they could. There would be just enough light to see where they were going in an hour.

"No thanks," pushing the flashlight away and looking again at Emilio, "How do we know who to talk to."

"Don't worry, they'll find you. Listen for coyote calls," Emilio turned away. His mind moved on to other things, the money he would be getting and the party he would be going to mostly. Jan took one last look into his mind, and realized that she had gotten all the information that she was going to get from him. He knew nothing more. It would be great to get his address, but most people think about the house, not the house number, or in his case the apartment. What she was able to get was the area in which he lived in Nogales, which would be helpful combined with his name and description; someone would later be able to tail him.

"Be ready to go in about twenty minutes," his voice abrasive, "that's when the Federalies are the farthest away." With that said he left them in the dark.

Jan looked toward Gabby and motioned her toward the ground to relax before the trip began. The others joined them, not saying a word, all of them putting their trust in Jan.

Jan watched as each woman, or girl, readied themselves in their own way. Jan chose to meditate in order to maximize her energy. Reading their minds had taken more out of her than she had wanted it to. She had started out this journey already tired from the wait they had endured in the shed. Although she had been trained to go on very little sleep for very long periods of time; she also had been taught that she needed to make the most of what time she did have to rest. Ten minutes of deep meditation should be enough.

Her breathing began to slow and she could feel the rhythm of nature around her start to fill her head. Too soon she would be back in the city and away from nature and the rhythm that replenished her spirit. She barely noticed that Gabby had moved closer toward her and that Emilio was walking back toward them. It wasn't until his light shined into their eyes that she became aware of the group again.

"It's time. Go down that arroyo and keep following it. Stay low and when you get to the fence look for the looped hook at the bottom that keeps the fence closed," Emilio wasn't looking at them, just mentally tallying up the money he would get for the group. Jan was momentarily shocked, and for the first time her surprise nearly registered on her face. It wasn't the fact that he was thinking about the money that would be normal. No, it was the amount of money he was thinking about that baffled and shocked her. He wasn't thinking about five hundred dollars, or the extra thousand they would get after they had gotten them both across the border. Jan knew they were to be sold, but the amount the buyers were willing to pay surprised her.

The amount they would get for each of them was seven thousand dollars. Jan knew for sure now that they were dealing with some high rollers in the slave trade, the type that she wouldn't want anyone to get too deep into, including herself. "Get going," and they heard the coyote call, "Follow that call." It wasn't her first dangerous job, or the most dangerous one she had ever taken by far, but it was the first time she felt responsibility for any innocent person that had happened along her path. That was what the difference was, and the feelings Ward had made her start to face before they took the job on.

Jan grabbed Gabby by the arm and headed down the path with the others close behind. They could barely see the path in the moonlight, and twice Gabby tripped and nearly wrenched Jan's arm in the process. The path was a dry, deep wash, or an arroyo, which provided cover from the dropping temperatures in the desert as well as from other people searching out in the desert at night, looking for illegal aliens. Even though the arroyo was dry now, with just a little rain this could become a swift running river.

Glancing at the sky to check for clouds, it was clear for now. By looking at the ground Jan could tell that the wash had run not so long ago. The rains had been good lately. Just how long they would follow the wash once they got to the other side, was up to the coyotes, and springtime in the desert could easily bring unexpected rain.

The advantage to being in the arroyo for walking was that most of the path had been cleared by the running waters over time, but there was the occasional tree branch and the odd pieces of trash that had been left by others who had crossed, as well as a few larger rocks and car tires.   Given time, Jan might have found some information here that could be useful, but there was no time, and quickly weighing the benefits and risks involved, she knew that what she could find would not out weigh the risk of getting caught.

Jan glanced back and saw first Gabby and then the other three traveling companions just barely in the light provided by the moon. Jan was amazed that even though Gabby was scared, sore, and tired, she kept up. Jan didn't diminish her pace at all. She needed to get across. She now had her suspicions confirmed; they were going to be sold, although she had no proof or information as to who or what they were to be sold for yet.   Knowing that the information she needed lay just across that cattle fence, she continued to push on. Time would be the only thing that could keep them from making it across the border and into a world that no one else in the group but her suspected.

It took them less than ten minutes to reach the fence, and the closer they got, the quieter they got.   Jan moved soundlessly. Carefully feeling along the bottom of the barbed wire fence to find the looped piece, Jan contorted her body to let the light fall onto the fence. She could feel the group's anxiety grow with every second that passed. As her fingers released the fence and there was a small but audible click, Jan heard and felt a collective sigh of relief.

One by one they lay on the ground and slid across the rough ground under the fence and in-between the loose pieces of barbed wire. Jan waited until last to cross. They all ignored the scrapes and cuts they received from the debris that was caught on the fence from previous rains. In fact, as she read Gabby's feelings, she knew that all the danger she may be in was worth it. Gabby's feelings only echoed what the rest of the women felt. It was the thrill of just being in the United States. Jan had waited until last to cross and now pulled her bag through from the other side. Although she didn't carry much, she didn't want to be without what tools she did have if she had a choice.

Gabby was ready to stop and take in the moment, but Jan grabbed her and pulled her the length of the wash along with the others who were quickly and quietly following. The Border Patrol would be very unforgiving, and she didn't even want to try and find out how well her cover would hold. As she pulled Gabby along, they all heard the unmistakable cry of a human coyote. With very little reserve, Jan walked in the direction of the call. Now was not the time to have doubts or second thoughts, this was her time.

8

Once they had cleared the immediate area of the border, Jan stopped momentarily. She could tell that Gabby was having a hard time with one ankle and wanted to give her just a couple of minutes for a rest. No said anything for fear that they would be detected. Jan was up to date on all the surveillance out there, but if one was careful there was always a way around it. She knew her way around it. Motioning to Gabby and the others, they moved forward. They may be in the United States, but they were not safe.

Again she heard the cry of the coyote, and it was definitely not an animal she heard, at least not the four legged kind. Whoever made that call was the one they were to meet. Jan listened again, and then taking Gabby by the hand pulled her off the path and over to the west following the call. The three other women followed.

Jan began to check the area for people, other than the ones she was with. She wanted to know just how many were waiting for them before she got there. As her mind reached out ahead of the group, she found what she was looking for. One man stood alone, well armed, and waiting to catch a glimpse of them in the growing moonlight. The closer they got to this man, the darker his thoughts were. Jan was well aware of what type of world she could be entering when she took on the assignment, but the worst was proving true.

A quick thought of Gabby went through her mind, as she let the man's thoughts develop. Now more than before, she realized that Gabby was going to need her protection in the end as well as the other women. The walk through the desert might be the safest part of this journey. From what she could tell, they were to be sold to the highest bidder. It didn't matter to him what happened to them, just so long as he got his money.

They walked across the desert, just off the path. About twenty feet in Jan tripped over something laying half hidden in the desert. In the background she could hear Gabby gasp, and Jan turned to get a better look in the moonlight. What she had tripped over was not a branch or a cactus rib as she had first thought; it was a decaying human foot. By placing her hand over Gabby's mouth, Jan quieted her. Dragging Gabby and the others back to the path, Jan walked back over to investigate a bit further.

The body had been there for a while, and life in the desert had not been kind to it. From what was left of the remains, Jan could tell that it was once a young woman by the clothes. Bending over the body, Jan looked at what was left of the skull. Toward the back of the skull was a neat round hole, the kind not put there by nature. She had been shot and left here to rot. Without the help of forensics, she would not be able to tell if the bullet left in this corpse would match up with the man and the gun they were about to meet up with. There was also no way of knowing why she had been shot.

Looking nearby, she noticed some discarded items in the moonlight. These items had probably once been in a bag, but now were loose in the desert, caught under branches and in cactus needles. Jan moved over quickly to pick up a piece of paper that had blown onto a small bush. The bush had served as a shelter, so the paper had survived pretty much intact. She quickly scanned the text and realized it was a letter. It was from this woman's husband in Phoenix. As she read what she could, she picked up on the feeling of the letter and how much he missed her. He was excited about being with her soon, and happy that they had saved the money for her to make the journey.

There was a new feeling that Jan was experiencing, empathy for the victim. Recognizing it and tucking it away, Jan's mind shifted toward herself and in that moment, that split second of time, she dropped her guard. She was focused on the names on the paper she held.

Gabby screamed and the sound was quickly stifled. Jan

dropped to the ground fully cognizant of her surroundings again and looked back toward the group, stuffing the letter into her shirt. From where she was she couldn't see what had happened. Staying low and quiet she came back out into the open and down into the wash. There she saw that Gabby had been restrained, and her mouth taped, along with the others. Jan felt the man move in behind her and she did nothing to try and stop him.

Acting as if she were terrified, Jan began to open her mouth as if to scream. She had no intention of screaming, but she used it as a distraction. While he was busy trying to keep her quiet, or so he thought, she shifted her bag so that it would hang on her back. As he attempted to tape her mouth shut, she tried to talk.

"Are you the coyote we're to meet?" It was then he viciously slapped the tape on her mouth, rubbing it into place with a smile on his face. The man, without saying a word, grabbed her arms and strapped them together behind her.

"Yes. Now shut up, do you want to be caught?" Jan shook her head no, "Good, just follow my directions then," the man didn't have a heavy accent, and with the moonlight, Jan was unsure if he was white or Hispanic. Later she would pick his mind to get all the information she could. She felt her pack move and could hear him unzip the bag. She knew what she had in the bag, and unless he knew what he was looking for, Jan was pretty sure he wouldn't find anything that would cause him any concern. Zipping up the bag halfway he walked back around in front of the group. All the money that she was to use to get into the states was now in his hands. He had probably searched everyone else and relieved them of their cash as well.

He grabbed one of Gabby's' arms and one of Jan's and lacing a rope through each he continued stringing them together. When he was finished, he half pulled, half dragged them down the wash again. Jan had luckily been tied in the lead and was the closest to their current captor. The feelings coming from the back of the group were a mixture of fear, uncertainty, and just plain terror. Jan took this as her opportunity to read the leader, blocking out the other women in the group. She found a name, his name, Omar, and where they were headed, a skuzzy neighborhood in Phoenix.

They continued to walk for some time before they were allowed to sit and rest a bit. The walk in the desert was arduous as they tried to miss all the obstacles and move up and down the hills. Even using all she could see through her eyes and his, Jan had still brushed up against cactus and bushes. All of them had cuts and cactus needles located on and in their arms and legs. They had no way of dealing with any of these injuries as they were still bound. Once they were sitting, Omar removed the tape from their mouths one at a time and gave each of them a sip, or gulp, of water.

"Don't make a sound or I'll be forced to tape your mouths closed again. This time I may not undo them either. I'd take a moment to rest," he said to the whole group with his face was hidden from their sight, "I'll be back in about thirty minutes. Anyone want to join me?" he leered at them.

All eyes looked away, and he turned and walked off into the darkness. Jan notice the flicker of a lighter, and thought she could smell cigarette smoke. Carefully Jan laid back and motioned for the rest to do the same. It wasn't much time to rest, but it was all they were going to get. Jan closed her eyes and relaxed her muscles. She could feel the ache of the walk and the burn from the cuts, but she put all that aside and rested. The minutes flew by like seconds and then he was back.

"You're in luck. We only have to walk another two hours before we will get picked up. It's a good night. Now let's go," his voice was gruff, and his demeanor cruel. Jan picked at his mind again. He had walked far enough away to make a phone call without being heard. Now he was ready to move on and get them to the meeting point. Omar pulled Jan roughly to her feet and then the rest of them before he returned to Jan.

"Ah my dear, if only I had more time with you," and his hand slid down her cheek and onto her chest. Bile rose in Jan's throat but she did nothing to betray her character.

They walked on for almost two more hours without a break. Each of the women fell at least once or twice, all of them except for Jan. Each time one would fall, they would be showered with unpleasant explicatives and a forceful pull up that would soon leave bruises on their arms. They would then be pushed roughly forward to move them along again. Jan could feel the drag of the weight behind her as she pulled the others along for about an hour and a half. The pace was grueling and the end was yet an unknown. Jan shook off the feelings she was randomly getting from the others and tried to read just how much longer they would be on the path.

She couldn't read much as she was concentrating greatly on just keeping the group going and staying on the path. It wouldn't be long now before she would tire from all the readings and walking she had done. The terrain was not what she would call mountainous, but it was very hilly and the deep narrow wash only made the journey more punishing. It would have been a difficult walk for most of them to begin with; but it was as if Jan was the engine pulling along a train of women as they each slowly began to tire.

Finally she got a read on him and knew that it wasn't much longer until they were going to stop again. She wasn't sure if it was just a break, but it looked as if they might be getting a ride of some kind. Jan knew that he was looking for something, and as she tripped on a rock, she lost her connection and chose not to reconnect as she kept herself from falling. If she fell, then the entire group would most likely collapse.

He had most likely killed the other woman on a journey similar to this one. She wasn't sure why the other woman was killed, but now was not the time to find out if it was because of sheer tiredness. Roughly he stuck his hand out in front of Jan and nearly pushed her backwards. Looking around, he then turned and spoke to them.

"Wait," was all he said, and it was all they could do. Moments later Omar returned with a purpose, his face set, and Jan could tell he had found what he had been looking for. He pulled her roughly up and the others awkwardly followed. Without saying a word, he pulled them out of the wash and toward a taller Palo Verde tree near a rocky outcropping. Once they were closer, the shadows turned into an outline of a vehicle. They were loaded one by one into the back of an old Jeep. The ends of the rope looped and tied to the roll bars.

The Jeep bounced across the desert tossing them from one side to the other. The jeep moved over the rocky, sandy inclines taking its center of balance to the limits as they traveled. There were times that Jan was sure the Jeep would tip over. They traveled with no headlights, just the parking lights. There was good news and bad news that went with this. At least the walking seemed to be over, and that was a good thing for her compatriots, but the fact that he had a vehicle that could travel this terrain meant that they were doing well in this business.

Now that the walking had stopped, Jan tried to stabilize herself and pick his brain on what he knew again. Taking a deep breath, the clouds of dirt that swirled around them settled into her lungs. Stifling a cough, she pushed through all the discomfort she felt and reached out with her mind to touch his thoughts.

He was the connection, the supply person. He picked up the women at the border and took them into Phoenix. He then later arranged for them to be sold, and he and his friend were the ones who arranged delivery of the women. His cut of the money was substantial, and from what Jan could tell, the total take was about fifteen thousand per person. Not the largest amount of money this group could earn in the business they had become involved in. If allowed to continue, they may figure out that they were charging just a hair too little for the cargo they carried.

Mentally Jan smiled with satisfaction, as she knew that they had infiltrated the group before it had gotten too large. It should crumble easily with just a bit of a push from them. As Jan let that thought slip from her mind, the addresses for a couple of drop houses came into his. Drop houses were where illegal aliens were kept and hidden before they were moved out. Omar was in the process of deciding which house would be the best for this group.

As he mentally went through his choices, Jan discovered that they obviously had more cargo stashed away. Jan needed to look for proof of the addresses of these houses either on his cell phone, or anything she could find, when and if she was able to take a trip out and alone. Just because she only saw two in his mind didn't mean that there weren't more.

About an hour later they arrived at a paved road. Omar pulled onto the road and traveled down it only about two miles before he stopped. Pulling in front of a camper that was at least twenty five years old that had been left on the side of the road, he reversed into place with the tow hitch of the Jeep about a foot away from the camper itself. Before anyone could move, he jumped from the driver's seat and moved around to the back of the vehicle. This was the most risky spot on the entire trip. If any of them were seen now, they would almost certainly be picked up.

Wasting no time he grabbed at the rope and quickly cut both ends of it. He was truly more worried about being caught than anyone trying to get away at this point. Grabbing both ends of the rope he pulled out all of the people almost into a pile onto the side of the road. Half walking, half crawling they were pulled toward the camper and shoved down beside the door. Taking out keys, he unlocked the camper door and opened it fully, latching it to the side to keep it open. The rope pulled tighter as he leaned inside the camper to turn on a small battery operated lamp that was nearly out of battery, but it did allow Jan to catch a glimpse of the inside.

Omar pulled them all into the camper and then crawled under the table for the booth. Jan noticed that the old and worn seats had locks on them, and as he undid the first one the thoughts from his mind became clear. He threw off the stained worn pad and opened the lid of the bench. Illegal aliens were often hid inside parts of vehicles and campers, just about anything they could find to use, so without fighting, she allowed him to put her inside what she considered a self made coffin. Omar's thoughts were not being hidden at all, so Jan knew that the other side of the bench was where he was going to put Gabby.

Jan knew that one wrong move at this point and what only looked like a coffin would quickly become one. His mind was focused only on getting them into the camper and on his way. He knew that every moment he stayed here, was one moment closer to being caught. Jan needed to wait until he was less focused to read his mind better. The lid on the bench slammed closed and she heard the lock click in the darkness that now enclosed her. It was only a few minutes later that she heard the other side slam shut and knew that Gabby was now in place.

Slowly she watched through his mind, as he locked away the other women. Jan fought to keep all their fears and hopes out at bay. She had broken out in a sweat with the exertion but wasn't worried that anyone would notice. It only took about ten minutes to get them all into place and the camper door closed and locked.

First she looked for any other minds that might be in the camper and found none she didn't already know. She could feel the camper being hooked to the Jeep as it gently rocked. There was the faint sound of the engine, and she knew that his mind would be more relaxed. Without compunction, she pushed away the feelings of fear and regret that floated thickly through the camper and searched through his mind as he drove happily back towards Phoenix.

What she found was not great, but not bad, he was the one in charge here and anyone else they ran into didn't have a clue as to what was going on. He only worked with a few close friends and they were in Phoenix now. A drop of sweat made its way into her eye and without having her hands free she just had to endure the sting. He had done this a few times and so far hadn't even been stopped. He was one of the lucky ones.

Jan calculated that they had hours or so yet to be locked in this camper. The muscular and mental strain started to take hold and Jan knew she needed to relax. Her legs ached and her arms were numb. With her knees tucked into her stomach she tried to squirm, with no avail, to ease the pressure on her arms. Her eyes began to droop, and slowly sleep took the place of discomfort, dreams the place of thought, as they bumped down the road. She was only awakened when she was forced up against the back of the bench as he stopped and pulled the camper to the side of the road again.

Ward looked down at the table again and said nothing while the bodyguard patted him down. As Ward had known, the bodyguard didn't find any gun. Eddy glanced quickly at Ward and there was an understanding that could have only come from working together. Neither one betrayed their feelings. Eddy had stumbled upon, or purposely knew, who to contact and they had hit pay dirt. Ward took a quick read of his mind and found that he had run into an old acquaintance here that had turned him over to these people. Ward was going to let Eddy take the lead here and now. Ward rubbed his wrist as he took his place standing on the left side of Eddy in a battle ready position.

The door to the room closed to ensure that whatever went on

in this room never left it. There on the table lay Polaroid pictures of not one, but many different women, mostly Hispanic, but not all. Only one fit the description of who they were looking for, and Eddy was holding that picture. Ward assumed that the other women they were searching for were currently out of the mix. Ward took a moment to glance at the pictures.

Not one of the pictures had a name on it, or any other identifying mark. The women in the pictures were smiling and they were standing in front of an adobe structure, most likely in Mexico. They all seemed to be taken in about the same place and at about the same angle. Eddy said nothing to Ward, and continued to shuffle through the pictures, as if he were truly shopping for something special. Ward waited.

"Is this all?" Eddy started the conversation again. Eddy handed the pictures to Ward and he took them obediently. "You see anything special there?" There were two other Hispanic men at the table, one who Eddy knew only as Carlos. Ward had dealt with him and his men before; and from the calls Ward had made yesterday Eddy knew that Carlos would be at the casino tonight.

The other Hispanic man Ward didn't know at all. There also was one other man at the door, guarding the inside of the room. Ward could tell by picking up on the random thoughts that both the guards were armed well and ready to use what they had at any time. Business must be good. Ward gave the guards little thought at the moment. No one was looking at Ward but them, so he decided to start picking minds as fast as he could. With Eddy in the lead now it allowed him the down time he needed to take a good look into these men's thoughts.

"We will get new ones soon. On nights like this, they will transport as many as possible," he was referring to the presence of the full moon tonight. Focused, Ward didn't even let his mind sideline back to thoughts of Jan; if he did his part of the job well he would see her soon. Now was the time for getting all the information that he could. Without looking his way at all, Ward concentrated on the other Hispanic man at the table. The Hispanic man that had said nothing was definitely thinking a lot. He was unsure of dealing with a new client; it made him nervous and you could tell this by his demeanor.

He kept trying to think of a reason not to deal with Eddy and Ward, but could not think of a good one. Eddy had come to the table with a reference, a good reference. They had people in common. The gentleman doing none of the talking seemed to worry only about if they were good for the money. Ward watched as his hands shifted and played with the pen in front of him. His eyes darted between each of them being careful not to give his trust away too soon, and finally his name became clear, it was Enrique, Enrique Santos.

As he looked back at Carlos the thought crossed his mind of how Carlos' friend knew Eddy from some gang associations in Phoenix. Enrique seemed to take very little comfort in this information though. Enrique was the weak link, and the one that would be the most dangerous. He could make or break them. Ward decided to store that information for later.

With Carlos leading the conversation, Ward was able to take a better look at him while he read his mind. He wore good clothes, tailored clothes that were not just off the rack. His slacks were khaki green and his shirt was a pale lime green. He wore a simple leather jacket, lightweight, and black. Ward was sure this was to hide the presence of a gun that was probably tucked in the back of his pants, or secured in a shoulder holster. His hair was short and spiked with the dark tips bleached white. Everything about him said high roller. On his left hand he had about three gold rings and a very tasteful, but large, gold chain peeked out from under the shirt. Ward took this all in a matter of seconds, never stare; it would mark you.

The next hurdle was that in this type of business, surnames were not exchanged. It made it more difficult to track down people if one was taken into custody. It didn't take Ward long to discover Carlos' last name as he plodded through his mind. It was Lopez. He had been in the States for the last ten years. He was about thirty and had himself crossed illegally. He seemed to have a couple different places in which he would keep the women, but no addresses that were easily gotten from Ward's simple reading of him.

"I need pictures. I have a customer waiting and willing to pay good money if I have the right girl. What I need to know is am I doing business with you or should I move on?" Eddy was playing the part well.

"No, not yet. I will have them by tomorrow, or after we complete the transaction. Not more than a couple of days. Don't you see anything you like here?" Ward picked up on a bit of wariness from Carlos, and Enrique clicked the pen numerous times.

"What good are promises? I could easily make do with some of these, but just starting out again I want the best you can provide. If all goes well I'd like to have my partner here start up places in other areas, expand the business. I want my clients happy. That means I need a reliable source," Eddy let his fingers move the pictures around one more time. "This one is good," he pointed to the picture he held earlier, "but I will need more than one just to supply his demand."

"Understood," Carlos smiled. His phone rang and he just opened it and listened before he disconnected, "Good news, come see me two nights from now. Same room and we'll have the pictures for you," Carlos picked up the picture Eddy had fingered. "Would you like me to keep her for you?" Eddy looked at the picture as if he were trying to decide and then looked toward Ward.

"Well?" and Eddy looked at Ward. He wanted Ward to help him identify the one and he was more than happy to do it. Ward looked at the picture with a stern face, and ever so slowly gave an affirmative nod.

"Yes and maybe this one also. I'll wait to make a final decision till I see what else you get in," at this Eddy stood up signaling the end of the bargaining, "Here's a couple thousand to keep them on hold," Eddy dropped the bills on the table, "In two nights we will discuss prices more," to seal the deal Eddy and Carlos shook hands. Eddy turned to leave and Ward followed. Enrique never moved and his thoughts never changed.

9

Neither of them spoke as they walked out to the car. It was late and dark with only the light of the moon to interrupt their thoughts, and the lights in the parking lot to keep them under surveillance. Ward got in the driver's side closing the door firmly and Eddy got in on the passenger side nearly slamming the door. If someone were watching them, and that was a given, then the illusion of money held. It was all in the look of the car and the way they carried themselves that seemed to ooze money.

This time, Ward revved the car engine and pulled out of the lot just short of spinning the tires. He wanted to be noticed. Ward could read Eddy's body language as well as his mind, and knew that what had just taken place inside the casino had taken a lot out of him emotionally. It was nearly one-thirty in the morning, and they had sat in with the white slavers for at least an hour and a half discussing details and looking at pictures.

As they drove away from the casino Eddy's shoulders began to slump a bit, and his head slowly dropped onto the headrest. His breathing was rhythmic and slow, his eyes closed to the world. Ward let him relax a bit as he pulled onto the nearly deserted freeway. He turned the CD player on and listened to the sounds of Sting as the engine reached cruising speed.

Ward had learned a vast amount of general knowledge in the meeting. Details would come later. Right now he needed to center Eddy's thoughts again so that they could discuss the details of the job at hand.

Eddy reached over to turn the music down about ten minutes

later, and he sat up straighter. Ward could tell that he wanted to, needed to talk, but wasn't sure how to start out. He could also tell that some of the stress he had felt when they got in the car was gone. Ward waited and let Eddy stay in safe territory at first.

"Saw you found Rob."

"Yah. Was a bit surprised he was there. Thought the last job might have just pushed him out of our circle," Ward had been passing good information to Rob through his contacts for the last couple of years. Jan hadn't known about it, and it wasn't until they started this job that she had learned about that part of his chain, "Guess I might have sold him short, but he's not too happy."

"Um," Eddy was remembering a time when Ward hadn't been happy with the choices Jan had made to stay in the department. He also remembered a time that Ward had worried her association with the department would endanger her. It must be very similar to what Rob was feeling now. The last assignment Jan had with the department had nearly killed her, Ward, and Rob. It was after that job that she had finally agreed to stay with Ward and leave the department.

It had been a leap of faith; since she didn't even remember who Ward was when she had made the decision. Eddy could only guess it was time for the shoe to be on the other foot. Ward, not paying attention to what Eddy was thinking, took the opportunity of the lull in conversation to change the topic.

"Can you handle this job?" Ward had taken Eddy's uncertainty as hesitation about the job. Ward was pretty sure that he could count on Eddy to help out no matter what the job, but he needed Eddy to make the commitment; he wouldn't do it for him.

"Yah," Eddy nearly chuckled, but it wasn't as if he found any of this funny, just in an amazingly morbid way, "If my life had never changed, this would seem normal. Funny thing though, that type of character doesn't seem to fit anymore," Eddy looked out into the desert as if he were searching for something he didn't expect to find. Peeking into his mind, Ward knew that his thoughts were focused on his current life. "Think I like it better this way."

"Will there be any problems with the contact you used after we finish?" Ward was concerned that after the job was finished there might be a backlash; it was the first time they had worked so close to home in a while.

"That weasel, no, no worries with him just as long as we get the whole bunch. And anyway he knows me by another name," Eddy waved at an imaginary object as if he were brushing away the thought. "Did you get any clues about how many we may be dealing with?" Eddy knew that Ward had an uncanny talent for getting a feel for things. He didn't know how, nor did he want to know.

"Seems to me that they are the ones in charge from the looks of the money they have to throw around. New money though, not dealing with a large syndicate yet, although it could grow quickly. I'm sure that's what they are hoping for. That's where we came in. They want to grow. Those two didn't seem related, but it could be by marriage. We'll know more once Rubber gets us some information. Whatever happens next we need to make sure we have seen Jan and whoever else they have, before we even negotiate an amount," Ward stayed matter of fact, and even surprised himself about how easy it was.

In some ways it was just like old times, only better. Once he saw Jan he would have more information, even if they didn't talk. Eddy would be safer not knowing about their being able to read minds; at least that's what Ward thought.

"The deposit should at least keep them there until we get back," Eddy turned toward Ward, "The one woman fit the description of who we were looking for."

"Makes me wonder where the others might be right now," He didn't want to try and guess. Depending on who they sold them to, they could be anywhere by now. Next time he would try and get more information on their client base from their minds. Ward had needed to get the general set up first before he could move on to the next level. Even as he spoke, a plan was beginning to form in his mind,

"When we talk to them next, you will need to keep the conversation alive so I can watch their body language. Focus on their successes more. Don't get too nosey, that may tip them off. But the more you can get them to brag the better," Ward had slowly trained Eddy over the last couple of years to be the type of partner that any mind reader would value. Eddy could work with the best of them now, and he didn't even know it. Ward smiled, "We can't afford to lose the contact and it looks as if you're the boss."

"Yah," his voice held less enthusiasm than before. Ward was a bit concerned, but didn't voice it. It wasn't that Ward was unsure of Eddy. Over time they had both taken the lead in different jobs. This one just hit closer to home for Eddy than the others had.

Eddy enjoyed working with Ward. He was treated as an equal and he had never had that experience before. What bothered him was the type of job it was quickly becoming. It was a messy business they were getting into. It may drive some of it away for a while, but not forever. Sometimes the enormity of the crime world overwhelmed Eddy.

At one time that world had welcomed and taken care of him, but to Eddy that was now a lifetime away. At times like this it amazed him that he had escaped it. Ward was also doing a bit of soul searching. Since he had been on his own it had become part of the job. Sometimes he found silence was the best way to communicate, even between people who couldn't read minds. Some things were better left in their own heads and not shared.

It used to bother Ward that he didn't belonged to either world. The change for Ward had been just as difficult as it had been for Eddy. It was something he had come to terms with slowly after he left the department, and with Eddy's help. The crime world was not a comfortable place for him to hide out in, nor would he have been welcomed if his intentions were not to join them completely.

A man he had once considered a brother, had intentionally implicated him in the crime world, and faked his own death. This had been the first steps for him to leave the department. The man then had the gall to invite him into the crime world he had become involved in. When Ward resisted, he then tried to drag him forcibly into that type of life, not one time but many times. Each of these times he had avoided it, although it was narrowly sometimes, and he had some of the scares to prove it.

After leaving the department Ward had also tried to live in the regular world. Just a normal person; live as any person would with a regular job and all. He had quickly realized that world was not for him either. It was too mentally cluttered for him to stay in it for long periods of time. He had been changed. His future forever changed by people who no longer controlled his world or would protect him from the other. He had struck the only balance he could to survive. Eddy had become his partner in the real-estate business, and they did well, very well. Ward had used his savings to start Eddy's company and he was a very silent partner in it. Together they had built up the business to the point where neither of them had to work.

Neither of them really ever had to work again if that is what they wanted, but they were both drawn to something else. Ward knew that it wasn't the same thing that called the both of them to begin with, but in the end, it was enough to put them together. He watched the straight dark road fly by, and the lights of the city come closer as his speedometer inched up past eighty miles an hour.

"We will get them," Ward let the words hang in the air, purposely not saying who they were. Eddy said nothing. Ward continued expressing both of their thoughts, "We will get them. Put them all back where they belong." The conversation ended as quickly as it had begun. Ward again focused on the road as his words trailed off aimlessly into the silence. As they inched into the city, Ward took off on the exit that took him directly into the downtown, and drove toward Eddy's condo mindlessly.

Pulling up to the gated community in which Eddy lived, Ward leaned out and entered the code to open the gate. Ward pulled up outside of Eddy's condo and stopped the car. Eddy didn't make a move to get out. He sat still. Ward didn't intrude on his thoughts, he knew that Eddy would share them in good time, and he should have the right to privacy, and to phrase them the way he wanted to. It wasn't more than a couple minutes before Eddy, without turning to look at Ward, spoke.

"Who's our contact this time? Will it be Rob," Eddy wanted to know just who to call if things got too bad. Eddy knew that part of the job was to get the information into the right hands so that the proper actions could be taken. After the last job, he learned the number he needed to contact the department directly. He just didn't know if he should use it.

"Yah, or Bill.   Rob's got our cover set up so that the

department can't find either of us, and it needs to stay that way," Ward never contacted the department directly. It would be suicide for him.

"This is a messy one. I don't think I need to tell you that," Eddy started speaking then stopped. Ward waited, he knew there was more, "How deep are you going to let her get?" Ward had known this could become a problem between them. They had worked together before and Eddy had gotten to know his boundaries and abilities. Ward had worked with Jan before and he knew the extent of her abilities, as well as her boundaries. He had no doubts that if she felt she was in extreme danger at anytime, she would and could get out. Eddy had only worked once with Jan and it was under Ward's strict direction.

It would be a leap for Eddy to trust him to know what and how much Jan could take, and the fact that Jan would also know, but strangely enough that wasn't the problem. Eddy was really nervous about the fact that they might not even meet up with her. Ward could tell that by his words and body language, he didn't need to read his mind. He also knew that it would take a couple of jobs for him to gain any comfort level with Jan and her training. On the last job Ward had treated Jan as frail and helpless, and at the beginning she was, not at the end, and not now.

"You have to trust us on this one, she will do fine, and we will break this ring up. We have worked like this many times before. She's good, maybe even better than me at this," Eddy got out of the car without speaking. He didn't close the door right away. Eddy bent over and looked inside the car again.

"See you in the morning," Eddy stood up and closed the door. He turned and walked up the sidewalk to his place. Eddy had bought it about a year ago wanting to be closer to the downtown activities, and nightlife. Eddy loved sports, and whether it was Diamondback baseball or Sun's basketball, Eddy had tickets. The Coyotes hockey team had just moved out toward Glendale, a suburb, and that had left Eddy with some mixed feelings as now he had to drive to two sporting events outside of the downtown area, hockey and football. For Eddy, being in the middle of things made him happy.

Ward took off and headed out east to Mesa, another suburb

of Phoenix where Eddy had arranged an apartment for Ward in one of the complexes they owned together there. Ward knew the place and was looking forward to getting there. Ward merged onto the freeway and was on his way. He saw the lights of the police car sitting off to the side and slowed a bit. As he passed it he saw that the officer had a man standing on the side of the road taking a sobriety test as his wife, or companion, waited impatiently in the car. Ward drove past and thought nothing more of them. In the morning he would have to ask Eddy for some work clothes.

Jan had been jolted awake when their host had pulled the jeep and trailer off of the road and onto the shoulder. Keenly aware of the danger they could be in, she had decided to let herself into his mind even though she was still tired. With a deep and calming breath, she could easily see that they had been pulled over by a highway patrol officer. That was better than a border patrol agent, but the time of day was still wrong.

Looking into both of their minds she could tell what the scenario would be, and what the trigger for the officer to search the trailer would also be. Jan saw the officer look at his watch and discovered that it was about four thirty in the morning. It was the first time since being put in the shed that Jan had gotten a good idea of what the time really was.

She was still pretty unsure of where they were, but with any luck that would soon become clear. Jan could see the area but no signs to confirm or deny a place for her. Omar was very relaxed and had his lie ready. Jan couldn't help but smile, it was always fun to mind read a lie; they looked very different than every other thought. It was a good thing that was a mind reader's secret.

"Good morning officer. Is there something wrong?" Omar seemed to be smiling. There didn't seem to be any of the usual nervous habits when stopped. He was calm and relaxed. His fingers held the wheel loosely and he leaned on the window frame. Jan believed this could work.

"Isn't it a bit early to be out?" the officer was looking in and around the truck with his flashlight for anything that might be cause for alarm. The fact that no one else was there was beginning to send up red flags in the officer's head.

"I happen to agree with you, but my sister wants the trailer for her family to go camping with this week, actually today, and I couldn't change her mind," Omar offered just the right amount of information, not too much, not too little.

"Did you know that the right taillight is out?" that had been why the officer had stopped him in the first place, and the fact that he thought he might have caught a live one.

"You're kidding. I thought I had that all fixed. I've been working on it for the last two days to get it ready. If it's not one thing with this old trailer it's another. I should just junk it but then what would she use to go on vacation with that mob. No one wants her kids to stay twice in one place that's for certain," Omar even managed to get the head shake right and the frustrated tone of voice just perfect. Well planned and practiced. Jan could feel the sympathy in the officer. Letting a small sigh of relief escape from her lips, Jan knew that they were not going to get searched, at least not this time.

"When you get there, just get it fixed before you let your sister have it. I won't sight you this time," the officer started to walk away, "Good luck."

As the officer got into his car, Omar eased the jeep and trailer back onto the road. He smiled, as the officer's car became a small speck in his mirror. Jan could tell that it hadn't been the first time he had been stopped, but he had also never been searched. He was proud of this fact. Again Jan tried to see the terrain through his eyes and found that the surrounding desert was changing as well as the type of road that they were on.

Fear began to press in on her again, but it wasn't hers. She could feel that at least one or two of the girls were awake, and they were scared. A couple of them had figured it out, but she didn't want to focus in on their fear. Fear was a powerful emotion; it could overwhelm all other thoughts and keep a mind reader trapped.

Jan needed to refocus and concentrate on where they were going. She knew they would have to get there early in the morning so as not to attract suspicion. Through his eyes she could barely see the lights of a city, she wasn't sure if it was Tucson or Phoenix right at this moment, and then she saw a landmark come into his view on the left hand side of the road. It was the outlet malls that were located about an hour out of the center of Phoenix. Jan now realized that she must have been asleep for at least two to three hours for them to get this far. Omar's thoughts were wandering, unfocused and were beginning to give her a headache. She decided to reconnect with him in about forty-five minutes when they got to town.

She began to focus in on her companions in the trailer again as they started to wake. They were scared, no doubts about that, all of them. One at a time she looked through their minds to try and gather more information on them. Gabby she knew already, and she was the most relaxed. Jan decided that her calm was based solely on the fact that she did not feel completely alone. She knew Jan, not for long but it was something more to grab onto than the others had.

One by one Jan went through their minds. The stories were mostly the same. They were going for a better life for themselves, their family, or to meet up with their families after they had found a better life. None of what was happening now had been in their plans or expectations. Out of the five of them, Jan was sure that only three of them, including her, really knew what they had gotten themselves into; the others were just scared. She then remembered the letter she had tucked in her bra.

At least these women and girls would have a chance to meet up with their families as planned, not like the one woman that still lay in the desert. The worst part was that she was sure that the family would not take it well, but at least she had found one of the women they were looking for. She frowned and her brow puckered as she reminded herself that not all endings were happy.

Jan could sense the ache in all of the women's muscles. This only intensified her discomfort, and after looking through all their minds, she decided to start into a routine of tensing and releasing each muscle. It took her fifteen minutes to go through the isometric muscle routine. She had used this routine other times when she had been confined, and it had been part of her training to help keep her muscles and mind fit. When she finished she felt a bit more relaxed and ready, even if she could still feel all the tension around her, she had better control. Pushing away all other thoughts it was time again to look into Omar's mind.

They were just entering the outskirts of Phoenix, and from what she could tell they were headed straight into the downtown area. The sun was just coming up over the mountains in the east and even though it was cool in the trailer she was again breaking a sweat. Focused only on where he was headed she watched carefully. He went west out of the downtown area on Interstate 10 and then got off on the Nineteenth Avenue Exit.

In this area of town it was possible to find all types of housing, but mostly the old shacks that only posed as housing for people with just enough money to be able to say they owned their own home, dysentery and all. Turning carefully he pulled the trailer into an alley behind a house. In the backyard was a group of shacks all built on the same small plot. Jan pulled out of his thoughts when she got a feeling that they would soon be getting out.

Jan wondered just how many were still housed in these shacks and even inside the house. Just how many had traveled through this drop house? With any luck the house might contain some information that would be helpful. She would need to get a chance to do some exploring, without being noticed. It was at that moment she felt the trailer stop and heard the door to the trailer open again. Omar latched it to the side of the trailer again to keep it open and out of the way. She had no time to look for others.

She was not the first one to be let out of the small space she had been allotted for the trip, and she could feel the pain and fear as each of the others were dragged out of their hiding spots and pushed out of the trailer landing on their faces and sides. Most could barely walk with their stiff, sore muscles, so they were dragged from the place they had landed and into what Jan could only guess were the shacks that she had seen in the backyard. Jan didn't try to read anyone as there was too much fear and pain in the air for her to get a good read of any of their minds. Using the other skills she had been taught, she listened and waited to see what was out there. There wasn't much outside noise, and occasionally she heard Omar mumble and gruffly pull or push one of the women. All of a sudden Jan felt him coming her way. She was as ready as she could be. She heard the lock being opened and then the lid was lifted. There was no smile on his face, in fact, no emotion at all. This seemed almost routine to him; all he was handling was cargo.

"Time to get out" and he grabbed her by the arm. With a hard pull on her one arm he wrenched her out of the little box in which she had been placed. Jan had tightened the muscles in her shoulder to keep her arm from being dislocated. She didn't allow Omar to see that she had more muscle control than the others, so she stumbled, tripped, and fell to the floor. Omar kept pushing and kicking her toward the door. Then he pushed her out the door. Jan tumbled down the two steps to the ground, and collapsed onto her left side in the dirt keeping her right side as free as she could.

Omar followed her out and pulled her toward the shack where he had put the rest of them. The shack was no disappointment. It was small and dirty with barely enough room for four people to lay side-by-side in, and all five of them were now being stowed in it. The windows were boarded up allowing very little light to creep through the cracks. The door was a bit more substantial than the one in Mexico. Even if the door hadn't been more substantial here the guard that she saw roaming the yard was definitely a deterrent.

She could tell as she was pushed into the shed that one of the girls had a question, and was ready to voice it. Since the tape was still over their mouths it was difficult. The woman started to mumble and then to create even more noise so they would notice her. Omar went over to her and roughly ripped the tape from her mouth, seeming to enjoy it. A small whimper escaped her mouth as the welts began to form, and then she looked Omar straight in the eyes.

"When do we get to go to our families?" although she was serious, Omar just laughed.

"Keep your voices low or immigration will find you," it was a demand. "We are your family now, doll," Omar's smile sickened Jan. It was the last impression he wanted to leave with them until he decided to open the door again, "Until we sell you."

10

As the door to the eight-foot by eight foot shed rattled closed and a padlock clicked into place there were no sounds coming from the people trapped inside. She was sure it was the shock that kept them immobilized in the beginning, all of them except for Jan. Each of the women, or girls, had been left with their bags. They had already gone through each bag thoroughly and taken anything of value. Jan knew that the items in her bag could mean the difference between life and death, and was very happy that she still had it; it would be invaluable tonight. Not knowing how long they would be kept here and fearing that if she left it too long there would be no way out, Jan had decided that she had to do her sweep tonight. There was a stream of sunlight starting to seep into the shed from many different places as the day continued.

These sheds, Jan had seen at least three of them when they had dragged her toward this one, were nowhere near what would be called watertight. There were holes or cracks in the ceiling as well as the boards that covered the small very utilitarian windows. The walls were two by twos covered with rough wood that looked as if it had been used many times over for many different things. They had probably been old storage sheds at one time that the coyotes had bought from others after the sheds had seemed at the end of their usefulness.

Many places had been badly repaired more than once. The floor was bare concrete and had not been swept for weeks, if not months and a thin layer of dirt covered the floor along with filth, human waste, and bugs. The smells in here would have been overpowering if the cracks and holes that existed in the shed had been covered. These sheds were temporary housing for when they first brought in the illegal aliens, and not as places in which they planned to imprison people for longer periods of time.

Jan could hear and feel, and read the guard outside of the shed. From the reading she got she knew there would be a guard on duty most of the time. She would deal with him only if it was necessary. This was only a minor complication to Jan and the completion of her work. Right now there were other things she needed to do.

Jan went to work quickly on getting these women out of their shock and back to reality. She first started by untying their hands. Gabby was standing motionless and her face was frozen in a look of horror. As their emotions began to thaw, Jan could feel them. Using what light there was in the room; Jan gently pushed behind Gabby and took a good look at the ropes that held her hands together. They were only simple knots, easy to undo. Turning around she untied Gabby quickly and it was only then that Gabby began to move.

Gabby whimpered silently as she rubbed her wrist and rotated her shoulders after she was untied and then she carefully removed the tape from her mouth. Jan was sure that they would all sport some red welts where the tape had been removed. Jan slid around in front of Gabby and turned so that Gabby would instinctively know that she wanted her hands untied as well. As Gabby worked quickly on her knots Jan could feel tears falling on her forearms. She was silently sobbing, and that fact pained Jan.

Compartmentalizing those feelings for a later time, Jan noticed that a couple of the others had taken cues and started undoing each other's knots, some crying like Gabby as well. The shock was beginning to wear off and they wanted to be able to at least move and communicate, all but one. She stood pressed into a corner. There was no emotion, thought, or panic coming from this woman, and that worried Jan. Shock was a funny thing. It could kill you just as fast as anything else, and leave no marks. They had been through a lot and this young woman looked like it. She was too young and inexperienced to handle what she had just been through.

Jan pulled her bag around front and pulled out another shirt she had, placing it over this girl's head and arms. When Gabby saw her do this, she copied Jan's actions. Soon the others followed and she was beginning to warm. Jan looked for other injuries and found that she had deep cuts and scrapes, but nothing as serious as the shock she was facing.

The space was tight and the conditions oppressive. Checking her pulse and eyes, Jan made her take a sip of water from the jug she had in her bag. This water contained extra electrolytes and would help her recover faster. Making sure that she had done all she could to help out the girl in the corner, she now turned her attention to the others. Jan could tell that one of the women, the one with short black hair, wanted to out of here and would try soon. Jan was pretty sure that unless this woman picked the right time, if there was a right time, it would end in tragedy. It was one more thing she would have to watch out for and she made a mental note of that.

It was then that the silence they had shared was shattered. They all heard the scream that was too quickly stifled by another sound. Jan visibly winced. It was a sickening thud, the sound of a bat or board connecting forcibly with flesh. It was a sound that was all too familiar to Jan. The shed that was nearest to them must have other women in it, at least one.

Up until that moment Jan hadn't given it more than just a passing thought. The emotions and thoughts in this shed had masked the others and she had plenty to do here. Jan had known what she volunteered for going across the border. She had even come to terms with having the others with her. She had not believed, or maybe it had just been a hope, that she wouldn't find other women still housed here.

That scream forced her to come face to face intimately with the fact that what she did would affect more than just herself and the people she was with. That terrified scream spoke volumes. Ward had made her come face to face with those issues before starting this mission. Could she handle failure if it should happen? Could she stand losing one person to save many? She made the choices now, not the department and it wasn't easy.

Pushing aside her thoughts and feelings Jan started the search for minds, any mind, to find out what was happening. Without concern for herself or the energy it might take, Jan ended up in the mind of the woman who had just been beaten and through her terror filled eyes Jan looked back onto Omar's face. It was a long time rule not to read a mind full of pain. There were many reasons for this; the biggest was the fact that pain itself came through far better than anything else and to read the other thoughts one had to take the pain as well. This made the reading less than reliable.

Jan had no idea who she was reading, but had known that she had been trapped in that shed for at least three days. The pain oozed from the other woman and overtook both of their minds, numbing their thoughts. Although Jan could not see the woman yet, she could tell from her thoughts that her mouth had been taped again and that the right side of her face was in so much pain that something had to be broken, most likely from being hit. Through her mind Jan could feel the swelling in her face and the throbbing pain.

Jan wanted to pull away, to leave her mind, but she was afraid that she might not be able to change minds fast enough. Jan Watched as Omar's hands gripped her upper arms and the pressure he used was more than was needed. Jan's face began to twist with the feeling of the pain. Omar's face was close to this woman's face now, and his voice was harsh and cruel.

"I almost had you for myself, but we found someone who wants you Makita. I think you'll like this one," his smile sickened the both of them. "They're going to take you to Vegas. You'll have a real good time there. Lots of work for someone as pretty as you," he let his eyes drop down below her face, and the meaning was more than clear. "Should work off your debt in three, four, ten years," and he laughed, "if you last that long." It was then that Makita started to sob behind the tape, her eyes blurred, and the immense sorrow and pain that she felt made it necessary for Jan to break from her mind. Slowly Jan again felt human, but not whole. Tired and with her reserves nearly empty she tried again, but this time for Omar's mind.

Not allowing herself to think, she quickly looked into Omar's mind. He was thinking of the contact, the money, and the place these two women were to be taken. This was more than Jan could hope for and not at all what she wanted. It was an easy read. Pushing the ugliness of the situation out of her head she went straight for the information she needed. His buyer was located not directly in Vegas, but just off the north side, easy to get to and business was by word of mouth.

He had sold many women to him before this batch, and there was a standing relationship with this buyer. He wasn't the first choice, but he took the leftovers. This was not his primary buyer, but he kept the cost profitable on those that didn't sell. The pick up and drop off spot was just outside of Nothing, Arizona. It was a small stop, not a town, located on a fairly well traveled road that carried many people to and from the gambling spots located in Nevada.

Hardly anyone stopped on this road, or at Nothing itself. If someone were to escape or make a break for it during an exchange, there was literally nothing around there but desert. It was a small gas station and store with a house located somewhere behind that. Total population, two. The next town was at least twenty miles away in any direction, with no reliable sources of water located anywhere in the desert that surrounded it.

The desert around Nothing was also pretty barren. It contained only small scrub with no shade at all. Reddish brown mountains surrounded the area in the distance, and rocky hills covered what was left. If someone escaped, it would surely mean death by dehydration. There was no place for anyone to run. No place anyone would want to run to.

She sifted through to the information she needed as quickly as possible, storing it away for the future. She could now place at least two buyers, maybe three, but the two faces she could see were pretty reliable. The local buyer paid more for his shipments, and they were to be offered to them first. She thought she saw another house, but she wasn't sure as that image faded. Then Omar's thoughts shifted and Jan rubbed her temples unable to pull out any more information. She was too tired to get anything more than what he was thinking.

Omar began loading the camper again with three women while Jan waited, hoping to see more on who this buyer was. This time his thoughts were more focused and Jan got a vehicle description and partial plate. Now all she needed was a chance to hand the information over to someone. Omar would take off in the next half hour with the women. Beads of sweat ran down Jan's face as she tried to keep the link and find the name of the buyer. All she could come up with was another picture of not the buyer but a horse trailer. It was a metal trailer with Nevada plates and was being pulled by an old gray, maybe primer color truck, a Ford.

Jan pushed herself harder to look even deeper into Omar's thoughts using up what was left of her energy. She began to unconsciously lean up against the wall, her eyes rolling back in her head and slowly closing. The effort was worth it for the information she was getting.

Another picture formed of Omar meeting with a man about his age and slightly taller. He seemed to be about twenty pounds lighter if Omar's picture of him was anywhere near accurate. His long shoulder length hair was wavy and black, jet black and his skin coloring was rich reddish brown. He didn't look to be of Hispanic descent, but with his elongated face and slanted eyes Jan could tell that his ancestry was definitely leaning more toward Native American. They were to meet in about two hours. Omar would have to hurry. Jan silently took a deep breath as a name appeared in her head, Joseph.

Barely breathing again, Jan watched Makita struggle as Omar dragged her toward the camper. Omar tightened up his hands to a point where the pain must have made her stop. He pushed her through the door of the camper and up the steps. Following her into the camper he pulled her over to the small bed in the very back of the twelve-foot camper. Makita didn't know how lucky she was that he didn't have more time.

Lifting the bed with one hand, and keeping a painfully firm grip on Makita, he lifted the board that covered the hidden compartment. With little thought, he threw her into the hole under the bed. The board banged into place over her head, and Jan saw the lock slide into place. It would take someone who knew the camper well to find the spot in which she was held. It was clever, too clever. Unless the person inside made noise, no one would ever find them.

"You better get used to this, or you'll just be dead," the words were cruel and the voice matched, but the statement was correct.

Omar took the other woman from the guard, and placed her in

the same compartment in which Jan had been trapped. The other woman was too sick to struggle. Jan would have liked to read her thoughts, but knew that the switch between minds was impossible. Jan was unaware of her health, at this point. Her energy level had reached a very dangerous point, and she was losing her color, and her footing fast.

"I'll be back in time to meet up with them," Omar walked away from the camper and toward the front of the truck.

"We may have a problem," the guard wasn't being too clear.

"You know what to do with problems," and then Omar got into the truck and gave even more orders to the guard, "Tell Enrique if he doesn't give me an answer on the one soon I'll . . ."

Jan was easily jolted from Omar's mind when Gabby touched her shoulder, and a shudder ran through her body. During the time she had been reading both Makita's and Omar's minds she had slowly slid down the side of the shed. She was pale and looked as if she were about to collapse. Gabby had watched her the whole time and was now worried that she was going to lose her only link to another human being in this terrifying situation.

Gabby gawked at her and Jan could only imagine what she might look like. She usually never let herself get to this point, but there were times that the information and the rewards were worth it. Taking a couple of deep breaths and smiling she looked again toward Gabby as her color seeped back into her face.

"I'm tired. I'm hungry," she rested her hand on top of Gabby's to reassure her. Gabby allowed herself to smile just a little, "We need to sit down and get some rest." The others had already found themselves a place to be in the shed, sitting, standing or whatever was as comfortable as they were going to get. The young girl in the corner had more color in her face, and Jan was now less worried about her condition. One of the others had untied her and sat next to her rubbing her arms to increase circulation. Looking into all their faces made Jan's thoughts circle back to the ones she had had earlier.

Until now, Jan had been able to push aside her emotions and feelings. Feelings, as they had been taught, were a liability. When Gabby touched her, it had brought it all back in a rush. There had been a reason that Ward had never pushed her toward this. In the department, they had learned many skills that had made them not only mind readers, but agents extraordinaire. One of the lessons they had learned early on as agents was that they were the good guys trying to catch the bad guys. It had been the simple truth, but the next steps in these lessons were not as easy to learn.

They had been told in training that as good guys they were expected to complete the assignment to a satisfactory end, no matter what the cost. It was cut and dry, they were given the assignment, the goal, and what was necessary. They were not expected to think or decide what might be acceptable losses. They were taught to distance themselves from their emotions, turn them off, because nice guys, or gals, rarely finished alive in this business. They were just tools and their humanity was not a factor, it was a liability.

For years she had separated the assignment from the person, the person from the feelings, and herself from herself. Over the years the separation had become less clear for Jan. It had been a slow process and one that had happened without her being aware of it. After working many assignments with her partner she became comfortable with him.

Acting as a father figure he had watched as her relationship with Ward had started, and later on as her affair with Ward, according to the department, had ended. He had been urged by the powers that be to remind Jan of her duties. Rob had warned her about Ward both at the beginning of the relationship and during it, and the warning was not just from the departmental side of things. To this day she could still hear what Rob had told her after one of their assignments, before she took a short vacation, "Remember what they taught you, nice guys don't survive in this business, just watch yourself." She assumed he must have known they were meeting, but she never confirmed or denied Rob's suspicions.

All the trainers had been right about one thing. Nice guys and gals didn't survive, and now she knew just what she, and Ward, had lost when they were in the department, their humanity. Ward had had a couple years on her to slip back into his skin and get comfortable with it. He had given her a push to start the process. Without that, she would have been emotionally and mentally lost right now.

Uncontrollably, her mind slipped back to one of the more dehumanizing testing sessions she had endured. She had known that she was safe, in theory, but she had been interrogated, tortured and humiliated for days. It wasn't until about six hours ago that she had begun to question it. She stood in the back of a now pitch black room, blindfolded and bound to the wall. It had been hours since anyone had been to see her. For all she knew, it had been days.

Her muscles had stopped aching ages ago and were now just numb. This had started off as a testing session, but had something gone wrong? She had been dropped on some tropical island with nothing but her knife and a coded message and told to make her way to the beach. Once on the beach she would be picked up by a small group of SEALS and taken aboard a ship out in international waters. Jan would then turn over the message to someone who would identify themselves as 'Twister'. She hadn't found the beach, what she had found was a group of thugs with automatics waiting for her. She couldn't help but wonder if this was still part of the test or a factor no one counted on.

For all she knew this would be the first of many times she would have to endure this before she could go on to the more mentally stressful exercises. Up until now she had trained with many of the Special Forces branches. There were no lasting scars, no visible marks that she could or would show anyone, but she had achieved the ability to emotionally remove herself from her surroundings and to accomplish the job at hand. She was strong and capable and she hoped that was what was being tested. When they thought she was ready, they would continue with the mind reading lessons and mental activities. The few others she had met on this bizarre journey had told her this was the easiest part of the trip. All she was sure of was that she would do anything to stay alive.

She felt more than heard the movement outside the room and then the door opened. Before she knew it a small fragile woman had removed the wrap that covered Jan's eyes and was untying her right arm. The woman had left the door open a crack and there was muted light seeping into the room. She placed her finger to her lips in the hopes to signal Jan to stay quiet. The woman didn't look like she was in good shape herself. There were bruises on her face and arms, and she looked scared. Later Jan realized it was part of the experiment, the test, and that it wasn't just random how she had looked or which arm she had untied.

She wasn't sure just what happened next. Men burst through the door as she untied her legs with her right hand and her left hand became free. Guns fired and she pulled the woman in front of her and used her as a shield to escape from the men in the room. Jan felt her body jerk backward as if hit and her body went limp. Without further thought Jan flung her lifeless body toward the men and jumped for the door landing on her left shoulder and rolling out. She sprang to her feet and sprinted down the hall using what little she knew of the mind reading skills to try and 'feel' her way out.

Fifteen minutes later she was on the beach without time to signal the boat. Behind her she could hear her guards pounding through the brush. Without further thought, and it may not have even been any thought at all, she rushed toward the waves and dove in sinking below the swells and fighting her already tired body. She heard the crack of automatic weapon fire and knew that the ocean itself would keep her safe as long as she could stay about four feet under the surface.

After thirty minutes of swimming she floated to the surface one last time. Each time she had come up for air she had tried to signal anyone that might be watching. Each time she had been disappointed. Now as she floated up for what she knew would be the last time, she didn't even try to signal anyone. She rolled on to her back and tried to keep her head above water. She hadn't even thought of the woman she had used and left laying dead on the cell floor, all she had wanted to do was to deliver the coded message. She fought to get the message to 'Twister'.

Her arms were slowing and her head began to sink. Jan knew this was the end. Closing her eyes she readied herself for what was coming. It felt more like a dream as she was scooped up out of the water and drug onto an inflatable boat with four guys in scuba gear staring down at her and what she thought might be two more climbing into the boat. Where they had come from she couldn't even imagine, but they were her pick-up crew.

On the boat was where she really got the reality check. Instead of meeting up with some mysterious contact named 'Twister', she met with her trainer Sam. She knew then that she had been had. The woman was most likely alive and she hadn't just nearly escaped death, but was pulled just before it happened.

"Congratulations, you've passed," Sam said calmly. She wasn't really mad, she was furious, but she didn't let it show. First of all she was too tired, and secondly she wasn't going to give him that satisfaction, "Now let me introduce you to your next associate," with that a woman stepped into her view, "Her name is Pat." With that she had taken her final steps out of the world of humanity. It had been the job that had been the most important item. Complete the job no matter what, or who.

In the back of her mind she gave Ward a smile and the thank you he deserved. He had allowed her to take the baby steps she needed back into the world. Now, even though the job was important so must be the people it affected. They were there for them as well. Soon she would again be able to thank him for this chance he had given her to be human once more.

Gabby tapped Jan's shoulder again this time leaving her hand there. Jan turned to face a very scared young girl. The pain of what Jan had just seen happen to Makita and the fear she could feel from Gabby threw her back into what was now her reality, and discomfort. She could read all of the questions that Gabby wanted to ask. She knew all the questions that Gabby was too afraid to ask. And she also knew that Gabby knew the reality of the situation. It all came flooding into her head and was almost too much.

Gabby didn't blame her, but that may come very soon. Jan let her thoughts go by and let her mind shut down. Jan tucked the new feelings away to be analyzed later; right now she needed to focus on her character. This time it would be both the job and the people.

It wasn't hard for Jan to fall back into character; it would save Gabby. Jan was drained by all the mind reading she had done. She was weak and her pulse rate too high. It would take her longer this time to rejuvenate. Even in the morning light that was beginning to creep in, she knew she must look pale and drawn. Jan took a breath and again she let herself pick up on the others in the room. Taking in some of the fear of the others she was able to face Gabby with the look she knew would convince her that she too was scared.

"What's happening?" was the only question that Gabby was brave enough to ask.

"I don't know, but something is not right," Jan glanced at the other women. No one wanted to talk, and share their fears. "All I know is we have to stay together," and in her head she thought, 'and hope that Ward is as close as we are.'

"Do you think," and Gabby never finished her thought.

"Yes, I think we are in trouble. I don't think they ever wanted to help us," Jan noticed one of the other women moving in the background. She was the one that had been sitting next to the young girl in shock.

"I think we need to get out of here." Her voice was low so as not to alert the guard. It was the first time she had said anything.

"And go where?" Jan's question was valid, and in a world of illegal aliens that was the trouble, where to go. "Do you know where we are, or where to go? If we are caught then they will send us back and I don't have enough money left to cross again."

"I don't know, but I do know that I don't want to stay here. It is bad here," the other woman sat down by the girl in shock, not saying a word, "They will hurt us if we stay."

"There is one problem," Jan took a breath and looked at all of the women, "the guard outside has a gun. I saw it when they put me in here, and I think he would use it if we try to leave," the women looked toward the door and then Jan could see the realization of their helplessness dawn on their faces. Jan hated to crush their hopes, but she needed to keep everything under her control to keep these women safe.

In the past it was simple, now with the new emotions life was becoming complicated, and not so guilt free. She was sure that escapes had been tried before, some even successful, but those weren't the thoughts she was getting from the men outside, or the other women that had been in the other shed. She wasn't doing hard readings but it was getting too much. She had to shut off soon.

Until now her feelings about the woman in the other shed had been kept in check. By just a twist of fate she had made a contact with others trapped in this prison and then chosen to ignore them. She realized that in the last few minutes she had made a choice of whose life was more valuable, who was to be injured more or less, or even die. In the past she wouldn't have had feelings about this. An uncontrollable shiver ran through Jan's entire body as she realized this. Gabby started to rub her arms thinking that Jan was suffering from shock.

Her feelings were less of hopelessness, but of wonder. How had she been able to so easily dismiss the value of a human life? What had happened to slowly erode away the shell the department had erected to protect and distance her in situations like this? Could the lining have started to collapse once a relationship with Ward started? Had the department known that would happen? Was that why there was a policy stating no relationships of any kind existed? There was no way to second-guess it now, nor did she really ever want to.

Whatever had happened to change her, refocus her, reprogram her, she liked and embraced it. There was only one problem to it. Jan now felt the guilt that was associated with just having to sit and wait for the right moment as she let innocent victims be placed into a deadly situation.

In a corner of the shed their captors had placed a jug of water and she realized just how close they were to dehydration. Jan leaned over and picked it up. She first smelled the water to make sure that they were at the very least not to be poisoned or drugged. In the back of her mind she knew that all toxins didn't smell, but she also realized that right now they were the meal ticket and to kill them would be useless. Jan took a small sip and then passed the jug to the next woman. She didn't need to say anything, and they smiled at each other. Once the jug had made it to all five women it came back to Jan. After about fifteen minutes Jan was pretty sure that all she could possibly get from the water was a case of the runs, and she took another sip.

Slowly, as exhaustion took hold of the rest of the women they curled up together and fell asleep. Jan, although tired, was very restless. Her mind would not let her body rest. She watched as the others curled up on the floor together for both the mental support and security, and noticed a small but adequate space in the opposite corner. She moved silently over to that small space. She didn't need much room as she began to stretch.

Jan faced a small crack in the boards that covered the window. She could see the sunlight that tried to make its way into this darkness. She could imagine the many colors that filtered through the sky as it rose up over the horizon. Her muscles had taken a beating over the last few days and she knew that the assignment was nowhere near the end. She took a large breath in and slowly released it as she began her morning routine of Tai Chi.

Pushing all other thought from her mind she let the slow and steady movements lull her muscles into a deep relaxed stated that would tone and prepare them, and her, for anything. Her mind once again connected with nature, moving to its rhythm, and relaxation was no longer what she hoped for, but what she had achieved as she finished and went to rest in the pile as well.

11

Ward woke up restless and early the next morning, looking at his watch he realized it was just before sun up. Having barely slept, he still couldn't come up with a good reason to stay in bed just staring at the ceiling. In all the years he had worked as an agent and then later on as freelance, he had never known himself to sleep well on an assignment. He always got enough rest to complete the job, to stay focused, but never a relaxing sleep. This job was no exception.

Throwing the covers back, he placed his feet on the ground. Dressed only in lightweight boxers he got out of bed, stretched, and ran his fingers through his hair. The bedroom was small but adequate, more than he was used to on an assignment like this one. There had only been a few times over the years when he had gotten a good stay in a five star hotel or resort, most of the time it had only been in nondescript out of the way places.

A year ago Eddy had made mention to Ward that this complex had been up for sale. It wasn't a large apartment complex but it had about seventy units in it. Using the other complexes they had acquired two years prior as collateral, they bought this one. Eddy was right. It had been a great investment. It was barely empty and seemed to keep a steady quality clientele. They had been able to keep the rent reasonable and for that the management on site was thankful. It meant less turn over.

The income was also nothing to sneeze at. When Ward had asked Eddy to find him a place, he hadn't expected this. Since they owned the complex, Eddy had made a call and checked with the manager to find out if they had a one bedroom that was open. Eddy wanted Ward, and Jan, to have a place they could come back to in Phoenix, a home. Right now, both were essentially homeless here. Eddy had been in luck.

He had the managers move in the necessary furniture to make it furnished and livable. The managers weren't told that one of the owners would be living in the place, as Ward had been the silent partner in all of the business doings. As far as they were concerned Ward was one of Eddy's friends and they were working out the rental agreement.

Ward glanced around the apartment and thought about the place. It was in a well-established neighborhood in Mesa. The trees were large and the entire complex was set off the road giving it a welcoming look. It also blended into the surroundings and the architecture well. It was more stable. Smiling, Ward thought that this place might be a keeper.

The only piece of furniture in the bedroom was the double bed; in the living room kitchen area there were the basics. Eddy had brought in the computer, a small laptop, even though he knew that Ward would use his own most of the time to get the information he needed. The managers had made sure there was a television with a cable hook up, and the standard appliances one would need to survive in the kitchen. The entire floor plan was only a little more than five hundred square feet; but more importantly it had a connected garage.

He walked over to the window moving the vertical blinds enough to peek through. He noticed that the view from here was into a small courtyard with large, older trees. Ward smiled inwardly. It was a hundred percent better than his last place. It was also totally unavailable to him ever again. He walked out to the living area and opened the sliding glass doors out onto it. Normally he did his Tai Chi routine outside on the patio or balcony in Mexico. This balcony was far too visible for anyone located in or around the complex. He had checked the frig quickly last night and found a jug of milk and box of cereal in the cupboard. Eddy was always at a lost as to what to put in for food. Eddy called take out cooking, and the milk and cereal in the frig was the most Ward had ever seen in Eddy's frig. Most likely just to ward off hunger pangs if necessary. Ward decided to skip breakfast for now and pick something up on the way to Eddy's.

The muted colors of the sunrise began to fill the room and it called to Ward's spirit. Moving to the center of the living room where he could see the trees he faced toward the incoming sunlight and slowly started into his Tai Chi routine. He chose only to run through a short routine to just loosen up his muscles preparing him for the day. Although Tai Chi was an ancient form of exercise, many of the moves were related to the other ancient arts of self-defense. As his mind focused on the moves, he could feel his muscles respond to the movements and begin to relax as the world slipped silently away. Pushing all other thought from his mind he continued on soundlessly. His mind and muscles in sync and quieted, Ward could sense nothing more than the sunlight, and he was once again in tune with nature.

Finished, he walked into the bathroom and turned on the hot water in the shower. He quickly shaved as the water warmed. When he got into the shower, Ward carefully placed his cell phone on the sink counter in case of an emergency. Climbing into the shower he let the warm water wash over him before he began to soap up trying not to think about where and what may be happening to Jan. He knew that she was able to take care of herself. He put his head under the spray of the warm water. Ward could barely hear the sound of the cell phone.

He didn't waste any time getting out of the shower and reaching first for the phone. Ward checked on the number and identity of the caller as he grabbed a towel. Wrapping it around his waist he quickly answered the phone in one fluid movement. He had been expecting the call this morning, although the timing was just about five minutes off.

"Hey Eddy,"

"Got everything you need?" Eddy had waited as long as he could to call and check on Ward. He was never really sure of what Ward did on his own. It wasn't sleep. Ward got way too much done. Ward kept pretty much to himself even though Eddy knew he was probably more of a friend to him than anyone had ever been. What Eddy had learned about Ward he had picked up by observation. He knew that many times when they were working together there were plans that would change overnight. Part of his job was to help gather all the pieces together and be ready for anything. And the most important thing he had learned, there was no one he could trust more than Ward.

"We'll get started early this afternoon. Before I get to you I'm going to need a set of work clothes. I'll stop and pick some up. Have a set packed for yourself though," he paused for only a second; Ward let the conversation die for a minute. Although they both wanted to get started, it wouldn't be until the afternoon when they could really do anything, and the waiting would be the hard part. "I'll need to check the wires before I get there, so don't expect me any time before one."

"That'll give me time to roam around and check what's on the street," Eddy knew a few of the gang kids in the area and they knew him, at least they thought they did.

"See you at one," and Ward ended the call. He sat on the edge of the bed ignoring the little drips of water that ran down his chest. Dialing the number, he waited and then entered the password. Soon he was connected to the World Wide Web through his phone. He knew it would take just about as long if he used the laptop. He logged into the Border Patrol computers. It had been a busy night at the border. They had picked up about six different bands of illegal aliens and some of the coyotes in charge of them. Ward paged through the descriptions of the people, and the names and found that none of the fifty-five people that had been picked up matched Jan's description.

A sense of relief and worry passed over him at the same time, and he pushed it away just as quickly. He had learned after the first couple of jobs on his own that there would be time later to deal with the emotions that he could no longer continue to ignore. Now was not the time for it though. Routinely he checked through all the other departmental databases, and then Ward checked all the newspaper sites as they sometimes got the stories out before the official reports were filed. The papers weren't always a hundred percent right, but they could be useful. An hour and a half later Ward was dressed and on his way.

Ward had only brought a couple changes of clothes with him, and all were the same style of clothing he had on yesterday. He grabbed a black button down short sleeve shirt with black jeans. He clipped his gun on the waistband at the small of his back and left his shirt untucked. In order to hide the gun completely he would need to move it into his specialized holster that he had brought with him. Right now there was no need to hide it, just conceal it, as they were not going to the casino until tonight to meet with Carlos and Enrique.

There was a door in the back of the apartment beside the refrigerator. It led to the garage. Making sure the front door was locked; he casually placed a small piece of paper under the bottom hinge of the door. If anyone got in he wanted to know about it. Today was a new day with new surprises. He had already left other traps in the apartment that would allow him to know if anyone had been in. This one was for the intruder to find, so if someone did invite themselves in, they would know they had gotten caught and be less likely to look for more.

Going to the back door by the kitchen, he left and set the door. This indicator though was not obvious. Carefully Ward placed the corner edge of the welcome mat on the door. It was not enough to make anyone take notice, but if the door were to be opened then closed it would just ever so slightly be under the door, simple and effective. He walked down the dark narrow stairs and into the garage.

Jan was awakened by the sound of a car leaving. It was hard to tell what time of the day it was. She could still see sunlight, this time brighter and more intense, but had no idea on the position of the sun. It was significantly warmer in the shed now. She slowly moved so that she would not wake the others. Jan still felt tired. When they had been placed in here there was only one guard and Omar. Omar was gone, and now if she was right, so was the guard. It wasn't as if they would be left to roam around, but with the trip they had just taken, they expected them be exhausted. Carefully Jan moved toward the door and checked for any thoughts that might be lurking anywhere outside of it. She could sense nothing. Knowing that the opportunity might not come around again Jan decided that now was the time to go and investigate.

Jan gently gave the doorknob a turn and then pushed the door open about two inches. The door was chained shut, and a padlock dangled on the end of it. Putting her hand inside her bag that still hung against her back she found her picklock pen. Using the point of the pen she worked the end of the padlock her way. Holding it with one finger she then undid the pen and within seconds she had the lock open. Giving both a mental and visual check she could tell that she had not woken anyone. Carefully she slid out of the shed and into the bright sunlight.

Squinting, she first checked for dogs and found that there were none. Looking back at the shed, she realized why. Even if the walls from the inside looked weak and ready to fall down, they had been reinforced from the outside. Newer boards were not nailed on over the windows, but riveted into the steel frame of the windows. These boards continued on toward the edge of the shed's frame and were again riveted in place.

When she had first seen the shed these had just looked like haphazard boards, but with closer inspection it would be impossible to break out of a window. It would be easier to go through the wall, but how many women would know that. Before she left the shed, she relocked it. It was important that they assume that security had not been broken, and the last thing she needed was for anyone to escape and raise the alarm.

Without wasting any more time she headed for the house, trying to stay in what shadows there were. Once at the back door she checked again and knew that the house was empty. She easily let herself into the kitchen. Jan worked her way through the house in record time. In the first three rooms she had found nothing, as there was nothing to be found. The house was not well kept. Dirty dishes lay all around the kitchen and the morning paper lay on the floor. Walking into the living room was very much the same. There was trash throughout the room. Pizza boxes lay on the floor, and beer cans beside the one couch. The television was the focal point. It was state of the art and at least forty-two inches.

She went down the hall and glanced in the first room on her right. The bathroom was revolting, and as she looked through it she found nothing that would even link these two with anything more than disgusting personal habits. Moving cautiously down the hall she approached two more doors. She looked in the door on the left and then on her right and saw two small and well-used bedrooms. Deciding to save these till last she walked to the back of the house. Opening the door she noticed this room was tidy. Walking over to the dresser she opened the top drawer, and smiled. It was here all of the interesting stuff was kept.

Three hours later Ward pulled up to the gate of Eddy's community. It had been a good morning and he had much to show for it in the trunk, along with some of his old and trusted goodies. He had stopped and picked up a set of used tools, an old dirt stained white tee-shirt, tan work pants with holes in the knees, a baseball cap, and a large faded cloth that might have been a handkerchief or bandana in another life but now was very nondescript. After he had tucked these new items into the small trunk, and the cloth into his pocket, it was now time to stop for a quick breakfast that would also be lunch.

Pulling the Z3 into the parking lot in front of a square concrete box of a building that no one could remember what it's original color was. Ward carefully parked the car in the back, away from the view of the street, and hidden by the building. The place looked old, closed and maybe even condemned, though the faded sign outside the establishment declared the restaurant or bar to be open and operating. The restaurant, or bar, had been there for years, and relied solely on return business, or word of mouth. There were no windows, which meant that he could not be seen from the outside. The lighting inside was poor, making it hard for anyone to see or recognize him. Having stopped here a few times before, Ward knew enough to order only the huevos rancheros, eggs and salsa, with extra salsa.

He watched as the person down the bar from him ordered a shot and a beer. In less than five minutes his food appeared with hot fresh tortillas and rice and beans. He polished off the meal quickly and left the money for the bill on the bar along with a good tip. This early in the day he had been about the only one in here, but as he left, it was beginning to fill up.

He pulled up to Eddy's gate at five minutes to one, and was pulling into the guest parking area at exactly one. Eddy was standing in the shade, and as Ward pulled the car into a parking space he walked up and got in, throwing a small bag behind the seat. Like the day before, they both knew where they were going.

"Checked all the channels, nothing. With any luck she's here and we will see her shortly and get the information from her about the other side of the operation," Ward knew that Eddy needed to know almost as much as he did to do the job right. It never paid to keep your partner in the dark. When Ward took a breath Eddy jumped right in.

"From what I could get on the street this morning there wasn't much going on last night, and no one has put out trailers on us yet," Eddy watched as the gates opened again to let the BMW gracefully slide out.

"Good, that may not happen until we meet with them again tomorrow. I'm pretty sure we will be followed then," Ward pulled out of the drive and onto the road. As the car's speed increased he began to talk again, "They'll definitely want to check us out and then we'll lose them. You'll check out the goods later and I'll be doing surveillance."

"Same plan as always?" Eddy knew the routine.

"Almost, but I'll fill you in more later after we know where they want us to be," and that was enough for Eddy right now.

"Think Rubber's got anything yet?"

"We'll find out," Ward smiled slightly, and without further conversation they headed toward the south Phoenix area.

It took only about twenty minutes and Ward eased the Z3 southwest off the interstate. It was a little early in the afternoon, but if they waited any longer they would stand the chance of Rubber rabbiting away. If he had a chance he would try to avoid Ward, even though he knew he couldn't do it. As Ward had the day before, he started to drive up and down the roads looking for the old and tired ice cream van. It was just about an hour before the kids got out of school, and a prime time for Rubber to be up and ready to make a bit of money, legally. The day's temperature was a bit above average for Phoenix, in the upper ninety's.   He would do a good legal business today, and probably an illegal one too.

Ward could read Eddy's thoughts, and he had the same questions. After driving around for forty-five minutes they still hadn't found him. There weren't many people just sitting around, and only a few cars in the area. Both Ward and Eddy had been visually searching the neighborhoods as they drove, and Ward was pretty sure that they hadn't missed him. No matter what had happened before though, Ward knew that Rubber had never left him high and dry. The feeling in the pit of his stomach was becoming harder to ignore it.

"Stop," Eddy's tone was sharp, "I thought I saw his van down that alley." Ward didn't say anything, but the pit of his stomach wasn't doing very well. Throwing the car into reverse he went backwards until he could turn into the alley.

"Are you . . ." and Ward didn't have to finish before Eddy answered his question. The feeling was only getting worse, and this time he wanted to make sure that Eddy had some way to protect himself if necessary.

"Definitely," that was the answer Ward needed. Pulling up behind the van, Ward could only sense one person in and around the van. Ward wondered if Rubber lived out of his van and maybe this was where he spent the night. With that thought though, came another flip in the pit of his stomach.

"Be careful," was all Ward whispered as they both got out of the car. Ward's eyes darted around the area to make sure they were alone. He could still read no one but Rubber, but what he was getting from Rubber made no sense. It was as if he were dreaming. Vivid images were flashing through his mind alternating with moments of complete blackness. Sounds that had no connections and words with no meaning came through. Ward wondered if Rubber was asleep or just high, sometimes they looked the same.

With Eddy on one side of the door and Ward on the other, Ward knocked. When he didn't get a reply he again knocked and this time called out Rubber's name, "Carlos, open up," the images just kept coming. Ward pulled out the old cloth he had bought earlier from his pocket and tried the locked door. Suddenly the images he was getting from Rubber stopped and Ward's mind confirmed what his stomach had been trying to tell him.

"Damn," Ward ran for the car's trunk as he pressed the release button, "Something's wrong in there."

Eddy became suddenly more aware of his surroundings and he searched the area for any face that might be taking any interest in what was happening around the van. Ward was back in a flash with his emergency bag. Ward handed the bag to Eddy and went to work on the lock. It took only seconds. As he flipped the lock up, he pulled out his gun. Although he was sure no one else was in the van, he couldn't be too careful. Pulling open the door he went into the van, gun in the lead and head down. Eddy stood half in the doorway and half in the road, highly aware of everything that was happening with his gun at the ready.

The van was a mess, more so than normal. All the cupboard doors were open and the items strewn about the van. It looked as if the freezers had been turned off for at least three hours. The contents were beginning to seep out and run down the sides of the cupboards and into the mess, pooling on the floor, or what Ward could see of it. On the counter lay what Ward could only surmise was Rubber's stash, torn open on one side and spilled on the counter and floor. Searching what he could see of the floor with his eyes he noticed a foot under a spilled box of cups. He wouldn't be visible to anyone looking in. Ward tucked his gun into the back of his jeans quickly and grabbed the emergency medical bag from Eddy.

"Don't touch anything," he told Eddy as he put on latex gloves. Glancing at Eddy, he noticed that Eddy had already put on his gloves. Being careful not to disturb too much, Ward stepped over a pile of cups and plastic spoons toward where Rubber's head should be. Ward found an arm and checked for a pulse, and found a very faint, thready one. He turned his head and opened one eye. The pupil was almost nonexistent. Ward quickly inspected each arm. He found what he had hoped he wouldn't. There on Rubber's arm was a needle mark, only one. Rubber had good stuff and he wasn't stupid enough to overdose. Picking up a few items that lay about it didn't take long for Ward to find the empty syringe someone had used to inject what could be a lethal dose into his system.

"Turn the car around and call 911. He needs more help than I can give him," as Eddy went for the car, Ward did his best to give him what care he would need to hopefully make it to the hospital. Ward started to count off the seconds in his head. He didn't dare give him much of any medication without a toxicology report, or some information as to what was in the needle they used. He could tell that Rubber was still breathing and hadn't yet vomited or had heart failure. He started an IV and gave him an injection. He left all the packaging attached so that when the emergency crew got here they would know what he started.

Putting his medical kit away and continuing to count off the seconds till he would have to leave. He turned Rubber on his side, putting him in a position that if he did vomit, then he wouldn't aspirate it and die. His face was bruised and very pale. With the vitals Ward got and what he could see, it didn't look good for Rubber.

Ward could hear the car rev outside, just once. It was Eddy's signal that he was ready and in position. Ward took the pulse one last time and decided that even if he were to stay he could be of no more use to Rubber. Grabbing his stuff he quickly made his way out of the van. Leaving the door open he hopped into the passenger side of the Z3 and Eddy quickly took the car out of the alley. Eddy maneuvered the car through the neighborhood streets quickly and onto the main street. In the distance they saw the emergency response vehicles heading down the road. Eddy pulled the car over and waited for the fire truck and police car to pass.

"Was he?" Eddy didn't finish.

"Not yet, but close, too close."

"That's what happens when you work with drug addicts," Eddy's head shook a bit as he pulled back out into traffic.

"Only wish it was that simple," Eddy glanced toward Ward for a second, the thought already in his head. Ward didn't allow him time to voice it though, "Oh yes, Rubber was an addict, but he never shot up, no other tracks. He was strictly a nose guy. Who ever did this to him gave him what they hoped to be a lethal injection. They didn't plan on us showing up before he expired. With any luck we weren't too late, but I couldn't be sure. It'll be close," Ward thought back to what he could have done differently. Cars passed by and without even noticing them on the road, Ward took in every face and some of their thoughts. There were moms on their way to pick up kids, or drop them off; businessmen trying to make a meeting and wondering if they had time to make a quick stop; teenagers wanting to get to the mall.

After about two minutes of quiet thought he decided to pull it back together. There was nothing he could have done; some people sealed their fate long before he got involved with them. Rubber's situation may have nothing to do with them. He did lots of things that would and could rub people the wrong way, but that's not what instinct told him.

"Think it had to do with us?" Eddy drove under the freeway and turned into the doughnut shop where they always met. Not sure of what was going to be their next move; he decided that a doughnut and coffee should be his. As he put the car into park, he turned to look at Ward. Ward waited to make his comment until the engine was shut off.

"I'd be surprised if it didn't."

12

Jan noticed that everything was neatly in place and although there was a bed in here, she could only guess what it was used for. The room resembled more of an office area to her. Near the table was a single dresser. On top of the dresser were a piece of paper and a pen making it the perfect place to conduct business. Someone just visiting wouldn't see anything out of place. Jan on the other hand didn't think this, compared to the other rooms and how they were kept she knew what she had found. The other rooms were only a cover, or just an area for them to spend time while they waited to sell their stock.

Jan made her way over to the dresser and looked at the three drawers. Opening the top drawer, Jan carefully, but quickly, pulled out each item of clothing in the drawer and laid them meticulously on top. It was imperative that they go back in the way they came out. It was what was under those clothes that made Jan start taking notes in her head.

Being careful to keep track of everything around her with all her senses, she began to pull out the rolls of socks. Jan had noticed that the sock balls were larger than they should be. Most of the time these would be of no interest, but they were too thick to be just socks. She undid the sock ball. The first sock ball she unwrapped held a thousand dollars, and each pair after that also contained the same. Jan only counted the money in three rolls of socks before she just counted the number of balls in the drawer. When she finished she had counted twenty sock balls. Carefully placing everything back the way it had been in the drawer before she had searched through it, Jan opened the next drawer and again found a couple pairs of shorts and a shirt covering other items that had nothing to do with what the bedroom was really used for.

This time she found a small black notebook. The book was old but the information was not. Most pages contained numbers, addresses and first names. Jan noticed that some of the addresses had been changed, but the name and numbers were the same. On some of the papers she noticed that there were stars, and notes. Reading through all the information as fast as she could and memorizing the addresses, she learned that their abuse of women was not solely limited to the coyotes that had transported them across the boarder. From what she could tell they had started to network and contact other drop houses for business.

Some of the drop houses were beginning to sell the women to them. Jan could only summarize that the ones that questioned what they were doing the least were marked with stars. There were also other marks next to the address. Some addresses had a cent sign, others two or three. Drop houses that sold their cargo for the least were ranked with these cent signs, she guessed. Lastly there were ones that had dollar signs connected to their names.

The money in the drawer above, Jan guessed, was used to pay the coyotes on the Mexican side of the border as well as for those women they chose to buy off other coyotes that were holding women hostage. It took Jan only minutes to memorize all six addresses. The rest were numbers, probably future contacts for him. Phone numbers would be of little use to any government agency as all of these people worked off cell phones anymore, and usually used assumed names. Raids of the other drop houses would most likely be far more profitable for an agency as they might get names, not just numbers. Repeating the addresses in her head one last time as she placed the book back in the drawer, she would write them down later when she was back in the shed, if she had a chance.

Unless she was found outside of the shed, Jan should have nothing to worry about as they had already been searched and it would be a waste of their time to do it again. Jan placed everything back in the drawer and slid it closed. There was one more drawer.

Opening the last dresser drawer she didn't find any clothes on top at all. There were many newspaper clippings, and each one that she pulled out had to do with immigration and how the border security was changing. There were other articles on coyotes. Jan could only guess that the papers were one of two things, research or pride. She didn't need to determine which one it was right now. In the bottom of the drawer were three large manila envelopes. Jan pulled out the first one and opened it on top of the dresser.

At first as she spread the contents of the envelope out on the dresser she was able to distance herself from them. There wasn't anything but photos in this envelope. All the pictures were the same, all were porn, and most of the subjects had probably at one time been their prisoners. Jan looked through the pictures without emotion. The pictures were taken in a variety of places, some here in this bedroom, some in the sheds, and others in places she had not seen. Quickly grouping the pictures, Jan could tell that each woman had been photographed in many different positions and places. Jan's stomach turned. There was nothing flattering or humane about them. It was just another step they were ready to take.

There were markets for these pictures, as sick as they were, as well as the women. Since it looked as if the pictures were taken over a period of time Jan could only guess that the women who were not sold immediately were subjected to this type of degradation. Picking up the next two envelopes she noticed that on the bottom of the drawer was a bit of drug paraphernalia as well. Jan guessed that this was used to get the women to pose.

Jan went through the other envelopes quickly and found the same type of photos in each, as she placed the photos back in the last envelope another theory began working its way through her head. What if they didn't buy the women from other drop houses, but just, for a lack of a better term, rented them? Jan could feel someone approaching the house and seconds later she could hear the familiar rumble of the jeep and camper combination. Quickly she placed almost all of it back in the drawer as she let her mind keep track of the person who had just arrived, Omar.

Omar had approached the house from the alley. Omar glanced at the sheds. All looked the way it should and he started to walk toward the house. Juan wasn't there; he figured that Juan had gone to take care of the other problem when he was sure that all the women in the shed were asleep. His new cargo was safe; he had just made another ten grand, and was feeling pretty good about things. Omar looked again at his watch as he stepped onto the back patio. Omar opened the backdoor and walked into the kitchen. He went toward the refrigerator ignoring the mess that encompassed the room, opened the frig, and grabbed a beer. Making his way through the kitchen and into the living room he walked over to the front door. Looking out the side window, Jan could feel his impatience. He was waiting for someone. As he stood there sipping his beer he saw a black SUV turn the corner and smiled. Putting his beer down, he unlocked the door.

Placing her hands on either side of the drawer, Jan slid the last drawer closed silently. Taking the corner of her shirt Jan wiped the parts of the dresser she had touched. She moved toward the window that led to the side yard. As she approached the house she had noticed the side yard was only about three feet wide, and the last time it had been mowed or cleared was probably about three years ago. This information she had tucked into the back of her head incase she needed it, and now she did.

Unlocking the window she opened it up fully, popped out the screen, and throwing her leg over the windowsill she pulled herself smoothly up and over, all in a matter of seconds. Once outside she closed the window all but a crack and put the screen back in place. She crouched down below the window amongst the tall uncut and dry grass using it as cover. If Omar was meeting someone, it was likely that it was business related, and business seemed to be conducted in the room she had been in. Since he didn't seem to be worried about the sheds right now, she wasn't going to hurry back to her little cell.

This was always where it got sticky in any job she did. If she stayed, the guard could be back at any time and it would be discovered that she was missing. Even though with her mind reading skills she would be able to see him coming, it might not be soon enough to get back safely. Balance that with what she could learn, and it was a toss up. She had found more information than she had hoped for in the house. It always amazed her how careless some people could be with information that they wanted no one else to have.

It was powerful evidence that wouldn't be ignored by any agency it was turned in to. What Jan didn't have were the buyers' names. She decided it was time to take the next step. All the she was getting from Omar was that he was going to meet and try to sell his current stock. Jan took a deeper look into his thoughts to see if she could find out where the guard was, and more importantly, when he would be back. With frustration, on both their parts, she discovered that it was just as much of a mystery to him as it was to her. Jan looked down and watched as the line of ants started up her leg. She brushed them away as the men in the SUV approached the front door, and she waited hoping there weren't any mice.

Omar let the two men in and greeted the shorter one with a handshake followed by the traditional hitting of the two fists together. It was obvious the taller man was there only as a body guard. He followed his boss dutifully as they started through the wasteland that was once a living room toward the back bedroom, stepping over the trash that lay about the floor.

"You need to clean this place up," the shorter man stated as he walked through the room.

"It's a cover man," Omar dismissed his comment quickly.

"It's laziness man," and Jan could tell that he had a disgusted look on his face. Jan took a look at the stranger through Omar's eyes. He wore good clothes, ones that were not just off the rack, but nicely tailored. He wasn't afraid to show he had money. His slacks were a rich brown and his shirt was a pale tan with a very light checkered pattern. He wore a simple suede jacket, lightweight, that matched the pants. Jan was sure this was to hide the presence of a gun that was most likely tucked in the back of his pants, or a shoulder holster. His hair was short and spiked with the dark tips bleached white. Nothing about him said poor. Jan thought she could see a hint of a large, gold chain that lay just under the collar of the shirt. She stayed in Omar's head for the moment to try and get his name.

"We got some good ones this time," Omar sat just opposite of him at the small table in the bedroom, "and they all made it this time." The guard stayed alert at the door of the bedroom. Omar started to pull out the pictures in the last envelope, the ones that had been taken of the women in Mexico before any of them had known what was going to happen.

"I hope better than the last time. I finally just dumped the last one; it was costing too much to keep her. I have a client that wants to pick up a few of your girls. He's already picked out one, but needs more. Looks like a good source with good references," Jan finally got it, Carlos. Carlos took the pictures, and Jan changed minds, "Not bad. Better than the last bunch." Jan read his mind as he looked through the pictures. Through his eyes she could see her picture come up, and then Gabby's. "These two are good," and he threw Jan's picture and Gabby's picture across the small table, "This one too." He looked through the other pictures again. As he looked at the pictures, Jan looked at his mind.

He purchased women and then resold them to whomever for whatever. It had started out as a small local operation but was turning slowly into a large and profitable one. He was beginning to make connections not just here in town. All he could see were dollar signs in his future. In Jan's eyes he was the main target. If they could stop him then the rest would crumble, for a while at least. Jan's breathing slowed as she searched harder to try and get pictures and names of his buyers, and then suddenly she saw the buyers in his mind. She knew one pair of faces well. Jan smiled to herself; it was nice to work with someone who knew just what to do. She wasn't sure how they had connected so fast, but it didn't really surprise her. He had promised she would have backup.

Looking closer into Carlos' mind, they had left it open as to how many women they really wanted to buy. Ward wasn't going to leave anyone behind, and she knew it. With this in mind, Carlos threw another picture across the table indicating that this one would also do. Four, he had chosen four of them. All Jan needed now was for him to pick the last one. Ward had left it open, no it had been Eddy, as to how many he would need, but hadn't been open enough. He put the pictures down, and Jan's heart sank. They would be leaving one behind.

"Our costs have gone up, and so have the risks. I want more for this bunch," Omar knew he was a shaky ground, but with the mention of a new buyer he figured the timing was right, and his stock was good.

"Now Omar, I could still have this stock of yours just rotting away in one of my houses in a couple of months if he doesn't like them," Carlos smiled, but he didn't mean it. The smile went no farther than his thin lips. "This is the best you've brought to me in a long time but if the business is just getting too hard for you I could find someone else."

"I've got the best set up. You know that. We've never been caught, or even stopped. I've always given you a fair price for what you've gotten. Never made you take the whole lot if you didn't like what you saw. It would take you at least six months to find another deal this good, and this flexible. What would your new buyer say to having to wait?" Omar knew how to play his cards, and he was right. No one here knew about his contacts in Mexico. He had planned his operation well, and she knew he was ready for an increase in business. By reading both Carlos' and Omar's mind, Jan could tell that he also secretly agreed with everything Omar had just said, but didn't let it register on his face. Jan transferred her weight onto the other leg as she took a break, bushed away the ants, and continued to listen as sweat dripped down her forehead.

"What type of numbers are we talking about?" Carlos began to tap his finger on the table. He wasn't willing to pay much more, but he also didn't want his source to dry up, not when things were beginning to get good.

"Not much, just another two grand per body, that's all," Omar knew he might be pushing it, but if he never tried, how would he ever become rich. He sat back in the chair confidently, like he held all the cards, and looked straight at Carlos. The grand was his payoff; no one else would have to know about it.

"I might be able to manage that, one condition," Carlos paused only a minute before he continued with the conversation, "I get a return policy." This time Carlos looked straight back at Omar. This was not the response Omar had expected. He had expected a counter offer of five hundred. He was prepared to accept that, but this he had to think on a minute.

"Never thought about having a return policy before," Omar's

mind began to focus. "You know I couldn't give all the money back, I still have to cover some of the cost, but I think that we can come to an agreement."

"If I give you twelve for each, I need at least ten back for the ones that don't sell," it was not Carlos' final offer. Carlos put his hands on the table.

"Nine," was all Omar said.

"Deal," and Carlos put his left hand into his jacket to get out his wallet as he shook hands with the right. Omar smiled. Even if any of the girls were returned, he knew he had the buyer in Vegas that would take almost anything. He usually got six for them with him, but this way he never had to settle for another loss.

Jan watched through Carlos' eyes as the money switched hands. Then she heard it, and felt it at the same time, Juan was back. Because she had been so connected with the men in the room she hadn't seen him coming in from the back of the house.

The bodyguard in the room had heard it as well. Noticing the bodyguard and the slight movements he made, Omar got up and went over to the window that looked out onto the backyard. Looking through Omar's eyes, he confirmed what Jan was feeling. What happened next would determine if Jan made a break for it, or stayed. She had enough information to break the chain, but not enough to stop it yet. Ward might have it, or he might not. If she made a run for it she could also endanger Ward and Eddy with no way to directly connect with them. She also knew that the dealer in Vegas was one piece of the puzzle she wanted, and didn't have. Jan held her breath, and stayed still, she wasn't done yet.

Juan walked over to the shed. She could tell that he had had a hard day from the way he looked through Omar's eyes. She wanted to find out what he had been up to, but now was not the time to switch minds. She had overextended as it was. She needed to see what he was doing and where he was going. It could be very confusing if she had to make a run for it and was looking through Omar's mind. Omar flipped the latch on the window, and she knew that he was going to call to Juan to come into the house. Would it be soon enough, and would he listen? Jan could see the keys to the shed just inches away from the lock. She saw more than heard the key clicked in the lock and the padlock swung open.

"Juan, come in here," Jan held her breath as Omar's call to Juan made him turn his head looking toward the house. Giving a nod, Juan locked the shed back up without even looking inside, and walked toward the house. Jan slowly let her breath out. It had been a gamble, and so far it had paid off. Once Jan was sure that she was in the clear she pulled fully out of Omar's mind. Keeping low Jan headed back toward the shed.

She wanted to listen in some more, but was afraid she would blow her cover. She was lucky once; she wasn't stupid. Going around the back of the shed, pressed close to the wooden fence, she was able to approach the door to the shed unseen. Quickly and silently she worked the lock and slid into the shed. It was dark and hot inside, and from what she could tell, no one was awake. Jan stood there and stared for a moment.

The sigh was nearly inaudible. One of these women had not been chosen to move on. One of them had not been picked to go the safest way by staying with her. Later she would deal with having to leave one behind, now was not the right time. If they succeeded then she would be safe, if not, Jan didn't want to think about the consequences. She had seen some of the choices. Move the emotions off to the side to deal with later, not ignore like she had done too many times in the past.

Grabbing the water bottle she took a sip and tried to read the men inside the house again. She was able to pick them up, but to keep each ones thoughts clear was nearly impossible, she was almost too far away. Picking up on the information and not distinguishing which mind it had come from she read that the four of them would be moved in the morning. They had been paid for, and now delivery was up to Omar and Juan.

Juan was approaching; it was now easier to identify his thoughts from the others. He was going to check on his stock before they would be delivered in the morning. He was also carrying something. The closer he got, the easier it was for Jan to figure out what he had in his hands. He had another bottle of water and a box of soda crackers. It would not really be enough food for the five of them, but they had to feed them something since they were paid for.

When the lock on the door began to rattle the rest of the women in the shed began to stir and Jan began to stretch as if she had just awoken as well. With no words the door opened and the box and bottle were pitched in. Putting his head in the door he took a quick glance around the inside of the shed, taking a head count. Satisfied that everyone was still there, the door slammed closed and they could hear the lock click back into place.

The day was becoming warm, and the body heat in the small shed only magnified it. The heat and dehydration were beginning to take their toll. Most of the women didn't even bother to get up and move. Jan took the new bottle of water and gave it to Gabby first. Taking what was left in the original bottle of water she handed that to the woman on the opposite end of the pile. Inside the box of soda crackers were four wrapped packages. Jan handed one to each of the women, and left nothing for herself. Gabby looked at her strange but said nothing.

It was one thing for her not to eat, but most of these women survived on the barest minimum anyway. Jan had had good meals before Ward had left her at the bus station. She had eaten well knowing that this assignment might mean times of little or no food. It was important to Jan that she kept these women as healthy as she could for now. She now had an idea of what was coming their way. Once they were moved, they would again be given only the basics. No one ever wanted to see their investments die, that didn't turn a profit. Gabby offered Jan a cracker and she took it. The rest of the women followed suit. No one wanted to talk; it seemed that to talk might give this situation too much reality. Jan accepted no more than one cracker from each, and then just sipped water.

"Eat, eat," she encouraged them. Knowing her limits, she also knew she was nowhere near them. There had been many missions where she hadn't eaten for days, and she was ready to do the same now.

Juan stayed outside the door, just over in the shade with a beer in one hand and a piece of cold pizza in the other. Omar had been inside for the last thirty minutes, and had just walked out of the house and over toward Juan. Jan switched positions to the other side of the shed so that she could hear as much as she could. It was also easier to pick up on their thoughts. The exchange wasn't what she expected to hear.

"Did you take care of the problem?" Omar pulled over a dirty lawn chair and sat down in the shade of the old ash tree as well.

"Nothing to it. Didn't even have to use our stuff, he had his own," Juan smiled as if it were the part of the job he enjoyed. Juan did the dirty work, and liked it. Taking another bite of pizza he kicked his feet up on the old work van that he had used earlier. The green of the van gave way to spots of primer and bare metal. The dents only made the van look older than it truly was. Jan watched as he replayed it all in his head, right down to the fear in the face of the man he had injected with five times the amount of cocaine that he would need to kill him.

"Covered your tracks?" Omar didn't crack a smile. He didn't want one slip up. One mistake could take him out of business.

"He put up a struggle at first, but I made it look as if a drug deal had gone bad. Messed up the place, spilled his coke, and then gave him an overdose. No one saw me," Juan was looking up in the tree.

"I hope not. Can't afford to mess up now. We may need to increase business a bit. Carlos just made me a new deal. He wants more with the guarantee of a return for the ones he can't sell," Omar went on to tell Juan the details, except the extra money, and he listened quietly.

"So how many of the new ones did he want?" Juan put his feet down as he took more of an interest in how much they would be earning.

"Four, not all five. The guy in Vegas won't want any more for a couple of weeks, so we'll wait until later. It's the same arrangement for drop off in the morning. Will you be up to it?" Omar looked at the shed and then back at Juan.

"Sure, but can I use the leftovers for pics," Juan waited impatiently for an answer. Jan could tell that he got pleasure from this part of his work as well. She chose not to look too closely at the pictures in his mind right now.

"Just don't harm her or we won't get anything for her," Omar stood up, "And don't be late tomorrow."

"Isabel, are you all right?" Gabby was still concerned that Jan had not eaten very much food. She also looked as if her mind was far, far away from here

"I am fine. I just needed water. I'm not hungry. The rest of you need the food more than me," Jan was a bit miffed that she might have missed the moment to get the address, but she couldn't blame Gabby for that. She needed reassuring as well.

"When will we get out of here?" Gabby asked the question that was in everybody's' mind.

"It will be soon from what I can hear." Okay, small lie but it would have to be that way for now.

They sat in the darkness and in silence for the rest of the afternoon. They were scared and who could blame them. Jan was even scared. With all the feelings that surrounded her, how could she not give in to some of her own fears? As she thought about what was going to happen, she knew what was at stake. Jan was the last one asleep and she went to sleep huddled with the rest thinking of just that.

Awakened suddenly, Jan was unsure of the time of day when the door rattled and opened with a loud crash. In perfect Spanish Juan yelled through the open door.

"Everybody awake. Get up," he held an AK in his hand and was in no mood for anyone to question him, "Hurry up, we don't have all day." They all started to move slowly, and to grab their things. "Get a move on," the voice was rough and threatening. He gave them only seconds. Most of the women were still in shock from waking up. Jan wanted a closer look into his mind, but concentrated on getting everyone to the van quickly. Slowly they all walked to the door. Roughly he threw the one that hadn't gotten sold back into the shed, enjoying it.

"You're going to stay, no one wants you yet but me," and he smiled with his mouth, but leered with his eyes. The woman that now lay on the shed floor had been the one that had been closest to being in severe shock yesterday. Jan looked back, and then felt the barrel of the AK press into her ribs pushing her out the door, "You, he wants, so get moving. Everyone in the van, and don't say a word."

Once in the van Jan saw that the only seats were in the front. There was only the floor for them in the back of the van. Gabby sat so close to her she could almost feel Gabby's heartbeat inside of her own chest. The windows were painted so that no one could look out, and more importantly no one could look in. The only thing that separated the front seats of the van and the cargo area was a wire cage. It was originally for keeping paint buckets and other items from flying into the driver in case of an accident, but in this case, it effectively kept them from the driver. Juan closed and locked the door, and Jan noticed that the sliding door of the van could only be opened from the outside. The inside handle had been beaten away. As Juan got into the driver's seat, Jan got into his head.

It wasn't hard; in fact he was almost too simple, an easy read. She was able to see the area where they were located in Phoenix, and the instructions to the drop place. This would make it easier for her or someone else to come back and get those who were trapped here. This house was located off a small side street around Nineteenth Avenue and Roosevelt. Juan drove onto the freeway and headed out toward the west side of town. From what she could see in his head it would take about half an hour to get where they were going. They were to be sold quickly and he liked the idea. He would be done with them. A babysitter was all Omar thought he was, and he resented that. He wanted to get back and work on his web site.

Jan realized that her suspicions were correct. Where would a computer be in the house they just left? She hadn't seen one in the back bedroom where she had found the office, and the pictures. Releasing half a breath she moved deeper into his mind. The only other rooms she had not had a chance to go through were the two smaller bedrooms. This porn web site was not a joint endeavor between Juan and Omar. Jan made a mental note of that as the picture of the machine and the room appeared from the clouds she was looking through.

Juan was lost in thought as he routinely drove down the freeway, the AK lying on the floor just out of the reach of his passengers and just within his reach. It was interesting that Juan was planning on doing the same thing to Omar, cutting him out of the profits. Omar was a good partner, although he had always treated

Juan as an employee, but soon that would change. He had plans for those pictures he had taken. Omar had only been mildly interested in it when he had started; Juan wondered if Omar was gay but didn't really care. He thought Juan was just getting off on it, he didn't realize that Juan had a plan to make money off those pictures with the help of the Internet.

Over time Omar had begun to take an interest in what Juan was doing; he wanted to see if it would make any money first though. Juan was sure the potential of the site would be more than what they could make selling the girls. He smiled as he thought of the money he had already made. When he finished, Omar would finally call him partner, if he allowed him to.

Being careful to keep her eyes closed as she did her reading, Jan picked up on all of Juan's thoughts. Taking a small break Jan opened her eyes and thought about what she had read. Seldom had she ever seen things work that way in any world. All one had to do was look at the number of people in WIITSEC, the witness protection program, to understand that criminals were just that, criminals. It didn't matter who they stole from or hurt. If you chose not to play by their rules, well then, as they used to say, here are your concrete goulashes.

Today there were different ways to dispose of people, and some were not as humane as the old goulashes. Jan took note of the sign as Juan pulled off the freeway onto the exit ramp, Forty-First Avenue. She watched as Juan drove north of the freeway for about five minutes and then turned off the main road. It was early in the morning and the traffic was busy. People were trying to get to work as life was happening all around them. Some people were even coming home from their third shift jobs just hoping to get a little sleep.

The neighborhood looked poor, not desolate. The people who lived around here worked hard for the money they had. Some were Hispanic, some Anglo, most tired. Some of the houses and yards were maintained, not beautiful, but lawns were mowed and houses painted. But for each one of those family homes, were two or three houses that either needed painting, fixing, or a yard that needed water or care. The streets were different here. There was a main road and then a three-foot divider down each side of the main street. On the other side of this divider ran an access road for all the little side streets. This prevented all the traffic from the smaller streets from emptying out onto the main street and slowing traffic. Every so often there would be a break in the dirty landscaped barrier and the cars that wanted to enter into the major stream of traffic could.

Juan pulled down one of these access roads and drove a couple of blocks before he stopped. Jan strengthened the connection again looking through his eyes and noticed that they were nowhere near a house, a side road, or the entrance back onto the main road. Juan sat waiting just three feet off the main road for someone. In town it wasn't as difficult to stay unnoticed as people thought. Most people were oblivious to what was happening around them. Jan focused and discovered that they were going to make the switch out in the open.

Seconds later Jan could see, through his eyes, a van coming from the opposite direction. It pulled up beside them stopping only when the two sliding doors were positioned opposite each other. Juan walked around the front of his van, and in-between the two at the front. The other driver did the same, except at the back. If the other women in the van thought that this might be a good time to escape, Jan could assure them that it was not. What room there was between the two vans was completely filled by the two drivers guns readied, effectively creating a hall between the two vans. The doors were pushed open and Juan looked into the van and spoke quietly, malice dripping from his voice.

"Get out," and that was that. His part of the deal was complete. Carlos had the items he had purchased. Juan was free of them, and now had time to pursue his porn site. Using the barrel of the gun he poked at them until they climbed from one van to the other.

In the back of the new van sat a very large Hispanic man with a gun, automatic, pointed right at them. It was the same man Jan had seen through Omar's eyes yesterday. These people were not going to lose. Jan was getting the feeling that the farther she got into this the more experienced the players got. As the door slid closed, so did Jan's mind. It was time to move to another head.

Jan placed herself up against the wall of the black panel van with Gabby beside her. When she had been looking in Juan's mind she had not needed to brush off the others' feelings, and fight her tiredness. Starting again was just that, starting again. Jan took a quiet breath and moved her mind slowly through the growing fear and anger in the van. Fear was black and oppressive. When she read fear it was like being trapped in a coffin surrounded by a thunderstorm. Little by little her mind moved into the gunman's. As the clouds cleared and the light seeped back in, she saw what was about to happen.

13

The black van pulled up to a house not more than five minutes away from the transfer point where they had met. They had taken a route through the side streets and alleys to get there. This neighborhood was about the same as the one they just left, fairly poor, but hard working. In her mind she had seen the road sign for the street they had left as they turned, but this street name and house number still remained a mystery. She would get it later when she had more time to probe.

It was a good place to have a drop house; most people were more concerned with their own lives and not their neighbor's. The house itself was only about twelve hundred square feet and nothing special. It had three bedrooms that had been modified into prison cells. The only people in the house she could get a read on, besides the prisoners, were the bodyguards that Carlos and Emilio employed. Obviously they did many duties for which they were paid well. The living room had been changed into a makeshift bedroom and a small kitchen located in the back of the house kept them happy. Business was hardly ever conducted in this house. It was just a holding pen, a prison, until they got the orders to deliver their stock.

In their minds she could see that there had been only one time that a buyer had come to this house. It had been a trusted buyer. They had purchased a substantial amount of girls, and even though the pictures were helpful they wanted to look over what they were buying. That buyer had become a regular with them, and there was the hope that these new ones would also be regular customers.

Reading the minds of all the people around her, she had

found it easy to read Carlos. Once the women had been secured in the room, their jailor left taking his thoughts with him. It was then that Jan realized how tired she was. She knew that there would be another time that her talents would be needed, and for that she needed to take the time to rest. Before drifting off to sleep, Jan placed herself in front of the door. If anyone came in she wanted to be the first to know about it, not that she would be asleep for long.

Jan became aware that it was hot, and an ammonia smell, that of human waste, was overpowering. It wasn't comforting at all to know that there was enough air movement to keep from getting heat exhaustion or becoming asphyxiated. Relying on her internal clock, they had to have been in this small room for about five hours.

Her head was reeling with all the information she had learned in just the last couple of days. It was now time to risk writing it down. Before she picked her head up off the stained and putrid carpeting that passed as flooring, she reached out with her mind to see if anyone else was awake. They had been lucky so far. They had been kept as a group, except for the one, and Jan chose not to think of her just yet. Locked in the small ten foot by ten-foot bedroom, windows boarded closed, and door securely locked, Jan could tell, as she searched the house with her mind, that there were others. They were scared and hurt. A thick black shroud hung over this house in her mind. That in itself would drain her energy quickly.

A quick count of independent thoughts brought the number to eight women altogether. Limiting her search to just their room, Jan discovered that there was only one other awake in the room. It would be the best time to take out the pen and paper from her bag. The other woman barely took notice as Jan began to scribble down the names and addresses she had memorized yesterday in coded form. Jan took the information back even further. She wrote out the directions to the holding pen in Mexico, and the names and descriptions of the men that had first picked them up. The more she wrote, the more interested the other woman became. As she was noting down the transfer spot and the area of the new house they were trapped in, the other woman came over.

"What are you doing?" it was just innocent curiosity, and nothing more. She was getting bored with doing nothing, and there was no one else to talk to. Jan knew that she had graduated from high school, and even had some higher education. Her family had been murdered and her house burned in Ecuador. She had decided to try for a better life in the States. She hadn't counted on this. There had been warnings from others who had tried the trip, but no one talked about being bought and sold, only caught and sent back.

"I'm tired of doing nothing. I thought I'd write a letter," one Jan would personally deliver later.

"It's not going to get to anyone," her voice flat and lifeless. By now, all had guessed that the journey they had purchased was not the journey they had wanted, or one they would escape from.

"I know, but I have to do something to keep me from going crazy. I can't even tell what time it is. Maybe someone will find it later and help us," Jan had begun to write down the descriptions of the vans and the trucks as she spoke. Even though she had told the other woman that she had no idea of the time, the one thing you tried never to do was to let your awareness slip away. It was how captors got the better of their prisoners. Jan had kept tabs on what the time was, and was pretty sure she was only about an hour or two off. She would guess that it was getting close to evening. If she planned to leave and drop off the information, she would need to be constantly aware of the time.

"I'm Maria," it was the first time any of the women had reached out to someone else in the group that they didn't know. Maria had watched Isabel and Gabby talk and share. She was pretty sure that they hadn't known each other before now, but for some reason Gabby had trust in this woman.

"Isabel," Jan started to fold the paper into long thin lines.

"Thank you," Jan wasn't sure why Maria had thanked her. Maria saw this in her face, "for yesterday when you gave me your share of crackers. I was very hungry." It had been the last time that they had received food or water from anyone.

"It's nothing. I wasn't hungry," Jan smiled. "Why did you cross?"

"The same reason as you I assume, for a better life," Maria sneered as she looked around the room, "Some better life." Jan knew the dark and depressing past she carried with her.

"It will get better," Jan tucked the paper into the strap of the bag and refolded the material to hide it. Maria watched with a growing interest.

"You're different," red flags flew up for a moment, "You seem calm, like you are ready for anything they do to us. Your life must have really been rough." The red flags went down again. She was attributing her resolve to an entirely different background than the life she had really led. What Maria couldn't have known was that Jan's background was even rougher than she could ever have imagined.

"That's why I had to try and come. Whatever happened, life could only be better," and that was the truth, not for her, but for all she could reach.

"I'm from Ecuador, nothing for me there. I have no family or home anymore, so I had nothing to lose when I tried this trip," it was more information than Jan had expected. They both smiled. Her character, resolve, was stronger than Gabby's and could be a real asset to Jan in the end.

Metal scraped metal. They both heard it at the same time. The sound was barely audible, but in the silent world in which they now existed it filled the room. The door to the bedroom was being unlocked. They both turned to stare at the door and the conversation they had begun quickly came to an end.

It was early evening and Ward had just picked up Eddy. Both were impeccably dressed, and both were carrying their favorite pieces. They were going to grab a bite to eat before they went out to the casino. Eddy had suggested a new place for Mexican food as well as for rumors on the west side of town. Seeing that they had time, Ward drove over to Fifty-Ninth Avenue and Thomas. It wasn't quite a restaurant and it wasn't quite a grocery store. It was more of a market place where one would be able to get something to eat, groceries if needed, other items of necessity, and listen to what was out on the grape vine.

Earlier in the day Ward had checked all the data bases again and this time he looked for any reports on Rubber. All he could find was a general admittance to a hospital of someone that fit his description, but they had no name to connect to the person. The last report they had was he was in critical condition and they had no idea of whether or not he would pull through. It was too early to tell. The only people that were paying any attention to this case, Ward discovered, were the local police because of the amount of cocaine they found in the van. They had found nothing else but the needle, the cocaine, and a mess. The police had assumed that it had been a drug deal gone bad.

Something told Ward that it wasn't a bad drug deal; too much had been left for it to be that. It sounded good and it looked good for the papers, but that wasn't what happened. If Rubber happened to survive, Ward was sure he would not be able to count on him for quite a while if ever again.

The other databases were pretty calm. Border Patrol was the only one showing any activities that could even be linked to their case. It seemed that they were trying to locate drop houses in the Phoenix area. According to the reports though, they weren't getting very far. Ward smiled. With the information that they would pass on, the raids could be a lot sooner.

"We should be able to pick up some of the local gossip in this place," Eddy stated as Ward exited off the interstate at Fifty-Ninth Avenue.

"Good, the more information we can turn in on drop houses the better. Sources say Border Patrol is trying to set up raids, but they have at least another month's worth of work to do. I think we can help speed this process up," Ward eased the car to a stop at the light. It was amazing to watch people react to this car. Some openly stared, some just glanced quickly at it, and some even avoided looking at it at all.

"It's an outrage you know, a real outrage. They don't understand all the work you put into helping their operations move along. It's not right that they still have you on a wanted list. If they only knew what you did to . . ." Ward raised his hand, and turned to smile at Eddy. He then rested his hand on Eddy's shoulder.

"Life's not fair and we both know that," and this time his face got a little more serious, "I can't change who I am and they can't change who they are. We've been through all this. You don't need to start ranting about how hunted I am by all these agencies for things I have never done, and all the things I still do for them," Eddy always spouted about how Ward had gotten the short end of the stick.

"Yah right. So superman, just how are we going to find her and the rest of the bunch? Then get the others arrested?" Ignoring Eddy, Ward pulled into the parking lot of the market. Before the car came to a complete stop Eddy got out.

"Eddy, I'd know if she was near," Ward said to Eddy's back. Eddy seemed to calm down a bit, and waited for Ward to round the car before they walked in together. It was never a good thing to read your partner's mind all the time, and in that way Ward respected his privacy. Mind reading was done only when necessary to get the information and other traditional means would not work. Ward was pretty sure, though that the reason for his mood had something to do with the return to the casino tonight. Ward followed Eddy through the masses of people in the store and toward the back where the cafeteria area was located.

The air was filled with music and chatter that was about twice as loud as the street noise that they had left outside. Piñatas hung all around. The colors filled the eyes and assaulted the senses. There was a mixture of smells, not all of them pleasant. The floor needed mopping from all the people that had been through the store.

Ward noticed that the store was divided up like a market place you might find in any Mexican town. They had put the taqueria in the back of the store along with the juice and take out stand. They had placed about six cast iron tables and fourteen plastic chairs in the back along the wall with patio umbrellas over all the tables to give it an outdoorsy look. In general the place was clean, but well used. In some ways it was exhilarating, in other ways it was exhausting. There was one piece of undeniable evidence. If you listened hard enough you could pick up some good tidbits in places like this.

Eddy got to the take away counter in back and ordered for the both of them, letting Ward listen. Ward casually walked over and took a seat at one of the old cast iron tables. Ward could smell the meat cooking in the back and if he hadn't been feeling hungry before, he was definitely getting hunger pangs now. The smell of the spices and searing meat took him back to Mexico for just a second and he let himself breath in deeply, only for a minute, as he fingered the chain that hung on his neck. Eddy walked over with an order of carnitas and all the fixings on styrofoam plates with two colas. Ward looked over at him, and the tray seemed to be overflowing with the food he had ordered for them.

"Anything good?" Eddy pulled another chair over.

"Only the smell of the food," Ward had opened himself up a bit, after the memories of Mexico, to try and pick up on any information he could. It had been a wave, a tidal wave, of emotions, memories and information. They both sat and ate in silence as they listened to all that was going on around them. Ward got nothing of consequence, a couple of possible drop houses in the area, but from what he could tell not the type they were looking for. It would be good information to pass on, may help Immigration in their investigations. The more addresses they could turn in the sooner the raids would begin.

As they continued to eat, Ward put one of his hands to his head and rubbed it. By the time they finished eating, Ward was close to having an overpowering headache, and he was ready to go. It had been a while since he had read so many people at one time. His training had prepared him for it, but now he could do so much more. Eddy noticed the stress lines on Ward's forehead and leaned in toward Ward.

"Let's go," was all Ward said. Eddy noticed the lines on his forehead didn't go away as they moved from the table and wondered if he was okay. He may not be feeling well, something he heard that disturbed him, or he had a headache. Eddy decided to wait a while before asking him. The last thing they needed was to be fighting off a dumb virus. Now would not be a good time for the flu, although he had never known Ward to be ill. Eddy knew that crowds were not Ward's favorite things and he avoided them when possible. He would attribute it to that for now.

Ward disliked large crowded spaces as much as Eddy disliked casinos. The worst place to be for a mind reader was in a large crowded space. The only thing that would be worse was when a mind reader had to open up his mind and read what the masses were thinking to pick up any information. It was hard, tiring, noisy, and made his head ache. The one thing Ward and Eddy knew was that at times it didn't matter what they liked or disliked, they did what was needed to get the job done.

"You okay?" Eddy waited until they were outside. The lines on Ward's face had started to ease, but they weren't gone.

"The usual. Too much noise, I was getting a headache, and the information we were getting in there wasn't all that good," Ward rubbed away the lines, and got into the car. Glancing at his watch, it was almost time to make their way to the casino, but they had a bit of time to waste before arriving. Pulling out of the parking lot, Ward headed east on Thomas instead of south back toward the interstate, and drove down Thomas road for a while.

At the stoplight of Thomas and Forty-Fifth Avenue Ward got a very funny feeling, it started in his stomach and moved throughout his body like a slow burning fire. He started to look around visually searching the area while he waited on the light. He was pretty sure he knew what those feelings were. It bothered him that he couldn't pin it down. Ward looked around again, letting his eyes scan the area more slowly. The ring that hung on the chain around his neck felt as if it was getting hotter and hotter. Eddy watched him and took notice when he saw all of Ward's muscles tense for a moment. Eddy started to scan the area as well, trying to discover what it was.

"What is it?" Eddy hadn't seen anything, or anybody out of the ordinary. He never knew how, but there were times that he missed the things that Ward seemed to easily pick up.

"Nothing," Ward replied with very little feeling, or conviction; his voice low and heavy. His face was still set and serious. Eddy didn't believe him, and had many different reasons to base his suspicion on. Eddy dismissed what Ward had said and continued to look until the light turned green and Ward drove off. The tension began to leave Ward's muscles, and he started to become more himself again, although not as much as before. Eddy knew it would do no good to ask Ward again. He would only tell him if he wanted to share it.

After an hour of driving they were at the casino. The last colors of the sunset were slowly fading from the sky as the darkness of the night overtook the light of day. This time when they pulled into the lot Ward could tell that they were being watched. He felt, before he saw, the bodyguard at the edge of the building. Ward nodded his head slightly in that direction and Eddy gave a nod of understanding.

This time when they got out of the car Eddy was in the lead, and Ward was a half a step behind him and to his side; the proper place for a bodyguard, or lesser partner to be. Eddy had taken the lead the other day and they had to keep it that way. Ward had had time to read the minds at the table and this time he planned to get a lot more information. A plan had started to form in Ward's mind and if it worked it would bring this all to a head very soon.

When they stepped inside the casino the tall Hispanic guard that had been just outside the building met them. He had also been there the other night at the first meeting. They were escorted to the back room, and once inside, they were frisked. Eddy's gun, which Ward had tucked into his back waistband, was found, but his gun was not. It wouldn't be good if they didn't find at least one gun. It would have made them look either naive or suspicious. Carlos and Emilio remained sitting at the table the entire time, and only when the guard gave a nod did they stand up and begin to speak to their guest.

"Sit down my friends. I have been wanting to meet with you," Carlos was excited, "I am sorry for the inconvenience, but as you know, we have to be careful." The smile stretched across his face. Ward could tell that he could hardly wait to make the deal. Emilio, on the other hand, was as nervous as Carlos was excited. He was going to be the wild card in all of this and the one to watch. Carlos pointed toward the table for them to sit. In front of them were placed a pile of four new pictures of the women they had attained, plus the original two Eddy had picked out the other day in a separate pile. "As you can see our supplier came through and we have something more to show you like I said. They are fresh, just got here. Aren't they pretty?"

"I'm looking forward to seeing what they brought in," Eddy picked up the pile of pictures. Gabby's picture was on top. He studied it for a moment knowing that he would need to pick more than one person. Eddy steeled his emotions as he flipped the top picture off. The next picture was Jan.

Ward showed no emotion either; he had already known her

picture had to be in the pile they were given. When they were walking into the casino he had quickly searched the bodyguard's mind for the faces of the women and found Jan's face there. He had mixed emotions, everything from fear to pride. Ward had settled on pride before he had compartmentalized the feelings. Eddy casually flipped her picture on the pile being very careful not to take more notice than he should of it. He looked at the other two, and none of them matched who they were looking for so he pushed them back across the table, fairly sure he had taken enough pictures to excite Carlos. "Before we go any further we need to have a few questions answered."

"Of course, of course, what would you like to know?" Carlos smiled spreading his hands out on the table palms down while Emilio fidgeted with the left over pictures. He kept nervously shuffling them with his hands. He glanced back and forth at Eddy and Ward.

"What's the price?" Eddy folded his hands together and rested them on the table. Eddy waited, acting perfectly relaxed. Eddy was playing his hand well. Ward sat still, confident of Eddy's skills, and picked at the minds of the two men at the table. The information he was getting was pretty good. Ward watched Emilio carefully, he didn't trust him, and he was easy to read, very easy.

"The price is very good for what you are getting. These girls are very good looking and they haven't been any trouble to us at all. Not like some we get. They followed directions well," Carlos used his hands while he talked and assured them.

"I don't want any damaged stock," Eddy looked right at Carlos, and nothing in his demeanor was pleasant, "or any of my stock damaged."

"Now would we do that?" The obvious answer was yes, "We want you to be happy." Carlos continued and Emilio played even more with the pictures. Carlos quietly put his hand on top of the pictures to stop the fidgeting, "Twenty per girl."

"Uhm," Eddy pretended to think as he picked up his pile of pictures again and looked through them. Ward leaned over toward Eddy and whispered in his ear. The others couldn't hear the whispered instructions to Eddy. They had been simple, he didn't need to say much, and Eddy nodded and continued to look at the pictures after Ward sat back up.

"I assure you that you cannot get a better price anywhere else for the quality. They will be able to work many years for you," without the other pictures to fiddle with Emilio stood up and began to pace. Ward hoped that Eddy would pick up on the clues and answer soon. Four pictures at twenty thousand apiece would make quite a tidy sum for the night. Eddy raised one eyebrow as he noticed Emilio in his peripheral vision. After taking a deep breath Eddy decided it was time to give them his answer.

"Eighteen only per girl," Eddy sat looking straight at Carlos.

"My friend, I can go no less than nineteen," and he was serious this time.

"Fine, but," Emilio stopped pacing for only a second and turned to look at the two, "it would be silly of me to carry around that much cash."

"I agree," Carlos was just a bit suspicious.

"I can have the cash by tomorrow afternoon. Let's say two," Eddy put the pictures down and looked back at Carlos, "Where would you like to complete the deal?"

"Now, I don't like to be suspicious, but just how do I know that you will not have," he paused, "let's just say other people there as well?" It was the first time Carlos had echoed any of Emilio's fears out loud. Emilio almost missed a step and tried to cover it up.

"I'll be there early, by one, check out the area before you meet up with me. I have no problems with that, but remember I don't want to be set up either so make sure you come only with your friends here," and at this he pointed to the bodyguard and Emilio, "no one new, and the items I purchased." It was now Eddy's turn to spread his hands on the table, though only his fingertips touched the table, never his palms, "Or else," and he let the statement stand on its own.

"Alright," Carlos planned to do just as Eddy had suggested, and he smiled. It would be Emilio that wouldn't be so easy to get to relax, as he began to pace a bit faster.

"Where do we make the deal?" Eddy was hoping that this was okay with Ward. He was sure that this was how it was supposed to go down. There were no signals from Ward to change anything he was doing, so Eddy continued to deal. Ward sat beside him quietly, and deep in thought from what Eddy could tell.

"There's a small busy market place on the corner of Thomas and Fifty-Ninth. Do you know it?"

"Yah," Eddy smiled, "I know it." They had just been there.

"We should both be comfortable there. Now, shall we say until tomorrow at two?" Carlos had picked that spot especially. Meeting there it would be harder to catch them if there was a set up. They could easily get lost in the crowd, get away, and back to safety. Carlos also knew it was close enough to the house to have an escape route. They could be back there before anyone could even track them. Emilio looked at Carlos and relaxed again for a moment. Ward looked at both of them and committed the final bits to memory. He had gotten what he had wanted to know, plus extras.

"Two," everyone stood up and shook hands. Ward and Eddy were escorted out of the casino, but not before Ward had been given Eddy's gun back. Ward saw a familiar face at one of the machines as they walked across the floor. Without even looking in that direction he carefully shot out a thought for him to catch.

He had learned the basics of how to send a thought when he had been kidnapped and experimented on ages ago, and over the years he had perfected it. Memories of those days were painful, and it was the betrayal from one he never suspected that hurt the most. He rarely ever used this skill. If reading a mind was invasive, then planting thoughts in someone else's head was down right unethical. Ward had only used the skill a few times, but now it was important to help alleviate a friend's fears. It took only seconds for him to do and some of the message back contained surprise at receiving his thoughts, and the rest was a bit of relief. Then Ward and Eddy left the casino.

As they left the casino this time, Ward suspected that they would be followed and he was right. Eddy and Ward picked out the tail quickly. Ward said nothing. Eddy watched the tail silently as well. It was a black SUV, the make of the SUV was indiscernible at the distance it was following, but they were fairly sure that it was a Ford Explorer by its shape when the moonlight bounced off of it just right. When they got to the Ray Road off ramp Ward carefully guided the car onto the ramp and towards the stoplight.

Ward was waiting for the Explorer to follow them off the interstate and onto the ramp. Once the Explorer had gotten off the interstate, Ward made a left turn onto Ray and then went into the neighborhoods on the lower west side of town. The homes he was driving through were fairly new and fairly expensive. Eddy knew exactly where they were going. It wasn't the first time Eddy had seen Ward use this place. When they knew they were followed and wanted to keep the tail, but only to a point, they used this place.

It was a gated community whose roads quickly disappeared past the entrance allowing the residents privacy, and it made for a good hiding place. They knew no one that lived in the community, but Ward did know the 911 codes for any gated community. After making a right and then a quick left they were there, and more importantly they hadn't lost their tail.

Ward pulled up to the gate and rolled down the window. His fingertips could just touch the keypad, and Ward entered the code while watching the rearview mirror. As the gate slid open the black Explorer passed behind them. Ward smiled a wicked little smile and waited until the Explorer had gone far enough past the gate to make it impossible for him to slip into the complex right after them. Ward pulled in and let the gate close. As they turned left down the road they saw the Explorer reverse quickly and try to make it to the gate before it closed. It didn't, and the men sat messing with the control panel trying to come up with a combination that would open it while their prey drove off.

Ward drove to the back of the community, up a small hill and stopped the car. Switching the car lights off, the only light came from the street lamp about ten yards down the road. It gave only enough light to easily see the occupant's eyes, but not really enough to make out all the facial features of the car's passengers. They were out of sight of the entrance, and Ward was sure that the black SUV had little hope of getting into the complex. They would wait him out from back here. Ward looked toward Eddy, his wicked smile only getting larger. Eddy could see Ward's eyes and the white of his teeth through that smile. It could only mean one thing.

"Are you up for some grand theft auto?" Ward's voice was

barely more than a whisper. Eddy returned Ward's wicked smile with his own lopsided smile his diamond earring sparkling from the little light there was. Finally, they were going for action and not just talk.

"Thought you'd never ask."

14

It was about three thirty in the morning when they parked the car in an industrial area near the airport. The night itself was dark, but the immediate area was aglow with streetlights and security lights from the various warehouse, storage, and parking facilities. The lights blocked out the rest of the stars that might have made an appearance through the city lights.

Ward and Eddy were parked about three blocks from a plumbing contractors' storage lot and his nine trucks he did business with in and around the valley. Of all the contractors he had checked out, this one had been the most promising. Ward knew they had a fleet of eleven trucks and workers often took the trucks home to be able to get an early start on the next day's job. This would make the disappearance of a vehicle less noticeable to dispatch in the morning. Getting out of the car, Ward and Eddy didn't look like they had earlier in the evening. They had significantly changed their appearance for this job.

When it had been safe to leave the gated community, at about one in the morning, they had gone back to Eddy's place to change. On the way over Ward had explained the details of the plan to him including the ones for later that afternoon. Eddy just looked straight ahead and nodded in agreement. Smiling, he memorized all the details Ward gave him quickly. He had some questions, but knew that the plan was sound and would work as long as Jan was fit enough to do her part, and catch the cues he gave.

That was what worried him a bit. This would be the first real job that Eddy had worked with her when she was at a hundred percent.   Ward swung the car into the drive of Eddy's gated community and entered the code.   Eddy's home wasn't the first choice of places to go, but the apartment Ward was in was too far away to keep to the timetable.   Once parked, Ward moved around back and pulled his shopping bag out of the trunk of the car.   Then they both went inside to change.

Ward changed quickly into the clothes he had purchased at the thrift shop earlier that day.   He tore the sleeves off the old T-shirt giving it a more authentic look and put it on.   Once the pants were on and the gun safely hidden away, he put the hat on his head.   Ward looked somberly in the bathroom mirror and gave himself a nod of approval.   Eddy walked out of his bedroom and looked just as if he were ready to walk back onto the construction site where he sometimes hung out for fun.   Since they had become business partners and property owners Eddy didn't need to work, but he sometimes enjoyed the banter of the people he met there.

Ward walked out of the bathroom and looked over at Eddy.   Ward smiled one-sidedly and pointed to his own ear.   Eddy gave a full on smile with teeth showing, and didn't even bother to acknowledge Ward's gesture as he walked out the front door.   The earring that hung in Eddy's ear at all times didn't seem to fit the character of two workmen hired to complete a plumbing job.   The problem was that Eddy rarely took the earring out, saying it was a good luck piece.   Leaving it in would make him easier to identify, but that would be a fight for later Ward mused as he followed him out the door.

They sat in silence three blocks away from the service truck they would use as cover.   For this part of the job they didn't need to talk.   They had done this type of work before and both of them knew the routine.   When they got out of the car Ward leaned over the top and again pointed at the earring before they closed the car doors.   Eddy smiled again, and shook his head no.

"I don't ever take this out," his voice was low and deep as he leaned over the car and looked Ward straight in the eye.   It was his badge of honor for making it, not only out of the crime world, but also making it in the real world.   It was his luck.

"Not even for Jan," Ward new the words hit below the belt.

He thought he caught just a slight wince on Eddy's part, but his words were effective.

"Not playing fair tonight, huh," was all Eddy said as he removed the earring and put it in the glove compartment of the car. Ward took the box of old tools up out of the car trunk and the tool no good car thief would be without, a slim-jim. Eddy was still surly and wasn't smiling as they walked the three blocks to the fence in silence. Ward was sure that as soon as Eddy was absorbed by the job he would forget the earring and be happy enough.

Ward had picked this company because their employees sometimes took home service trucks, but more importantly none of the service trucks were on a GPS tracking system that had recently become popular with larger companies. By the time the truck would be missed, hopefully they would be finished with it and have it parked three blocks away where the car was.

They walked up to the side fence, in-between the streetlights and went unnoticed over the fence and into the back lot. Ward took a quick look around for security cameras as he landed squarely on the ground, and he only noticed the one. It was attached to the main building and had a very limited range. Eddy landed squarely on the ground and crouched low looking and listening for dogs. He hated dogs, not all dogs, but guard dogs. When he was comfortable with the fact that there were no dogs he let out a sigh of relief. Ward snapped his fingers once and Eddy looked quickly at him. Ward pointed to where the camera was and Eddy shook his head no. Ward knew that it meant there were no dogs. It was a routine that they had been through before.

Ward pointed to the only truck that wasn't completely in the camera's view. Moving soundlessly they made their way around the other vehicles and equipment until they got to the back of the truck. Ward adjusted his hat to make his face difficult to see, Ward made Eddy stay down as they moved around to the driver's door, the only part of the truck that might be caught on the camera. If Ward was seen and identified it was one thing, he was still on the wanted list, and they could just add another charge to it. He couldn't and didn't want to risk Eddy being seen, or caught on camera. He still had a life in the real world that Ward could never hope to have. More than anything else, he didn't want Eddy to be associated with him.

Ward pulled the slim-jim out of the toolbox and within seconds the door's lock yielded with a slight click.   He opened the door, waved for Eddy to get inside the truck. Eddy pulled his hat way down over his eyes to cover the shape of his face. The open truck door created a natural cover for Eddy as he crawled into the truck. It would be hard to recognize him even if caught on camera. As Eddy squeezed his large frame into the cab of the truck trying best as he could to keep the majority of himself below the dashboard and out of sight. Just above the dashboard an arm or a part of his back would pop into view and move across the cab. Ward slid into the truck after Eddy. Eddy got himself semi comfortable on the floor of the passenger side of the truck while Ward hotwired it. In a matter of minutes the engine rolled over and they were pulling out of the lot and onto the street through the gate.

Both kept their heads down as they drove out past the dispatch house where the vehicles normally checked in and out. When they drove past the camera, all that could be seen was the driver and a lump the size of a rather large black man located on the passenger side floor.

Ward pulled out of the drive and drove down the road. Eddy got himself up into the seat adjusting his hat at the same time, and smiling. At four in the morning they now had their truck and cover. Most of the streets were deserted and dark. No one was out that time of night that didn't have to be. There was the occasional taxi and the delivery trucks making their way to the stores, or into the airport. The moon had already set and the night would have been dark except for the glare of the streetlights that put a harsh glow over everything. Eddy began to think. He wondered if Ward knew where to go.

"We were at the same meeting and I didn't see anything that could lead us to their drop house. I know you told me we were going to stake out a house, but how did you find out which one?" A car went by them in the opposite direction. Eddy was just a bit curious. He had tried to notice anything at the meeting that might have been helpful, but he never saw any addresses.

"I just put a couple of things together that I heard from the market with the meeting place," Ward didn't take his eyes off the road, "and I'm sure that Carlos doesn't want to be too far from his base in case he needs an escape route. He may trust us but Emilio doesn't. I also saw a black Explorer matching the one that followed us cross our path earlier in that general area after we left the market. Seems like a good place to start looking," it wasn't the complete truth, but it was close enough to satisfy his curiosity.

"Now, let's see if I have this right," Eddy still wasn't sure about this part of the plan. It sounded feasible only if they had the right area and the right house, "We do some charity plumbing work outside a neighboring house to find out if Jan is being held nearby, and to find out just how many guys we might have to deal with. Sometime during this charity work, one of us or both of us will sneak up on the house to confirm our suspicions." The way Eddy said it, with a touch of sarcasm, even made Ward believe it couldn't happen. Ward glanced at Eddy and could tell that his disbelief was growing.

"You make it sound too easy. We'll need to do some looking around for that black SUV to find the right house, if it went back to the house. After that we can set up for the surveillance," Ward turned into the neighborhood and started to look at all the houses watching for a black Explorer. He was sure of the address, but he didn't want to seem too clairvoyant.

"You're just lucky that I go for your crazy schemes," and Eddy fingered the place where the diamond earring had once been. Eddy knew that most of the time what seemed a crazy scheme wasn't so with Ward. Ward pulled around a couple of corners and then down the next street. He didn't drive down the street Jan was on the first time around that would have looked odd. He took his time and ambled his way down streets looking in driveways for the Explorer. Ward made a few more turns as the darkness inside him grew, and then made it look as if he had accidentally found the house they were going to be watching. Both saw the Explorer at the same time. Silently he pointed it out with his finger as he drove past.

The Explorer was nicely parked under the carport out of the way of a house that was nothing special to look at. There wasn't anything that would distinguish it from any other house on the block. It was a thirty-year-old tan concrete block ranch house with an old sagging car port. The front yard needed more work than if the owner just tore it out and started over with it again. The house itself wasn't big, and from the looks of it there could be no more than three bedrooms inside. Ward knew it wasn't their primary house, but it was the one they used most frequently and where the guards stayed. The other house was only used in emergencies. Ward fingered the chain that had hung around his neck from the start of the mission. The ring that lay just under the sleeveless white T-shirt on his chest felt as if it was growing warmer again and he knew. Passing by, they could see that the lights in the front of the house were on, but the blinds were closed. Ward noticed no security cameras and only one sensor light that was aimed toward the drive and the walkway.

Eddy said nothing as Ward passed the house and drove once around the block. This time when they turned back onto the street Ward stopped the truck three houses down and turned off the headlights and engine on the truck. For the first few minutes they both sat in silence and stared at the house. Eddy, half stunned and half reconciled with what Ward had just done, was trying to figure out the floor plan as he waited patiently for more directions.

"I'll watch the house right now," Ward's voice was low and deep as he spoke, and his voice seemed to bubble up from the depth of his soul. His eyes never leaving the house as he continued to talk, "You keep your eye out for another house close by that needs some work on landscape pipes. I don't want to add breaking and entering to the list," without moving his head or varying where his eyes were focused he continued, "Try and get us as close as you can, same side of the street would be preferable." Ward drew in a deep breath and slowly let it out. The depth of the despair and fear he could feel emanating from the house threatened to drain him. Eddy took stock of the neighborhood, but not without noticing that Ward's breathing had slowed considerably and his gaze had become fixed and more intense.

"Wait, wait, slow down, I can't see a thing, remember," Jan giggled as Ward led her blindfolded down a set of steps and through what seemed to be a complicated maze. She had promised not to sneak a peek through his eyes with her mind, although he had had his thoughts blocked for most of the day. It was the second day of her two-week vacation. When she had gotten the vacation from the department, she had kissed Rob on the cheek and told him she was going to spend some time on marine research off the coast of San Diego. He had reminded her to check in with the office there and to call him. He was a constant worrywart as she could tell by the lines that had presented themselves on his forehead during their short conversation.

Regulations stated that she was not supposed to be out of his sight, or the department's, unless undercover on assignment for more than two days. Rob knew what she was going to do on vacation. Jan was pretty sure of that, and Jan knew that her secret relationship with Ward was breaking more department regulations than she could count. Rob and Jan had an understanding between them. The topic of her relationship with Ward was taboo. The last time they had discussed it Rob told Jan flat out, to end the relationship. Rob saw nothing but trouble and Jan saw something she was missing in her life. Reminding him that she would give him a call when she should, she had then set off.

"Careful here Babs," Ward's voice brought her thoughts back to where she was going as well as the item she had just tripped over. He had now eased her into a room and they were making their way to the other side of it, her in tow.

A smile encompassed his entire face and lit up his eyes. He knew it was all he could do to keep from letting the secret slip. For the last few months he had been planning this; not knowing exactly when it would happen, just being prepared. Earlier in the year he had completed a job for a family in Mexico. It hadn't been an easy one, as their son had gotten himself deeply involved in the drug world. Ward got him out and brought him back here, a place of safety. They were grateful, very grateful, and wanted to repay him for his kindness. Only problem was, they didn't have anything to pay him with, and Ward rarely accepted pay for jobs that righted wrongs. The Garcias had insisted though. It was then that this entire scheme had begun to brew in his mind. This way he could have them feel as if they were repaying him even though he was giving them a new life.

In his phone conversations with Jan he had been able to keep this from her easily. There was no way they could read minds over the phone. When she knew she was going on leave she called him. He suggested they go to Mexico again, just the Baja Peninsula. He had taken her there once before and she had loved it, so she jumped at the chance. They agreed where to meet and it wasn't long until they were on their way to relaxation and reconnecting both physically and mentally.

He had blindfolded her about half an hour before arriving. He had been careful to time their arrival for just the right moment of the day. It had to be perfect to work. The sun had just dipped below the horizon when he had pulled into a driveway and parked the Explorer. The sky and clouds were painted with vibrant reds and oranges that were accented by the darkening blue of the sky.

"What's the big secret?" Ward stopped only for a second to open another door. Jan could hear the ocean and feel the breeze on her face. It was hard for her not to feel his excitement even though she was trying not to pick up on any of his emotions as he had requested before they began their journey. The smell of the salt air seemed to wash away all the stress that had been building the last three months. Jan could only guess that he had found just the perfect spot for a vacation, away from all that could bother them, and it would only replenish them as nothing but nature could. As she stood waiting she mused that she really hadn't lied to Rob, for all intents and purposes she would be studying the ocean. At the time she had said it she just hoped it would be enough for him. She drank in the ocean air, "Come on, you can't just blindfold me and lead me anywhere you want. You have to let me in on the secret sometime," she teased.

"Uhm, interesting idea," and his voice rumbled low in front of her, "Just wait. I'm almost ready," and the next time he talked she could feel his breath brush against her ear from behind. His voice was still low, but this time he was much closer, "I just want all of it to be perfect." And with that being said, his hands gently pulled the blindfold away from her eyes and he wrapped his arms around her waist from behind. The view was spectacular, and Jan gasped at the beauty of the place as she looked out over a candle lit balcony onto the breaking waves and brilliantly colored sky. "Do you like it?"

"I love it," her voice merely a whisper. The beach was deserted and from what she could tell very few people ever visited it. "Where did you find this place?"

"Shh...," he wrapped his arms tighter around her, "I want this moment to be perfect." Jan didn't know what to expect, but she knew that this was the perfect moment. She relaxed in his arms and leaned against him. Her body melted into his and he gladly supported her weight. They watched, locked together that way, until all that was left was the blackness of the sky and the sound of the ocean. The twinkle of the stars and the glow of the candles only seemed to heighten their already intense feelings. She could feel his lips against her ear and his warm breath brushing past her cheek in contrast with the cool ocean breeze.

"Ward, where is this place?" Her voice was hushed; overwhelmed by the beauty she was drinking in with all of her senses. Ignoring her again, Ward kept to his own thoughts, still not letting her in. With as much restraint as he could muster he also didn't get into her thoughts.

"Isn't this the perfect place for wind to meet water?" Jan knew that he was referring to the code names they had picked ages ago. They had often joked that they would only be able to be together and happy when they found a place where the two met. With that in mind, she began to get suspicious. She suspected that the path he was headed down may be the same one they always walked upon, and she wasn't ready to commit to leaving the department, not yet. He had tried to convince her to leave the department many times, but the one thing he never gave her was his explanation for leaving. Walking out was unheard of, and by all rights she should bring him back in, after all he was on the wanted list. She never tried to though because he seemed happier, more settled, and department life was not for everyone. To Jan, the thought that they may be broaching this topic right now only seemed to sour the beauty and tranquility of the space.

"Ward," this time with a firm, but compelling tone, "Whose place is this?" Finally she had asked the right question and Ward turned her toward him. His face was so close to hers that she found it nearly impossible not to get caught up in his dizzying thoughts and feelings as he could no longer hold it back. He suddenly let her back into his mind and his thoughts came at her in a rush.

"It could be ours, all ours, if that's what you want," there was seriousness hidden the twinkle of his eyes mixed with a touch of hope. He held her close not wanting to let go.

"Ward, what do you mean?" Jan's forehead furrowed. His thoughts were a mumble of everything, including the heat that they generated between them.

"Babs," he paused, "Jan, we were meant to be together. We both new it from the moment our eyes met. We can't hide it, or change it. Marry me and let's make this place our own hideaway," Ward's eyes were serious.

"Ward," Jan wanted to laugh, to cry, and most of all to say yes, but her work, their life, didn't permit commitment like this, "Ward you know the rules better," Ward's finger tips brushed over her lips and Jan's words left her. She stood there silently looking into his hopeful eyes.

"You don't need to tell me rules; you wouldn't be here now if you followed all of them. I don't want to think of the past, it is only a dark shadow right now. The future is a story yet to be told and untouchable. I want to live in the present, the now. I want us to think with our hearts, for just this moment, and not dwell on all the reasons why we can't, shouldn't, and couldn't be together. If we live happily ever after for these two weeks, the next two years, two decades, or two centuries it would all be worth it. Neither one of us knows the future, but we do know our hearts." He waited, his lips so close to her lips that the urge just to kiss her was intoxicating. "I'm not going to tell you that you have to leave the department, and I'm not going to stop what I do, but," and he never continued. The waiting was nearly impossible, but she never pulled away.

Jan thought for a moment, pushing away all other thoughts, especially his. She had to decide if she could do it, live just for the moment and not worry about what tomorrow held. He was right, if he could live with it this way, maybe she should try. Two weeks of happily ever after would be worth every minute of it, and if she said no, then what? Just where did she think this relationship was going and was it a relationship she truly wanted? Looking into his eyes she opened her mind to his before she gave her answer.

"Okay, I'm ready; let's make this place our own."

Jan was smiling when she woke up. It had been a while since she had thought about the day Ward had proposed, and she didn't want to wake from the dream. She felt another mental push and realized just who had taken control of her dreams and her thoughts. She was still in the small, filthy, now dark room, but she wasn't alone. Letting her mind answer his, she acknowledged his presence with an open heart and mind, so that he knew the dream not only woke her, but let him know she was alright.

No words could describe the next few minutes when they communicated. They had long ago passed the need for words to communicate their feelings. The type of communication they did now was more efficient, much quicker, and it was more meaningful. It was more a mixture of memories and bursts of colors swirled with feelings. They both smiled as they drifted through each other's thoughts effortlessly, taking comfort in knowing that they were both together. Then they were ready to get to the business at hand.

Ward began by letting Jan know all that he had learned, and especially what he had learned from his mind readings. The list was long and matched some of what Jan already knew and had picked up herself. Jan gave all the information she had to Ward. No matter what was to happen next they had to be able to inform the authorities of where to find the documentation they needed to put these people away. They needed proof and both Jan and Ward had found what they needed.

Jan let Ward know that at least one or two of the women here would testify against their captures, maybe not all of them, but she would work on that. Jan also let him know that she had found only one of the three people they were looking for, and was sure the other was in Vegas. Then she passed on the information that one of the women she had crossed with had been left behind at the first drop house. He confirmed the information, and made sure the address he had memorized was correct. Ward let her know that one of the women being held in the house with her was the second one they were to locate. A wave of sadness passed over both of them when

Jan let Ward know that the dead body she had found in the desert was the last of the women they were looking for. She gave him what information she had on the coyote's buyer in Vegas, but it wasn't complete yet and she hoped to get more. There had been a number in the book she had found, but neither was sure whether that would be enough for the authorities to follow through on. No other feelings were shared during the exchange of information as it would have been a waste of time, and that was one thing that they didn't have plenty of right now.

Jan learned what the plan was for this afternoon. He was not going to purchase them, but by working together they would be set free, and the kidnappers taken into some kind of custody at the same time. With that type of disturbance they were sure to get the police involved. He gave her the layout of the market, and the basics of the plan. It would be imperative that they work with their minds linked at that time so nothing would go wrong. Split second timing would be needed in order to keep everyone safe. They had worked like this before.

Jan questioned Ward again about the Vegas connection, and he acknowledged her concern with the fact that most likely one of the men involved would talk and that would be enough. Jan and Ward felt a nudge in the arm, and for a moment they were not sure whose arm had been nudged. Eddy nudged Ward again, and Ward pulled away from Jan's mind but not before he left her with a smile and the warmth of his love that closed the distance between them. Jan could almost feel his embrace as he left her mind, and she smiled.

"Over there," Eddy had nudged Ward twice. He had known that when Ward was focused, it could take a mountain to make him notice anything. Eddy likened it to a trance like state. Then Ward smiled, and a questioning look came over Eddy's face.

"It won't be long now," Ward said. He noticed Eddy's head was just a bit slanted as if in a questioning manor, but Ward didn't explain.

"I've been watching that house over there, and it doesn't seem to have anyone in it. So there will be no one to check on whether or not they called a plumber." Eddy continued talking, ignoring Ward's last comment. He knew there was something else to the trance like state he had been in. He had worked with him too many times not to notice it, and he also knew he would never know what it was, "It's on the same side of the street with only one house in-between. It should be easy to stay undercover there."

Ward looked at the house Eddy was pointing out. The house was built in the same style as the one they were watching. It was old, and most likely there had been no one living there for a while. The paint looked twenty years older than the house and even with just the streetlight he could tell that the trim was peeling and in bad shape. The yard had died off a while ago and with what little water it got in times of rain the weeds had grown to meet the windows and then soon died. On the side of the house there looked to be an old water timer box for a drip system that no longer worked, for plants that were no longer there. It was a perfect place to hide, right in the open.

"It's perfect." was all Ward said as a smile spread across his face.

15

They had unpacked the old toolbox and tools that Ward had purchased at the thrift store. Neither had any problems with borrowing the truck, but the idea that they could accidentally lose the guy's tools didn't set well with either of them. The plan was to return the truck in the same condition they borrowed it with everything, and maybe more, in it. Walking toward the targeted house they found an old sprinkler system that had been put in when the house had originally been built. They decided to work on the pipes first that went around the yard, all the time keeping one eye to the drop house as they worked. Both had their hats on and a scarf neatly tucked under the back of the hat draping down onto their shoulders to keep the sun from eating them alive later on. It provided a way to hide their identities from anyone going in or out of the house as well.

They had been working for a couple of hours and the sprinkler system seemed to have some promise to work again. They had seen no one enter or leave from the drop house, and the sun was high enough in the sky that they were working up a sweat. Ward had contacted Jan again briefly to find out more information. He had learned that although they were being kept alive, like he suspected, the conditions were terrible and all were in need of food and water. Jan was doing okay, but much longer and she would be as bad off as the rest.

Ward looked at the room through Jan's eyes and as she slowly turned her head to scan the room he could see the squalor they were in. The carpeting that was in the room wasn't just one color. The original color was hard to discern through all the stains.

Some of the stains were obvious ones, others, the blood, held a story of their own. The walls were streaked with dirt, oils, and blood from others who had been trapped in there. What there was of a window was nearly impossible to see.

Jan had also collected more information as the two worked outside the house. She was able to pick up on the positioning of the house and the layout when Ward had let her look through his eyes. Jan had felt better after collecting this information and discovering what had been happening while she had been working this angle. No one else in the room saw her smile this morning. They had all been too tired and nearing dehydration.

Phoenix was an expansive city. Looking at the city from the air you could see pools and patches of lush green grass in many places disguising the desert and covering it for nearly a hundred square miles. 'The funny thing about a desert,' Jan thought, 'people may be fooled, but no matter how hard you tried to convince the desert that it wasn't a desert, it just didn't believe you.'

Last night the bodyguard had brought in water, a gallon for all of them to share, but no food. The thought of that night made Jan shudder. He had come in for more than one reason. Throwing the water jug to the floor allowing some of it to spill as it tipped and rolled before she was able to upend it, he then started to walk through the room, looking at each one of them in turn. His eyes were pinpoints and his jaw was set in a very unfavorable smile as he moved through the room rubbing his hands together. Jan read his thoughts and watched him carefully. He stopped near Gabby and licked his lips.

"Pretty little thing aren't you," his Spanish slurring as he let his hand touch her face, and then it began to move on to more objectionable spots as it slid past her neck and shoulder. Gabby pulled away and gave his hand a push. Pulling her knees to her chest quickly, she wrapped her hands around her knees in a futile attempt to protect herself. Before Gabby knew it, he raised his hand to hit her, but the punch never reached its mark. No one saw Jan move to begin with; the motion was fluid, silent and swift. Jan intercepted his hand pushing it harmlessly to the side. Since he was high that had made it easier for Jan.

"Why you meddling," he never finished his question as he

raised his hand toward Jan. Jan didn't want him to suspect that she may have had training in self-defense, so she allowed him to backhand her across the face. Braced for it, the hit was not as hard as he intended. Years of work had taught her how not only to give a punch but also to take one and minimize the impact. The slap would barely leave a mark and would be just a touch tender for a couple of days. "Stay out of the way you bitch or you'll get a lot more than you're asking for. Then again maybe I," Jan moved away, not too far, so as to draw his attention to her. She had felt the approach of another man and by reading his mind knew that this would be all over in just a couple more minutes.

Another man, the other bodyguard, leaned in the door at that moment, "Are you crazy. Get out of here before we get in trouble."

With a snarl at Jan he left the room and Jan knew that next time it would not be as easy to get him to leave. Soon, they would be the ones that were free and their captors would become the captives. She had left that incident out of her report to Ward for so many reasons.

Maria yawned and pulled Jan away from her silent thoughts. Not one person in the room had thought that they would become part of a slavery ring. Just a bit of light came through the boarded windows highlighting the filth that surrounded them. Jan began to stretch and then stand. Maria watched as Jan went through the complicated Tai Chi routine, but never said a word.

Since last night she had suspected that Jan was different. Maria watched Jan move with a practiced grace that demonstrated that this was nothing new to her. She was balanced, and her muscles betrayed her by showing how powerful they were as Maria watched. As Jan finished the routine and came back to center with her feet spaced shoulder width apart, knees slightly bent, elbows out. Maria stood up, careful not to wake the others as it was early yet, sleep being the only kind of escape they could get.

"Who are you?" This time it was more of a demand. Her eyes fixed on Jan and her expression serious.

"What?" Jan hoped to defray her suspicions, but knew with a look into her eyes and mind that she may have just blown her cover.

"You're not who you said you were. I know that. You did that too well," Maria stood her ground, "You also pushed that punch away with ease, and even took the hit with barely a mark. Now, who are you before the others wake up?" Her fear was immigration, Border Patrol, or anyone that would turn them in and send them back.

"A friend," Jan's smile was small but confident, "I came to stop these people from selling women to others, but I work for no one you need to fear." Jan was not going to let her in on Ward yet, if ever.

"Why should I trust you?" Maria had moved toward the right a bit and was looking Jan over to try and tell if she was telling the truth. It had now become personal. It didn't matter what was going to happen to her right now, all she knew was that she wasn't going to be sent back. Maria looked into Jan's eyes demanding the truth.

"Because I am the only one who can get you out of this right now," Jan turned to what little water was left and took a small sip, "That and the fact that I will do everything I can to keep you in this country." Maria said no more. Jan knew that the friendship they had started to discover had helped a bit. The fact that Jan was willing to go through all this with them, and that she had no one else to trust also helped. They sat quietly waiting for the day to begin and sizing each other up as the rest of the group began to wake from the pile they were in.

Jan could feel Ward's presence near her even though they weren't in constant communication. She knew he was watching the house. Jan could only tell him of two bodyguards that she had seen and felt, but there could be a third, or any number of people who came in and out of the house during the day. They had been in the house such a short time that Jan had only read the two. With the transfer this afternoon though, there could be more coming. Ward let Jan know that he had seen no evidence of other people entering or leaving, and they were working their way toward the house to get a better look. Taking a quick look through his eyes she could see the broken sprinkler and Eddy working hard moving toward the edge of the property as he inspected each piece of pipe. Eddy and Ward had been careful to dig up the pipe and inspect it as well as the house at the same time.

Jan went over the plan in her mind again. Ward's plan was to meet this group of traffickers in the specified parking lot. He would be one of the guards on the exchange, Eddy being the boss. Jan would be the last out of the van and on Ward's signal would push all the others into their vehicle and get the door closed. The three of them would then take the bodyguards down and leave them there for the police to find. If there were only two bodyguards and Carlos, it would be even. Jan would be the one to take out Carlos, as he would most likely not have his weapon at the ready giving her the upper edge.

Eddy would take down the van driver from his vantage point. The other guard on duty would be left to Ward. He would need to be dealt with first and Ward would be in position to do just that. Ward had warned Jan about Emilio, but figured that he would run and not put up a fight if he even came. Jan had assured Ward that she was physically and mentally ready for this part of the mission, and the plan was sound. After all the information was completely passed, Jan slipped out of Ward's mind and into Eddy's.

She watched Eddy work on the pipe and survey the area. Jan waited, and finally got what she wanted. Eddy looked up to see where Ward was, and that is when Jan got a good look. It didn't matter what Ward wore he always looked good. His hat was covering his hair, and the bill was pulled over the top of his eyes. If there was any way to identify him, Jan couldn't find it. Jan could see his muscles relaxed and ready to move. He was in perfect balance, and a sight for sore eyes.

Then Jan felt and saw something that she shouldn't have. Eddy had started to move, and he was too close to the house she was in. Even though he had moved without a sound, his large frame had caught the attention of at least one of the guards. Jan realized it was too late for Ward to stop Eddy. They had spotted him. By the time she found Ward's mind he had discovered the same thing, and they had both read what the guards were going to do. Ward quickly moved in the opposite direction. He couldn't stop them from picking up Eddy, but with any luck he could keep them from killing him. Jan got up and went toward the door to see just how easy it would be to open.

Jan tried the doorknob and found it was locked. Not a problem she thought as she pulled the pick from her bag. The lock yielded without a sound and as Jan opened the door a crack she found that it had also been chained in two places. Without the proper tools this would take a considerable amount of time to undo. Maria noticed the change in Jan and so did Gabby. Before they said anything, Jan turned and put her fingers to her lips to quiet them.

Jan went over to the window to try and open it. The inside latch released easily and the glass slid open with just a bit of force as the sound of dirt and metal scraped. Jan had known no one had heard the noise but them; the guards were almost on top of Eddy right now. Jan fragmented her concentration as she worked to keep Eddy's image, his and the guard's thoughts in her mind as she planned her next move.

The boards on the outside were a bit more of a challenge and a slight curse passed through her mind. With time, Jan could have easily removed enough boards to get out and away, but there just wasn't the time. Ward quickly let her know that the door would be where he would expect her to be, but not to come out unless he needed her. It would be easier to remove the hinges than to take out the boards. He also let her know that she was not to break cover yet, Jan may be the only one with a cover if things went south.

While Ward had been watching and reading the people in the house, Eddy had slipped behind the house next door and made his way to the back. Eddy wanted to see inside the house and try to discover just how many people they were holding. They had agreed earlier that when they saw a clear spot they would slowly work their way toward it to get close to the house. Ward had done this type of observation before and many times with Eddy. Eddy hadn't counted on one of the guards moving toward the back of the house as well to have a smoke. It had been a long night and the guard wanted to walk outside and get out of the smelly house.

Eddy moved onto the back patio toward the sliding glass doors. The blinds were pulled closed except for a two-foot area at the opening of the door. Eddy pressed himself up against the house and moved across the glass toward the opening. It was at that moment he saw him, but it was too late. The sliding glass door opened and the guard stepped out on to the patio. Eddy stood still hoping the man wouldn't turn around, but it was only seconds before he did. This guard had been at the casino just the night before, but now he was definitely tired and cranky as he pulled a knife on Eddy. Eddy wasn't sure, but the bulge under his shirt suggested that he was also carrying a gun. Eddy raised his hands, making the only choice he could, staying in character as he was approached. The knife was dangerously close to his throat. Even though he was still hoping he wouldn't be recognized, the hope was fading fast.

"Who are you?" It was less of a question and more of a demand. The guard was about four inches taller than Eddy but weighed about the same. He took a closer look and a hint of recognition flashed in his eyes. He just couldn't place where he had seen him before.

"The plumber. They called me to fix the irrigation at that house," he pointed to the house he was supposed to be at. His accent was pure New York, "I think their leak has undercut this house and I thought I should find out." Eddy slowly pulled his hat a little lower. Then it set in. The guard recognized him. Ward moved toward the back of the house, but stayed out of sight.

"Hey, I know you," and he pulled out his gun, pointing it straight at Eddy, "You're no damn plumber. What are you doing here?" His manner had become menacing as the gun waved in Eddy's face, his voice hard and low.

"You got the wrong guy," Eddy held up his hands higher as a sign of submission and started to back away.

"Get over here," and he waved the gun to indicate that he wanted Eddy to get in the house. Not having a choice Eddy complied, but he didn't hurry in any way. Once inside, he would be at their mercy. "Where's your friend?" Eddy's face seemed set in stone and didn't give away what he was feeling at this point. Only Ward and Jan knew that he was chastising himself for blowing it.

"I told you, you've got the wrong guy, I don't know who you're talking about." Eddy was now at the opening to the patio door when the guard reached out, and spun him around putting the gun to his head, and wrapped his arm around Eddy's neck to keep him in place.

"If you'd like to keep your boss safe you'll come out," he said loudly to the air. Ward could also hear in his head the hammer of the gun being pulled back. Jan had managed to watch it from inside the room.

Both Jan and Ward were looking into the guard's mind, and at this point they didn't like what they saw. He wasn't kidding. Jan heard footsteps and knew that the second guard was on his way out. Quickly she warned Ward, and with that knowledge Ward stepped out of the shadows. His hands were in sight and his gun was in place. The guard smiled and pressed the gun into Eddy's temple.

"Come on over and join the party." The backdoor opened and the second guard looked out. His face sunk as he recognized who they were. He pulled his gun as well, but he was not as willing to use his as the one who restrained Eddy. Reading minds gave Jan and Ward the upper hand, but only slightly.

Without a word to each other the second bodyguard came over and patted Ward down. He didn't find the gun Ward had hidden, but took away the spare he had out. Giving Ward a shove toward the opening of the door, he followed them into the house and to the front room. Ward kept himself from looking at the door Jan was behind. He only sent out one message to her as he passed, 'Change of plans Babs.' Jan knew what this meant. From now on they went minute by minute, and Jan stayed connected to Ward's mind ready to do whatever was necessary. The door that kept her locked in could be broken through but that would mean risking a lot of noise and an injury. Ward knew that. Neither would be helpful, so she waited ready by the door with both the top and bottom hinges knocked out.

"Emilio was right; we shouldn't have trusted these two. It was too good," he wrapped his arm around Eddy's neck tighter restricting the amount of air flow, but not completely cutting it off, and pushed him down into a straight back chair. All the time he kept his gun close to Eddy's temple.

"Now wait, we don't know what they were doing around here, let's call Omar," he seemed to have a more level head. It had been the other guard that had attacked the women last night, and this guard had intervened then as well. He was scared. Ward thought about going for his gun but knew there wouldn't be enough time to get it before Eddy was shot, and that was a big problem.

"No, let's just waste them now and get out of here. You don't know who else might be on their way. They could be anybody. What if they are Border Patrol, the FBI, or local cops? If we kill them they can't follow us to the other house." He readied the gun and pushed it into Eddy's temple.

Ward stayed quiet, and Eddy stayed still. Eddy's face was ridge, blank, but Ward could feel his fear as if it was a fog that covered the room clouding everything else. The air was filled with tension and one wrong move would seal Eddy's fate. Ward stayed still not even moving the muscle in his jaw as he tried to sift through Eddy's fear and back into the other thoughts in the room.

"Don't you think we should try to get some information out of them first to see if we will be followed?" He tried to reason with him, all the while keeping Ward covered. The words made both Ward and Jan take notice, "Remember we will have witnesses in the back room."

Ward could sense Jan's mind but didn't focus on her thoughts. He used himself as a funnel for her; that way she could see just what was happening in the living room. None of the thoughts they could pick up on were good. Knowing that the only way to save themselves would be to create a need to keep them. Ward looked for an opportunity to embellish his cover and focused his concentration on Eddy.

"If you kill us now, we won't be able to tell you who we're working with," they both looked at Ward, and then looked toward Eddy. The guard let his arm loosen a bit, and Eddy gulped in air.

"You'll tell me. Who sent you here?" he directed the question at Eddy, but his patience was wearing thin as the gun wiggled at the side of Eddy's head. Eddy didn't respond, Ward and Eddy had played this game before, but the game had risks.

It was sudden, so sudden that Jan and Ward saw what was about to happen at the same time as it happened. It was too late for either to react. The bodyguard holding Eddy swiftly took the gun away from Eddy and pointed it directly at Ward's chest and pulled the trigger. The bullet made a sickening thud as it hit its target. It had only taken a split second, and Ward had had very little warning to be able to avoid the shot. Jan could feel the bullet hit and the pain from the shot seared through both of their bodies.

Jan fell to the floor at the same time as Ward was thrown

backwards. At the first feeling of pain Jan should have broken the connection, it was standard procedure, but they didn't follow that now. Together, they decided what was standard procedure, so she held on. Ward was still conscious and even through the pain she could tell a bit of what was happening.

"Now, tell me." As he brought the gun back toward Eddy's head he was met by the force of both of Eddy's arms as they flung up to easily knock the gun from his hand and him off balance. It was the opportunity Eddy had needed to break free, but he wondered at what cost. As he tumbled backwards Eddy grabbed one arm and flung him around in front of him. Eddy was standing now with the other man pinned in front of him. He glanced at Ward and saw the blood soaking his shirt. The wound was bad and Eddy knew that he would have to do something soon if Ward was going to survive.

"You idiot! Do you know what you've done!" The other guard was beside himself waving his gun and arms in the air. He wasn't able to get a clear shot off at Eddy and he quickly seemed to be losing his head about what was happening all around him. "You killed him! We've got to get out of here now," he leveled his gun at Ward's head. "Let him go or I'll finish your buddy off for good."

Strangely enough, that was the reaction that Eddy had wanted. He flung the guard into the other one and easily reached Ward before they got their balance back. Eddy pulled Ward's body toward the corner and behind the couch, ignoring the tightness in his face. The pain was unavoidable right now. Ward was now away from the line of fire, but Eddy was not. Seeing what was happening, the guard with the gun pointed it toward Eddy.

"You get the girls, and I'll get the van, and you better pray no one else heard that shot or else we won't even make it out of the driveway," he spoke out of the side of his mouth. Eddy readied himself for a quick roll and tuck to knock him off his feet but never got the chance. With a quick whip of the gun butt to Eddy's head he collapsed in a pile on the ground.

Jan didn't want to break the connection with Ward. She had to know if he was alive, and the pain let her know that he wasn't dead. She heard the commotion and pushed the pain to the back of her head letting it sit there to remind her that he was still with them.

Looking into one mind was hard enough but to look into two or three took a certain finesse especially now. Jan could see that they were going to be moved, not killed.

Quickly she grabbed her bag and motioned for the others to do the same. She prepared herself. Her bag was firmly anchored to her back as she crouched low looking right at the door. Her weight was balanced and she was ready to spring. At first, a thought seemed to seep into her head, and then it came through as a yell.

'Stay under cover! Have to break them.' They had been in tight situations before, death knocking loudly at their doors, but they had had back up then. Ward wanted her to continue with the job, but he didn't have the back up. Eddy was down.

Jan hesitated for a moment and again Ward tried to stress his point. This time no words came through. With this try only the pain returned crippling her just long enough to disable any plans she might have to try to come to his aid, and then there was nothing in her mind. She shut down completely.

Jan didn't see anyone enter the room, and just barely heard them. She felt a large void throughout her entire body. Her thoughts felt even emptier as well when she got nothing more from Ward. It had been like a switch, one moment she could feel his pain, the next nothing. She had felt this before, and it left her cold. Ignoring what was happening to the women next to her she allowed herself to be pushed along with little resistance. She tried to get the connection back. It made her look just as shocked and scared as the others.

Jan made one last desperate attempt to reach into either Ward's or Eddy's mind. No matter how hard she tried, she couldn't reach either as she was thrown into the black van at the back of the house at gunpoint. Mentally shaking herself she tried just for Eddy, and got nothing but the faint thoughts, dreaming. Her mind had begun to work again.

Jan knew that Ward could be protecting her from the pain by not letting her back into his mind, or, and as the other thought crept back into her head it put ice in her veins leaving her face expressionless and hard. It was as if a switch had been flipped and years of training took over as her mind began to plan on how she could bring them all in as the van skidded out of the rock driveway that lead to the alley. It was all too natural for her to shove her emotions deep inside her where they couldn't be reached. Only one thing refused to be put away before she faced it. Over the years she had been in many people's minds. With what she had gotten, or had not gotten from Ward's thoughts she was forced to wrestle with the idea that Ward could be dead. Right now though, she would have to leave Ward's future to Eddy.

16

The van drove through the city for hours to make sure that no one was following them. They were thrown from side to side, all except for Jan. Maria watched as Jan stayed braced up against the side of the van and her eyes seemed as far away as the small town she had escaped from in Central America. Jan focused on the conversation that she could hear on the cell phone to Omar and then to Emilio. None of the information they were passing on was new to Jan, and they had no idea whether or not they had killed Ward, but they had only injured Eddy. With that thought, Jan had hope for the both of them.

The guards had taken the file of information with them. Their thoughts let her know that they had toyed with the idea of burning the house down, and then decided against it, as it would cause too much attention. They didn't bother to let Emilio or Omar in on their fire thoughts though. The only evidence left in the house would be the condition of the rooms, and Ward's blood. That would be enough to raise some suspicion if it was found.

On the trip through the city Jan thought about what had happened. Running through the scene over and over again in her head as she listened to the two panicked men she had come to one realization. She was now in control of what was going to happen next. If he was still alive, and she allowed herself a moment to hope so, Ward would be in no position to attempt contact with this group again. The trust was gone, and his injuries were serious enough to need some time to recuperate. Jan began to run through the different plans in her head. Whatever she did, she now needed to get the entire operation turned over to the authorities. She had the information and the locations that both of them had collected. With the right people that would be enough to issue a search warrant.

There was only one way to make it happen, and that way would be to get in touch with Ward's contact and turn over the information. There could be two benefits from contacting him. He may be able to offer Ward help as well as turn this entire operation in to those who could put a stop to this. She would have to stay with the group to keep suspicion low. A plan was forming in her mind and she was beginning to push away the emotions that were left of the morning.

Maria sat opposite her, unsure of what to think. Earlier she had watched Jan collapse in the room in great pain, recuperate, and then she was dragged to the van only half aware of what was happening to all of them. Gabby tried desperately to stay beside Jan and had helped her into the van, making sure she was near. Gabby looked scared at the thought that her friend that had been so strong now seemed so weak.

Maria continued to watch Jan carefully throughout the ride. She had watched her transformation back into that very focused state she had seen earlier, and the fear and strain drain quickly from her face and body. Jan now sat well balanced and the movement of the van didn't seem to affect her. Jan turned to look Maria straight in the eyes. There were no smiles on either face and she did nothing to alleviate Maria's fears with the look on her face. The face she saw was one of determination, there was no fear, no panic, and Maria could tell, no feeling.

Maria knew something had gone wrong, she just didn't know what. Even if the look on Jan's face scared her, she was aware that Jan was the only one that could keep them safe. She didn't back away from her stare and gave a small nod to let her know that she would be willing to help if she could. Jan gave a small nod back to Maria. Gabby hadn't noticed either and Jan was glad of that. Young and innocent was not what she needed right now. Maria was more experienced and would make a better partner. Gabby would only fall apart if questioned.

As Jan put together pieces of how it was going to work she

hadn't paid attention to where the house they were being taken was. It wasn't important just yet. If she did get out, she could easily get the address, and Jan knew this town like the back of her hand. It would also be an easy piece of information to get from the guards' minds if necessary. The van began to slow and pull into a neighborhood. Through the driver's eyes she could see that they were in a middle class neighborhood again, but this time there were more middle to upper-class homes. She watched them drive down streets until they came to the new drop house.

This house was different, it had a garage, and the van was pulled inside before they were offloaded into the house. Jan had realized shortly into the trip that there were three more women in the van with them. These must have been the others in the house, locked in another room. She had felt them, but not given them much thought. She looked at them now as they were all dragged out of the van.

The condition of these three women was much worse than they were. Their clothes were torn and dirty. They were all in need of a good meal, plenty to drink, and medical care. Jan could imagine if they were in their care for much longer her group would look the same. There was also a vacant expression to their faces that led Jan to believe that a lot more had happened to them while in the custody of their friendly guards. Jan's mind skipped back to the night where these men had also almost victimized them. Only letting her mind linger on the thought for a split second she then noticed that one of them seemed to fit the description of another woman they had been looking for. When the woman turned to get out of the van, Jan saw the tattoo of a rose with a snake on her left shoulder.

It had been a major identifying mark that they had been given to look for. Two of the three women they were to find had been found. As fate dictated, all stories were not happy endings and one of the three they were to find was dead. One was still held captive here, and the last was probably in Vegas.

Jan got out of the van last, and could feel the muzzle of the gun jab her in the ribs as they were pushed through the house. It was the same gun that had fired the shot, but Jan didn't let this bother her. Her eyes never stopped scanning her surroundings and the guards were still too scared to notice just what she was doing.

This house wasn't much better inside, and Jan could feel the presence of more scared women here, two more. Gabby had stuck to her side like glue. She was young and terrified right now. Jan wrapped her arm around her in a protective gesture as they were pulled and pushed through the house. Jan's mind began to assess what her body could do as she carefully looked at all the places in the house that they were passing, she would need a way out and back in. Time was crucial now that the group was spooked. She had the location of the evidence, the way the operation worked, the women they were to find, the drop houses, and even more drop houses that Ward had unearthed unrelated to this operation. If possible she would turn the information over to Ward's contact tonight. She needed to find a way to get out and back in without being noticed

All of them were pushed into a small room toward the back and locked in. The condition of the room wasn't any better than the one they had left, but as Jan quickly surveyed the room she noticed that the window was only iron barred. Jan went through the room carefully and then back to the window.

The bars were only held in place with three padlocks, normally it would have been one or a simple lock accessible from the inside. Taking a closer look at the locks through the window she figured it would be the easiest way out for her. The high block wall around the house would afford her escape some cover just as it had afforded them cover for their operation as well. The window was only five feet from the wall, and with a jump she knew she would be able to get herself over the wall and into the other yard before they knew she was missing. If things went bad it was a good way to get all of them out.

Looking at the women in the room Jan realized not all would be able to get out this way if that were their only choice. She decided that she had to return. There was no way that all of them would make it quickly over the wall without being seen, and if she went missing that would completely spook the guards. There was no way she would be able to trace them again, and no way to know just how they would react.

It was late in the afternoon and Jan sat down beside Maria

with the intention of asking for her help. It was the first time that she had spoken in English for a week, the mission had moved fast, almost too fast. Of all of the girls and women there, Maria was the only one who might know any English. She had to be sure that no one else knew what was going to happen.

"Do you speak English?" Jan's voice was low and hardly carried past Maria's ear.

"Very little," Maria leaned over to Jan so that her voice would stay low as well.

"When it's safe to leave later tonight, I will go and come back as soon as I can. Do you understand?" Jan waited for Maria to nod her head. "You must stay here with the others and keep them thinking I am in the pile somewhere if they come in."

"You will come back for us?" The idea of Jan leaving scared her. Even though she felt she could trust her, she still couldn't figure out why she would want come back.

"I promise, I won't leave you, any of you here," Jan put her hand on Maria's knee and patted it to reassure her, "I can't. These men must be caught though," and Maria just nodded in agreement, "and I can do that myself."

They sat like that for about an hour, just waiting. Jan heard them down the hall, and read their minds. She put herself into a striking position just in case it was necessary as the door to the room flew open and the water jug was casually thrown in the room, and this time no one else entered. The door slammed shut and Jan began monitoring their thoughts again only to discover that they were watching the front of the house and the neighborhood to make sure no one was watching them. The backyard was connected to other lots on all sides and posed less of a threat.

Emilio had come to the house and they were keeping their vigil in the front room. Only one guard was near their door. That just meant she would need to be extra quiet when she left. Maria and Jan watched as slowly all the women fell asleep, not a restful sleep, but sleep. Jan nodded at Maria and pointed toward the door. Maria moved to watch the door as Jan pulled out the pen in her bag.

Jan moved over to the window and quietly released the latch. Slowly she pulled the window open with just a bit of a squeak to begin with and then found that it opened with ease. She popped the screen out and moved it to the other side of the window letting it drop to the ground. Jan wasn't planning to take the time to put it all back together before she left, but she needed it to not be obvious if any one looked in the room. With expertise, she quickly opened every padlock and then swung the bars open. Maria watched in amazement as Jan had the window open and bars off in less than five minutes. Jan waved for Maria to come over and help her now.

"Close the bars and window, but don't lock the locks, just make it look that way," Jan spoke in Spanish again so that nothing could be misunderstood. Maria grabbed Jan's arm before she could lift herself into the window frame. "I will be back as soon as I can," was all Jan could say to reassure her, and with those words she turned and jumped to the fence landing with her upper body and one foot over the top of the fence. Before Maria could blink Jan was over. Maria had been left with questions, and just a bit of anger. Jan could feel it, but could do nothing for it.

It had been easy, almost too easy for Jan. The yard she landed in had a swing set, and an array of balls and toys strewn across the backyard. If it hadn't been for the streetlights to help her it would have been like crossing a minefield. Jan stayed motionless in the shadows incase there was a dog either inside the house or in the backyard. Waiting for any little sound that said she had given herself away was the hardest part. After a couple of minutes had passed without alarms being sounded, she slowly began to move, assessing her surroundings.

Guiding herself to the back of the yard along the fence in the shadows, she had to find the best way out without going around to the front of the house. This would mean jumping a couple more fences. Standing completely upright in the back corner Jan could see over the fence and tell that both houses in back were dark. Lifting herself just above the top edge of the fence she could see the yards more clearly. In one there was a sleeping pit bull and the other yard was free from dogs. The choice was clear. Jan was over the fence in what seemed to be one effortless movement. Again landing on her feet and in a crouched position she waited, this time only seconds before she moved silently across the backyard in the shadow of an old mesquite tree and out the gate at the front of the fence.

Once out on the street, she took a quick look around and got the address and name of the street she was on. It would be necessary not only for her to get back in the house, but to give a location of the drop house she was in. From the information that she had read from them they were to move again tomorrow night, and to keep moving around until they were sure that no one was looking for them. With her bag on her back she made her way down the street looking for a car to borrow. Three houses down she found an unlocked car. Letting herself into the car she hotwired it and pulled out onto the street.

It only took her twenty minutes to drive to the contact's work address Ward had given her. It would be the only safe place to make contact with him. They had been so close to it in the other house that she had been tempted to slip out. That wouldn't have helped until she had gotten all the information so that warrants could be issued. She had taken some of the papers from the first drop house and a couple of pictures. Nothing that would be or had been missed, but it would be enough evidence to get a warrant. Looking at the time on the car's clock she could see that it was about three in the morning. There wouldn't be anyone there to greet her at this time of day, and probably no security either, just in and out and no strings.

Pulling into the church parking lot she looked for the signs that read office. Getting out of the car she made her way over to the gate that kept people out of the main gardens and away from the entrances. Jan was too tired to jump the fence so she quickly picked the lock and let herself in.

The gardens were simple. Grass and a few tall sycamores filled the space. There were a couple of benches, where she could imagine parishioners sat to eat and drink their coffee after service. There was the church itself and a couple of other buildings that emptied onto the courtyard. Following the signs to the office she walked up to the main door, after she had determined that no alarm bells would go off, she let herself into the narthex of the church.

About eight feet in front of her were the doors to the chapel that was nestled in the center of the building, off to either side was a hall that encircled the chapel area and contained the offices and various rooms. In the low light that filtered in from the outside garden through the rose colored windows, Jan could see the sign off to the side that pointed the way to the chaplain's office. Jan followed the hall to the left and then three doors down on the right. One was marked Office, one was marked Library, and one was marked Pastor. She tried the door and as she thought, it was locked. It was a simple inside door lock and yielded easily to her. After letting herself in, she turned on the light at the desk and looked around.

This room had no windows to the outside. The office was small, and even though it had been furnished comfortably with a couch and two side chairs it seemed more like a closet and not an office. Bookcases lined the wall behind the desk and they were filled past capacity. She walked around the desk and looked at the nameplate, Rev. William T. James. It matched the name of the man she was looking for, but she wasn't expecting any surprises else. Sitting down at the desk it was time to get busy.

Taking the paper out of her bag she wrote down the rest of the information she had gotten from Ward, as well as what else she knew as quickly as she could. Jan knew she couldn't just leave the information and let the photos lay out openly on his desk for anyone to find. He was after all retired from this type of work, and a reverend. She looked behind her at the bookshelves.

Letting her eyes scan the shelves she now understood why Ward had given her his service number. She saw the blue hymnal that sat directly behind his chair and got an idea. Pulling it down she placed it on his desk and opened it up to his old service number. Placing the information in the book and closing it she placed it carefully back on the shelf, upside-down. She then found a piece of paper to leave him a note. On the note she carefully worded what she wanted him to know, and to do.

"Padre," being careful not to use his name, but only his code name, she continued, "The Eagle is down. Unsure if he is endangered or extinct, please check on condition. Causes for the problem are here by number. Must get back, but moving soon. Thanks for the quick Rx," and then she signed the note, "Barracuda."

With the work accomplished she allowed herself to lift the phone receiver and dial Ward's number. There were four rings, a small click, and then there was nothing on the other end of the phone. Jan was unsure of whether or not the phone even connected. Not wanting to leave before she could get a hold of Ward, she realized that it might not be an option. What she needed to do was clear, and the last instructions he had given had been just as clear. She dialed one more time, and the same thing happened as before. Leaving the note on top of the phone she slowly got out of the chair, and put her emotions again in the back of her head, safely away for now. The job came first, relationships later. Following the hallway back to the front doors she looked into the chapel.

The chapel was simple. The clean white walls wrapped around the light colored pine seats neatly lined in two straight rows back from the alter area. The alter area was open and uncluttered. The table itself was draped with a plain white cloth. The carpet was old but had held up over the years well. Off to the sides were pictures of various saints.

She was not a very religious person. She wasn't sure what people thought they would find here, yet something compelled her to take just a couple minutes more inside the church. She walked into the chapel area and noticed a stand with devotional candles off to the side. Above it was a picture of Our Lady of Guadalupe. The feelings she had out in the narthex were even stronger inside the church and Jan walked over to the candles. Only one had been burnt and she silently read the paper that lay beside the candle stand. She had seen candle stands before and knew what they were for; it represented people's prayers.

It hadn't been until that very moment that she had ever thought about lighting one herself. Slowly she knelt and lit one candle for the women that had been abused and used by these people. It seemed the right thing to do, as this was their religious tradition, even if Jan had no religious affiliations. Jan got up and walked toward the door and then stopped. There was no way she could have heard the phone ring in the office she had just left, but it was. She turned back to look toward the candles and had a sudden urge to walk back to light another. This time she lit a candle for Ward.

One hour later she was parking the car back in it's driveway. From her bag she pulled out a ten-dollar bill and put it in the glove compartment. When she got out, she locked the door to make sure that it would not go missing on them again. Letting herself into the neighboring yard through the gate, Jan moved quickly to the back of the yard. Soon people would be getting up and she wanted to be back in place. She was back over the fence and into the neighboring yard quickly. Moving around the side of the yard she could see a light on in the house and she could see the toys that littered the backyard. It was just a dim light and Jan imagined a mother nursing her baby quietly in the night not aware of what was going on just next door or the dark figure that moved silently through her yard.

Jan perched herself on the wall and quietly dropped into the yard beside the window to the room in which they had been imprisoned. She waited, she listened, and she looked for minds. Two of the three were asleep in the front room; the other was located where he could see the door to the bedroom and out the front window. Jan undid the locks and opened the bars. Maria met her, and the smile on her face let Jan know that she really never thought Jan would return.

It was early in the morning as the pastor entered his church just after seven-thirty. His calendar was full and he had hoped to get a jumpstart on the day. Following the same routine he had for many years, he walked into the chapel first and over to the candle stand. Each morning and evening he lit a candle, and each morning he prayed for a different individual, or member of the church. Each time the candle would have completely burned before he had returned to light the next one. As he knelt down this morning he noticed that there were two candles still burning. He stood back up. Looking around he noticed nothing was disturbed or missing, and nothing was out of place. A strange feeling went through him. He turned and walked quickly to his office hoping to find an answer there.

He noticed his door was still locked, and he let himself think for a moment that he might be imagining things. Old habits were hard to break as he scanned the room looking for anything out of place. His eyes stopped on his desk. There it was, the note on the phone. He was now sure what had happened, at least partially, the candles were different, but he was sure of who had lit them now. He picked up the note and read it.

He knew who Eagle was and was surprised that the note wasn't from him. He had heard him speak of Barracuda a while back but had never met her. Placing the note back on his desk face down, he looked for the upside down hymnal on his shelf, and found it exactly how it should be for a drop. Picking up the book, he opened it to song 370, and there in the book were all the notes along with a couple of pictures that had been lifted from the envelopes as evidence for the police. He had seen worse pictures, but these were still ones he didn't want to be found with either. The pastor put all the information back into the book and closed it just as his secretary stuck her head in the door.

"Do you need anything Father?" she was smiling and had a very cheery disposition that matched her short round figure. Both her age and mannerisms said that she would be the perfect grandma, and that she was. She had just come in to work and before she stepped into her office to get her day started she wanted to make sure that there was nothing she could get him.

"Yes, thank you. Could you clear my schedule for the day?" He saw her questioning look, "I know, I know, but something has come up that I need to deal with. I'm going to make some house calls today instead," he picked up the phone to dial.

"As good as done and she pulled her head out of the door and went to her office. No more questions asked. That's what he liked about her. He first dialed a code, then a number and waited for the operator on the other end to answer.

"Good morning, USDPD, how can I help you?"

"Morning, I need to speak with Rob please, it's Bill," he sat at his desk and drummed his fingers as he waited for the name and number to be checked, and for Rob to be notified.

"Thank you, I'll put you straight through," and he heard the phone click through, and then the line began to ring again.

"What's up?" Rob was not known for small talk with others.

"We have a situation to deal with. When can we meet, and just how long will it take to set up at least four S.W.A.T. teams to raid drop houses?" He looked at the door wishing he had asked Donna, his secretary, to shut it as she left.

"Meet me at the 5 and Diner in an hour. Is there evidence?" Rob's voice sounded strained and anxious.

"Yes, good enough for a warrant and raid."

"The sweep will be ready for early this afternoon, just need to make a few calls to put them on the ready before I meet you. By the way, who's the info from?" Rob sat almost at the edge of his chair trying not to look anxious in a room full of mind readers.

"The usual source and one more that I'm sure you know," he knew that if she was linking herself with Eagle then her name may be on the mud list as well, and shouldn't be said. He also knew that if Rob was asking for a source then he didn't know about what had happened to Ward. That would be the next call.

"Later," and Rob hung up. The pastor hung up the phone, grabbed his cell phone and left the office with the hymnal under his arm.

"See you tomorrow Donna," and he closed and locked his door.

"Bye, have fun." She didn't glance up, and had no clue what he was up to. Which was the way it should be.

He started to walk out of the church and then stopped. He turned around and walked back in toward the candle stand. If she had felt the need to light a couple of candles, then he planned to keep his routine as well. Kneeling down he lit the candle right beside the ones that were burning and said a prayer, but this time it wasn't for someone in his parish. When he got up he was more focused, ready for what was to come. As he got in his car he dialed another number on his cell phone. It was a number that couldn't be reached from the phone in his office, he had blocked it, and he prayed for an answer.

17

For the next two hours Jan sat and undid the floss on her bag, and began to knot it. As the sun rose, the house began to grow busy. Not only could Jan tell what they were doing from reading their minds, she could tell by what she heard. They all could. Doors were opening and closing and the boxes were being hauled out to the vehicles as they hurriedly packed the house. The plan was to leave late in the evening when the sun went down and go to another drop house. Leaving in the middle of the day would be too risky. The women had woken up and were looking around at each other, fear in their eyes.

Maria and Jan didn't say a word. Jan hadn't told Maria what might happen, she wasn't sure. She knew the information had been good and the drop just perfect, but since this was all new to her she had to trust that the source would and could act fast on the information. Anyone that Ward dealt with would be able to handle it, but working with people one didn't know always left a margin of error. Jan had tried to take a nap earlier. If there was to be a raid it would have to be today, and if not, she wasn't sure what would happen to them. She would have to form a new plan. So she sat and knotted her floss making it stronger and stronger as she pulled the stitching from her bag. To others it only looked like a nervous habit.

One of the guard's thoughts, the one who had shot Ward, slipped into her mind. He didn't want to bring their hostages along. He would be happy to dispose of them and cut their loses. Emilio and Carlos wanted to take the girls with and start again with their regular customers elsewhere. They had too much money tied up in bringing them over. The discussion had been heated.

Carlos put his foot down and said that the girls would go with and the discussion was done. Jan looked through their eyes at what they were packing and saw all sorts of information that would cripple the ring further if found. The other bodyguard had no opinion; he was still scared and shook up from what had already happened. He was regretting his choices in life knowing that he had no way out of what was taking place now. The only thing they all agreed on was that by tonight they needed to be somewhere else. It was late morning or early afternoon and they were all very nervous. Jan hoped that they wouldn't change their minds and leave sooner.

Jan sat and undid the end of the white thread on her bag. Slowly she pulled out the cord and took great care to keep it from getting knotted with the rest. She had little time and she knew it. Maria and Gabby now watched her with quizzical looks on their faces. Jan looked at both of them and smiled.

"We need to slow them down," she said quietly.   Maria nodded and Gabby just looked at the both of them.   The other women were not near enough to hear what was happening. Maria stood up and walked over to the door.

The wind changed directions outside. About two miles down the road at a grocery store parking lot sat three large armored vans and fifteen men dressed head to toe in black S.W.A.T. gear. Three of the men had dogs on leads and were itching to move in as they walked around the vehicles in the lot. Radio traffic buzzed and all the men were intent on what was happening over the airwaves. They had already raided two homes that had housed illegal aliens and one that contained information on a white slavery ring. The men switched their weight back and forth between feet as they waited for the signal to go.   Every few minutes they checked and rechecked their equipment. Rob sat in a border patrol car in the same lot giving the orders and monitoring the progress of the other teams. So far no one that looked like Jan, or signals from her had been reported.

Rob picked up the list that Bill had given him earlier. Bill had made his visit short and left quickly heading in the opposite direction from his church. Rob could have had him followed, but there was no reason for it. Whatever had been so important was for him to deal with; Rob now had his hands full managing this task force. It had been easy to get Border Patrol to move, they always welcomed help from their department. It was the information they had been looking for, for the last three months.

Rob turned the list over in his hand again. Looking at the list of information he had to make a decision. He had to guess which house she might be in. Knowing Jan, he had looked at the last address on the list, and picked it to be the most likely site. This was to be his raid site. Closely monitoring the other teams on the radio, he waited for any sign of Jan. He needed to get to her before the authorities, to clear her away from the group. As of yet, no one had found her, and he wondered if they would.

Thinking about his job for a moment, he wondered how he would explain having an agent in the field. One step at a time, with any luck she wouldn't get caught. After all she was good, possibly the best. This address had to be the one she was at, before the raid he would send her a silent message. The officer with his face shield pushed up leaned into the car interrupting his thoughts.

"Whenever you're ready sir," Rob turned the radio down, and gave the signal to go ahead, "Let's roll."

Maria stood at the door ready. Jan pointed for Gabby to go over to the far corner and take the rest of the women with her. They would be out of range of any stray shots to begin with. Jan looked at the group of women huddled in the corner. There was no way to get them out before the raid, but they were the means to convict these people. Jan looked at Gabby and Maria again; she could feel the net from the S.W.A.T. team closing in and was glad that she had taken the chance on the contact. He had acted fast.

"I can't be caught," she smiled and looked at Maria and then at Gabby, "I don't have time to explain it all, but a raid is going to happen. Don't be afraid, I said I would do all I could, and I will. Do whatever the officers ask. Tell them everything, and be ready to testify in court if they ask you to. A friend of mine will try and help you stay legally in the country and that way you can get what you came for. He will know I was here." She quieted them quickly before they began to talk, "Maria, tell them that I came back as I said I would?" Maria nodded in agreement, and Gabby looked alarmed.

"She left for about an hour and a half last night and then returned while everyone else was asleep." Maria looked at Gabby and then back toward Jan, "We trust you."

"Good, because I think they are here," Jan felt very focused minds closing in around the house and at least one sharp shooter was across the street. She expanded her monitoring of the area with her mind. It was less exact for any reader, but a way to keep up on the operation. Jan could feel the S.W.A.T. leader outside with the mike ready to give the signal to move in, and there was a familiar mind in the car with him wishing her well and well away from here. The surrounding houses in the neighborhood had been quietly emptied just five minutes before.

She was ready as she felt the familiar rush of adrenalin pour through her veins. Jan walked over to the door standing on the left side of the opening. Nodding Maria started to beat against the door. When she felt someone coming toward the door she waved for Maria to move away and signaled for everyone else to get down. She smiled when she realized it was the guard that had shot Ward, and punched her. It would feel good to take him out. Danger and death were part of this game, but somehow karma always seemed to kick butt. She focused in on only his thoughts, seeing through his eyes, knowing what he was about to do before he even did it. When the door swung open she was crouched and ready, but he wasn't.

Standing in the door with his gun pointed toward the floor and finger in the trigger guard Jan leaped and jabbed her knee into his groin forcing him back about a foot and a half. Then she pinned him up against the wall. At the same time she caught and twisted his wrist to disarm him as he tried to move his gun toward her with one hand and with the other arm shoved it up into his throat. A shot was fired and went wild missing everything, but the men outside the house heard it. Jan felt the collective tension from in their minds push back into her mind as she withdrew from the guard's thoughts and pain.

Time was critical now. She easily took the gun away as the pain registered in his mind and his pants. He fell to the ground and she raised the butt of the gun upward and knocked him unconscious. Tucking the gun into her waistband she heard a familiar call from the microphone outside. She knew she had only minutes before they would storm the place. Quickly she took the cord she had created and looped it around his neck and rolled him onto his stomach. With practiced speed she trussed him up like a turkey ready for the oven. She had used this method almost all of her career. It was her calling card for Rob.

The guard, if he regained consciousness before they got in, wouldn't be able to move without slicing his neck open with the loops of dental floss. She was careful to leave him in a position where he couldn't be hurt unless he tried to move. Jan heard Maria and the others giggle as Jan propped the guard's legs against the wall and laid him on his side. Jan quickly wiped any prints she might have left on the gun and put it on the floor, out of reach.

"I have to go, remember what I told you. And what ever you do don't leave this room until the police come to get you," there was a commotion at the backdoor and Jan went toward the garage. No one in the front room tried to stop her. They were too busy trying to keep them out and destroy the papers. Jan heard the canister of tear gas enter the house in about three different places and the familiar hiss told her that she had only seconds left. She took a large breath and turned toward the laundry.

Jan made it to the garage before they opened the front door and she climbed up into the attic of the house through the opening in the ceiling. Sliding the board back in place, she quickly and quietly made her way across the attic and wedged herself into the tiny crawl space filled with insulation. Safe for the moment from the tear gas and the S.W.A.T. team she stopped to assess her situation.

Looking around she could see the attic vent located on the side of the house that was only five feet away. Once it quieted down outside she would be able to get out there and across the backyards again. Continuing to work her way in that direction she could hear the commotion in the house, along with the barking of the dogs. Men were yelling commands from behind gasmasks and the rest inside the house were coughing and sputtering. It took moments and the situation was under control. Jan could hear the fans being placed in the doors and turned on, lots of talking, and a shout went out for a medical team. She suddenly heard a loud laugh.

"Hey Sarge come look at this." The sound was muffled but Jan could easily tell what was happening by reading the minds in the room, the room she had just left.

"I don't think I've ever seen anything like this. Get the commander." He stood there looking at the women and the man that lay tied up on the floor, "Do any of you know anything about this?"

"No sir," Maria was the only one who understood the question that he had asked in English.

"Was there someone else in here?" He asked as he waved the other officers in.

"No sir," she remembered that Jan said she couldn't be caught. The other officers prepared to usher them out of the room.

"Get these people some water and something to eat. It doesn't look like they have had much of either for a while. Have the medics check them out," just then the commander walked in and looked at the man on the floor. Placing a hand over his mouth he stifled a laugh. Then he just smiled. Jan felt it, and she was sure that the thoughts were for her. Looking at the girls he studied all their faces carefully. He signaled for Maria to be left with him.

After everyone else had left, he walked her out. Maria took a deep breath and followed Rob to the opposite corner of the property. He handed her a bottle of water and a bag of chips. Many people were bustling around them and he just stood with his hands on his hips waiting. He handed her a tissue to wipe away what was left of the effects of the gas. When no one else was around, he asked her only one question.

"She was here wasn't she," and he smiled. Maria looked carefully at Rob. The smile seemed so knowing, so understanding, so much like the one Isabel had on before she left that she decided to give the only answer she thought was correct.

"She was and was not." Maria concentrated on the water, needing it more than the food, "But there was someone who told us you would help us stay here."

Jan nearly laughed when she heard her answer, and Rob laughed loud and hard. Rob and Maria were under the vent Jan planned to leave from. Jan wanted to let Rob know she was there, but there was a problem. Jan knew he could never explain her, so she would have to wait. Rob knew she was safe and that she was out of the way. That would have to be enough for now.

"You listened well," and Rob smiled again. He took her arm and walked her back over to the medics in the front of the house, "Whoever that person was, was right. I will do my very best to keep all of you in this country."

They were letting the medics come over to help deal with the women and more men went into the house to make sure the house was empty. Jan knew that one or two men would still be watching the house, but could not sense anyone near her. It was now time to make her exit before a go-getter got the great idea to check the attic for people. Carefully she popped the slats in the vent so she could drop out.

Jan put her head just up to the opening she had created and looked for anyone standing around. The fence next to the house on this side was much closer, only about three feet. Taking a chance she perched herself on the edge of the wall and tried to aim for the block fence three feet from the house. If she was seen she would have to make a run for it. With any luck, by landing on the fence first, she wouldn't break anything.

Leaning and launching herself out the vent she concentrated on the wall. She hit it with both feet and used it to bounce into a neighbor's yard landing on a rather large sage bush. As she landed, she heard the police dogs start to move and make a fuss. Rolling out of the bush she didn't take the time to assess if anything was broken, or just bruised. Running across the yard she heard the dogs coming up to the wall she had just maneuvered over and they were now barking a warning signal. Then she heard something. It gave her enough time to make it over the next wall and out.

"The back wall. I think someone just went over it!" Rob's voice rang out over the dog's barking. Jan didn't waste the moment he gave her, and she made it over two more fences and out to the street. It was still daylight and she would be noticed. Thinking about what she knew of the area she started to walk to the main street hoping to find a Circle K or Seven-Eleven. Her hair fell down onto her shoulders quickly as she took it out of the ponytail and ran her fingers though it. She needed a shower and a good meal. She also knew where she would find all of that and with any luck more.

Once at the corner she saw a Circle K with a pay phone outside the shop. Without a care of how she looked or smelled she entered the store and got change for the phone. Walking confidently up to the pay phone she picked up the receiver and called for a taxi. She was told it would take fifteen minutes for the taxi to get to the store so Jan went back into the Circle K, ignoring the stares, and picked up a sixty-four ounce cola. Grabbing a banana she walked up to the counter and pulled out her money.

"Ma'am, are you okay," the clerk couldn't be more than twenty years old. Homeless people abounded in the metro area, but rarely came out this way. Jan thought only for a second and then responded.

"You know, funny thing. I get asked that everyday. I just finished grooming about sixteen dogs, and you know what. It doesn't matter how hard you try, you just can't get that smell off you." Jan turned and walked out of the store. She would have laughed had she not been so worried about Ward. It had worried her that he never answered his phone. It was a long shot to think that the Padre would still be at the church, but she could phone him from there. Right now it was the only place she could think of to go as she watched the cab pull into the parking lot. She got in and the driver tried to hide his grimace. Jan gave him the address and a twenty. With the payment already in his hand he took off down the road.

The cabdriver gladly let her out in front of the church. He had made the trip in record time. After looking at the parking lot, Jan was getting a bit worried about going into the church and drawing attention to herself. There seemed to be a function going on. Jan looked over some of the back fences near the parking lot. It didn't take long until she found one with a pool and no one at home. Hopping over the fence she dove into the pool to wash off some of the past few days. When she felt half human again she got out and noticed a hose off to the side of the yard.

Walking over she found a bit of shampoo, dog shampoo, but right now she wasn't picky, anything would help. As she washed off she smiled at the irony. Shaking off the water, she dried quickly in the Arizona heat, and pulling out the unused clothes in a plastic sack at the bottom of her bag, she got changed. There was a slight odor to the clothes, but the fragrance of the dog shampoo covered it. She may smell like a poodle, she just hoped she didn't look like one.

Hopping back over the fence, Jan made her way back to the church and into the main building where all the activity seemed to be. Service was nearing the end, people were going up for communion, and all was quiet as the music played in the background. Jan waited at the back of the church in a seat off to the side while everyone else received communion. As she watched, she got an idea. Picking up a pen Jan drew a little doodle on her hand. The pastor looked toward her and noticed that she had not been in church during most of the service, and Jan just smiled.

He noticed that it looked as if she had just climbed out of the pool or a shower, and her face was unfamiliar. When he finished the service he made sure to keep an eye on her. Moving to the back of the church, he invited everyone to the celebratory buffet that was in the hall. The people in the church started to file out and shake the pastor's hand.

Some people made an effort to say hello to her, others just walked past where she sat. Once the crowds were gone she joined the end of the line. Soon she was face to face with the pastor. She offered her hand, and when he took it she rotated it so that he could see the doodle.

"Thank you," and she paused only a moment, "Padre." With this said he knew exactly who she was. He said nothing, just nodded. Jan understood. Slipping unnoticed over to the office she let herself in and locked the door. No more surprises, she wanted to know about Ward and then she wanted rest.

It took another fifteen minutes before she heard the door being unlocked. He slipped in quickly. She looked at her contact; he was tall, but not over six feet. He had male pattern balding that made him look more like a monk in his cassock than a priest. He hadn't let himself go slack over the years. He still worked out regularly.

"Barracuda I presume," he shook her hand.

"Padre," he gave an affirmative nod, "Jan."

"Bill. The dinner is not over yet. I can't leave. I only have a few minutes. Are you okay?" Jan nodded yes, "Do you need food?"

"If you can, otherwise I did have something to eat on the way here. I won't starve." He was at the door before she knew it and could stop him to ask about Ward. She looked into his mind and found nothing but a well trained thought process that would keep her out of his head until he wanted to let her in. Either he was hiding the fact that Ward was dead, or that he hadn't found out anything yet about Ward's condition. Jan was sure that if the news was bad, he would have told her if he knew what was good for him.

Jan was almost too tired to care right now. She had done all she could. Picking up the phone she dialed Ward's number, but again got nothing. The last week was beginning to wear on her, and she looked at the couch in the office. It looked so inviting and before she knew it, she had moved over to it and had lain down. She never heard the door open and only woke up when someone touched her shoulder. She reacted in the only manor she was accustomed to.

Her hand shot out to try and connect with the throat of the person. At the same time she rolled off the couch letting herself drop into a crouched and fighting position. The punch would have hit its mark but Bill had been ready. He ducked in the opposite direction and deflected the punch as a reflex action, and took two steps back. Her eyes were barely open, she saw who it was and relaxed again.

"Should have known better, sorry," Bill had placed the plate of food on the desk.

"You know how it is," Jan sat on the couch, "Did I hurt you?"

"Luckily no, I thought you still might be running pretty high on adrenaline yet. Eat up and in a bit I'll take you to him."

"Thanks," but in her heart a ton of pressure was released.

Jan could smell food, but she closed her eyes again and let the knowledge that Ward was still alive sink in. Taking the first few bites of food slowly she then quickly finished off the plateful and lay back down on the couch.

Her body was satisfied but her mind was still impatient as she drifted off into a fitful sleep again. The dreams were not restful, but terrifying. She was back at the drop house in her dream, and she watched Ward being shot replay over and over again in her mind.

She could feel it happening as well. The pain increased every time until it became nearly unbearable. She screamed out Ward's name.

"Hey," he shook her again. This time his hands carefully restraining any arm movements, "Hey, Barracuda, wake up." He had used her code name to jolt her mind into the present. Jan opened her eyes slowly to see a black T-shirt.

"Ward?" She was confused. She knew that she had not left the church, but who knew; Ward had appeared in some very odd places before. Then her mind cleared.

"Sorry, still Bill," he half picked her up and half carried her until she became fully awake, "I need to get you to the apartment before anyone else sees or hears you here. Luckily most of the people are gone right now; the last one is just pulling out of the lot. You must have been having one rotten dream."

"I'm still not sure which one is the nightmare," Jan had woken up enough to walk on her own now. "I'll walk now." As she said it, he let her slip from his hands, but still supported her weight. Her legs nearly buckled as they took on her full weight and if it hadn't been for Bill she would have fallen. Taking a deep breathe, redirecting her strength she was able to stand, and Bill let her go, "Sorry, took a spill over a wall earlier today, guess the adrenaline has finally worn off and it's caught up with me. You haven't told me much about Ward."

"I take it the raids went down without a problem?" Bill redirected. Jan was a bit frustrated, but didn't let on.

"Yes, thanks to you," Jan got into the car door that he opened for her. "You moved fast. Now, the information please."

"I'm not sure I should tell you just yet," Jan's heart sunk, "I know you were there when he was shot, a friend of his was knocked out as you well know. He came to after all of you were gone," Bill started the car and pulled out of the lot. "Ward was injured, lost a lot of blood during that time. When Eddy regained consciousness he got him into the county hospital under an assumed name as fast as he could." Jan had other worries now. How bad had it been? More importantly, did the department find him? "It didn't look good. A lot of blood lost before Eddy came to as I said, but the good news was the bullet missed most major organs. It was only the amount of blood loss that worried the doctors as well as some muscle tissue damage."

Jan had been listening and not paying attention to where he was going until Bill pulled off the freeway at the Stapley exit. He seemed to be lingering on the story a bit too long. Her tension levels were beginning to rise again. His thoughts let her know nothing. He had stopped telling the story and was now concentrating on the road. Jan still didn't know how or where Ward was. Bill pulled the car into an apartment complex that was set back off the road. As he parked in the visitor's spot he turned back to Jan and continued.

"Earlier today I got a hold of Eddy on Ward's line. He was waiting in the hospital for Ward to leave. Once the gunshot was reported, Ward wanted out as soon as possible and Eddy was more than happy to have me pick them up. I was a bit worried taking him out before he should be discharged. Now," he paused and Jan thought she saw a small devilish smile playing at the corner of his lips, "Ward is here." She didn't want to raise her hopes so she tried to look deeper into his mind, "No, don't get ahead of me. I've worked with a fair number of your types and I see what's in your eyes," and his mind was closed just as tight as anyone working in the office could have gotten it.

He got out of the car and she followed suit. Without saying another word he walked up the nearest set of stairs to an apartment door. Jan followed. The complex itself was well kept and there was a garage available as well. It would be the perfect place to hide out.

He knocked. As he waited he turned toward her and this time she did see the wicked smile. "Well, I've followed my orders," as he stood aside and let her come up to the door. She held her breath as the door started to open. Bill went down the stairs and waited at the bottom with his back slightly turned toward them, affording them just a bit of privacy. Jan didn't see him go down the steps. She was completely focused on the door in front of her that seemed to be taking forever to open. She could only hope that it was Ward on the other side of it and not Eddy.

18

It had been the first time he had allowed himself to rest all day long. Ward lay on the bed staring at the ceiling. Every inch of his body ached, he knew that he should have been resting all along, and would have made anyone else in his care do just that. But he wasn't his doctor. It had been over twenty-four hours since he had talked with her. Worry wasn't an option, Jan was good at what she did, and he knew that. When they worked together things always turned out well. All the information he had collected today had reaffirmed just that. The raids had taken place, the ring broken up, and even the Vegas police were setting up for a raid later tonight. It had been breaking news at six. All seemed perfect. Ward couldn't help but think, 'If everything was so perfect, then where the hell was she.'

By all rights she should have checked in with someone by now. He had expected to be notified by Rob, Bill, or even Eddy. He had gotten nothing. When Bill had called earlier that evening he had expected him to say that he had her. All he seemed to want was to let him know he would be over to watch the news later, and to check on his condition. Eddy had tried to reassure him that if there was bad news they would have already gotten it. Ward had been so stressed that he ordered Eddy to go and get rid of the car and bring back the Explorer. He was tired of being babysat.

With Eddy now out of the way, Ward tried to take a break to ease his nerves, but still the ceiling taunted him. For hours he had watched the ceiling fan spin around as his body punished him for all he had done to it.

In his tortured silence his ears picked up on the footsteps that were coming up to the door. Glancing at the clock he knew that it was Bill, and the knock gave him away as well, two short, two long, three short. It was Ward's old number. He was too drained mentally and physically to want to try to read the minds, the reason for the code. He rolled carefully out of bed gritting his teeth at the pain. Ward moved toward the door, but for his liking it was too painful and too slow.

Jan was standing and waiting. It seemed to take hours but once the door opened, relief nearly overcame Jan. Knowing better though, she never showed anything but a warm smile. Ward stood there with his left arm in a sling strapped to his bare chest, and grey pajama pants hanging loosely around his waist. She could see the large bandage that covered the wound, and could tell that there was still some seepage. He looked pale and was moving slow. His face was set in an emotionless expression fighting back the pain, jaws clenched until he saw who was at the door. Slowly he began to return her smile.

Neither one moved, they just stood there looking at each other as they wandered in and out of each other's thoughts. They both realized how good they looked to the other, much to their surprise. Jan had thought she looked a mess; her hair had dried with a funny cowlick in it and her clothes were not the ones she would have normally. They were old, and they had a smell, although she couldn't tell, because all she could smell was poodle, but Ward saw none of that. His eyes held a spark and a fire that had always drawn her to him.

Ward was sure he looked tired and weak. He had gained consciousness in the hospital and his only worry had been that the department would find him, or the cops would connect him to the shooting in the house. Through her eyes though, he could tell that no other sight could have looked better to her than him standing there, alive.

"Nice job," was all Ward said. It was all he needed to say; she could see it in his eyes and his mind.

"Had a good support system," Jan smiled, "Looks like you took the worst of it."

Ward thought back to the hospital when Eddy had informed

him that the shooting had been reported. The time clock had started ticking then. Ward had gotten up, ignoring the pain, and read his chart. It was promising, no internal organ damage, muscle tissue had been damaged, and he had already been sutured up inside and out as well as given two units of plasma. One dose of antibiotics had been given intravenously, and he would be due another in about three hours. Carefully he slipped out the IV needle, and got dressed. Eddy had slipped out and been waiting outside the closed door. When Ward walked out of the room Eddy had thrown a coat over Ward's shoulders and they had walked out of the hospital together, gotten in Bill's car and that was that.

Once Bill got them back to the apartment they sat and tried to figure a way to find her and help out. The only scenario they could come up with that would work was to wait. It was the last thing they wanted to do, but the only thing they could do, since the raids had been set in motion. They had no clue as to where she was, only the copy of the list Bill had made. Like Rob, Ward knew that the last house on the list was the place she probably was, but Ward also knew Rob would be at that raid. Jan was good, but that didn't stop him from worrying about her getting clear. He had spent every minute he could on the data banks trying to find information on what was happening.

With Bill and Eddy's protests ringing in his ears, he continued to work, until it was obvious even to him that he had to stop. Rob's plans were easy to find and looked comprehensive. Ward had gone back and forth between worry, exhaustion, and pride as he read about the raids at around two in the afternoon. She had done it, gotten the entire ring caught. The only thing he couldn't find was Jan.

Ward had expected her to show up earlier in the day and with every minute that had passed he could feel the lines of stress grow deeper in his face. Eddy had tried to get him to rest. He was worried as the color slowly drained from Ward's face. When he couldn't get him to take a break he tried to get him to take some of the painkillers, but Ward would have nothing of it. All of that now forgotten, the worry and fear melted away as he looked into and through Jan's eyes.

"Did I miss anything?" Eddy bounced up behind Bill. Bill

turned in time to see Eddy. The smile on his face was broad and his expression was one of relief. Eddy gave Bill a small nod. When Jan had shown up on his doorstep, Bill had called Eddy. They had arranged the meeting that night as a surprise.

"The look on his face was priceless. Looking at her has probably done more for him than anything you might have forced down him this afternoon," they both knew that Ward had taken nothing but an antibiotic that he had to, and even that had been a battle.

"Sorry I missed it," Eddy spoke in a low tone to Bill, "He was about to take me out if I didn't get out of his hair for a while."

"If I had tried to hold her off any longer, I may have been the next casualty," Bill smiled and then turned his attention back toward them.

"If you don't hurry, you'll miss the news," Bill broke the silence.

"Care to come watch it with us?" although it was a question, it wasn't really an invite and both Bill and Eddy knew it, but ignored it with a couple of goofy smiles.

"Why thanks. Kind of them to invite us in don't you think?" Eddy gave Jan a wink.

"Oh yah," Bill agreed. "Just never know what might have happened today and in any case we will only start drawing stares if we stay standing out here," they turned and walked in past Jan and Ward.

"Nice guys," Jan looked back at Ward.

"The best," and Ward meant it. Then he leaned closer to her, "They won't be here long," and he turned slowly.

Ward took hold of Jan's arm and led her into the apartment. Jan let Ward lean a bit on her as they walked in. She didn't take it as a sign of weakness but as a sign that he needed more recovery time. She also knew that Bill and Eddy were giving her that hint by inviting themselves in. Bill walked over to the TV and switched it on. Ward settled on the couch making only a small grimace as he sat down, and Bill leaned on the arm. Eddy looked at Jan and she moved over his way as the picture appeared.

"Any way you put it, it has been a busy news day in the

valley," the broadcaster went on, "We will start with a ring of drop houses that have been raided today." The news went on like that on every channel they flipped to. As Ward watched, Eddy tried to give Jan some information.

"He shouldn't have left the hospital, but we had no choice."

"I'm fine," Ward interjected from the couch over the top of the voice of the news broadcaster.

"No sense arguing with him. He wouldn't even know what a doctor is for," Eddy directed the comment at Ward but looked at Jan with a furrowed brow.

"I think I'll be in good hands tonight if you just leave and let me get my rest," Ward smiled. Jan put her hand on Eddy's arm and just gave him a smile and small nod. Eddy understood that she had the situation well in hand.

The reports were all the same. There had been raids on ten drop houses, two of which contained material that linked the coyotes with the trafficking of women. On the screen popped up the faces of six people picked up today. Jan and Ward smiled in recognition.

"You did good," Ward's phone rang across the room. Bill stood up to get it. Looking at the number he handed the phone to over to Ward with a smile.

"She there?" he didn't give Ward time to even say hello.

"Yes. Want to talk with her?" Ward looked over at Jan and she instantly knew who was on the phone. She took the phone; she knew the line was secure.

"Glad to hear you haven't forgotten me," Jan was remembering Rob's comment to Maria.

"Thought you might still have been around but wasn't sure. By the way, nice. Maria and the rest of the women will be all right. I think I will be able to work a deal for them to stay if they testify, but somehow they had already gotten that idea from somebody," Rob waited for a response from the other end of the phone.

"I wonder who gave them that idea?" Jan said no more.

"Oh, and Maria is the only one that will admit that there might have been one more woman that they kept hostage with them, but they all swear that she was taken away days before the raid," she could hear Rob take a breath, "Good thing too. Vegas will be raided tonight, but he probably knows that already. Mexican officials are looking for your men there. Thank the gang for me," Rob changed the topic, "Hear the bird was winged. Hope he's alright."

"Look's just fine to me," Jan leaned back on the couch and into Ward, on his good side.

"Well, just watch out for that fowl, okay. Still don't want to see you hurt," and he hung up. Jan put down the phone and looked up into Ward's face. Somehow he looked even better than when she had come in.

"Vegas is raiding and Mexico will pull the other coyotes in. The women will be staying and allowed to get in contact with their families here soon. We only missed one. Eddy in my bag you will find a letter I found in the desert near one of the women we were looking for. She didn't make it." There was silence for a few moments.

"You did nice work," Ward's voice was even, but his thoughts were not.

"We did," and their eyes locked for a minute. Eddy looked away from them and over to Bill. Bill had already focused on the refrigerator.

"Well," and Bill slapped his thighs and stood up, "I'm not supposed to be hanging around with wanted people and I don't think you are either Eddy. So, I think we should be going."

"Good idea," Eddy stood up and walked with Bill toward the door, "I think I'll just lock up as I leave."

"Thanks," Jan and Ward said in unison as the door closed behind the two. Without taking her eyes off him she leaned over and kissed him, letting the kiss deepen slowly. When she slowly pulled away from his lips, she glanced at his wound.

"It's not as bad as it felt, but you should have broken the connection," Ward had felt her there in his head the whole time and knew the only way to get her to continue the job was to block her out with the pain he had felt. He had then lost consciousness.

"Remember, we are a team now. I had to know," and she put her fingers to his lips to quiet him. "Think they will ever find the last girl in Vegas?"

"They have a chance now," and Ward sat back up, "We've

done all we can and Eddy will pass on all the information to their families. They also pulled in the one left at the first house."

"Good. I think," and Jan took a look down at herself, "I need a real shower and clean clothes."

"I was just thinking the same thing, but," and the wicked smile drew up at the corners of his lips up to meet with the twinkle in his eyes, "I think you could do without clothes after the shower."

The morning light seeped in through the vertical blinds and lined the bed. Jan awoke in some confusion to begin with, and then she felt the rhythmic breathing beside her. Jan felt her stomach rumble and remembered that she had something to eat last night at the church. Right now she was still famished. Getting out of bed she grabbed the towel she had dropped beside the bed the night before and wrapped it around her. Walking out to the kitchen she wanted to see if there was anything in the refrigerator. She got into the living room area and stopped. There was a brown paper bag just inside the door that hadn't been there last night.

Instinct took over. Carefully Jan moved over to the bag and picked it up. She noticed that a note was attached to the top of the bag in Eddy's handwriting and relaxed a bit. All it said was, "Hope everyone is rested this morning. Eddy and Bill." Inside the bag were a few necessary items. Jan noticed clean clothes for her, two sleeveless knit dresses, one black and one red. There were other essentials, lingerie items that went under the dresses in the bag.

Jan smiled and wished she could have been a fly on the wall when they went to pick them out. She looked at the item in the very bottom of the bag, an envelope. On the back was scribbled a phone number. Smiling, she opened the envelope. It was a gift card from a grocery store that delivered.

By this time Ward had reached the door of the bedroom. Looking at him Jan could tell that he had been awake for some time. He had changed the dressing on his wound, and she could feel the pain he was trying to hide from her. Jan held up the card, Ward just smiled.

"I was going to invite you back to bed, but I think I'm going to lose out to the grocery store," Ward chuckled as Jan smiled.

"Trust me, it's a hard choice," Ward watched as Jan moved toward the phone and called in her food order.

It took a couple of days before either was ready to make the trip to Mexico. Eddy had taken care of the car the night of the raids, and the Explorer had sat in the garage since then. The news continued to focus on the troubles of crossing the border, and the amount of people coming over, but there was no focus on the slave trade ring that they had broken up. None of the channels mentioned the obvious either; if illegal aliens were coming over, just what else was making it over the border? Watching the databases, Jan was able to determine that the connections in Vegas had been picked up and she had reason to believe that the other woman they were looking for had been found and taken into protective custody.

Ward sat in the driver's seat of the Explorer and waited for Jan to throw the two small bags into the back of the SUV. They had decided to keep the apartment on as a place to stay in the Valley. Besides, it would cost very little to keep up since Ward and Eddy owned the complex. Jan got in and they were on their way. Both were glad to leave the Valley behind them.

Later on in the afternoon they stopped at the little diner. The parking lot was dirt and the sign looked older than they were. They had stopped here many times before and both knew that the two cars in the lot belonged to the people who worked there. They sat at the same table as always and had the same order, chili and cola. When they left, they continued down the road until it was time to turn off onto a little used back road and wind their way to the border. Usually there wasn't any traffic around when they turned off onto this road; this time didn't seem any different. Suddenly Ward felt a cold shiver run up his spine, as if someone was looking through him. Jan felt the same. Without alerting the other, they both slowly scanned the area and saw nothing but a car way off in the distance.

Ward dismissed the feeling as leftover stress. Jan felt it might have been worry about Ward that caused the misreading. Continuing on their way to Mexico, it wasn't until they were five miles down the road that the feeling disappeared. It was a couple of days later, when Jan could completely dismiss the feeling of impending disaster.